The
Refuge

A Psychological Thriller

Jo Fenton

CROOKED
CAT

To Sandra

love and best wishes

Jo Fenton

Discover us online:
www.crookedcatbooks.com

Join us on facebook:
www.facebook.com/crookedcatbooks

Tweet a photo of yourself holding
this book to **@crookedcatbooks**
and something nice will happen.

To my Mum,
for introducing me
to crime fiction
(and for everything else
you've done for me).

About the Author

Jo Fenton grew up in Hertfordshire. She devoured books from an early age and, at eleven, discovered Agatha Christie and Georgette Heyer. She now has an eclectic and much loved book collection cluttering her home office.

Jo combines an exciting career in Clinical Research with an equally exciting but very different career as a writer of psychological thrillers.

When not working, she runs (very slowly), and chats to lots of people. She lives in Manchester with her family and is an active and enthusiastic member of two writing groups and three reading groups.

Acknowledgements

I would like to start by thanking my brilliant editor and friend, Sue Barnard, who has helped with early critiques, beta reading, and provided fantastic support through the editing process.

Massive thanks to my beta readers: Pauline Barnett, Helen Copestake, Katy Johnson, Louise Jones, Gayle Samuels and Awen Thornber, for making sure everything worked seamlessly and giving excellent advice where needed.

Thanks also to the remainder of the Manchester Scribes: Karen Moore, Grant Silk, and Claire Tansey, for all the invaluable critiques.

Technical expertise was provided by Jodie Baptie and Louise Doyle, and was very gratefully received.

Thanks to my lovely Writers United friends: Joan Bullion El Faghloumi, Sue Burrows, Libby Carpenter, Anya Stojanovic Chand, Lucy Goacher, Suzanne Harbour, Caroline Harris, Gareth Hewitt, Susan King, Helen Lane, Carol Lucas, Bean Sawyer, Laura Sillett, Lee Sloan and Paul Stephenson, for all your support, advice and feedback.

Huge thanks to my wonderful family: husband Ray, for reading my work, and giving advice, feedback and encouragement in equal measures; sons, Michael and Andrew, for putting up with me, and letting me discuss difficult plot points; and to the rest of my family for being so patient.

And finally, thank you so much to Laurence and Stephanie Patterson for accepting my books for publication and for your tremendous support.

The
Refuge

Chapter One

Mel

I'm used to guilt.

Nine years ago, my sister was abducted from home while I should have been looking after her.

Last year, my best friend was raped because I failed to protect her.

Five weeks ago, I killed the man who abused me and tried to steal my baby.

I have my baby back, and I'm sitting in our old common room feeding her under a baggy t-shirt. It's late morning. The new TV hasn't been taken out of its box yet, and the room is empty except for me and Emma. There's nothing to distract my thoughts from the terrifying memories, such as when Dominic burned my clothes and threatened to burn me.

Was I justified in what I did to him? I don't know. I'm relieved he's dead (and I feel guilty for that too), but I couldn't have gone back to how things were.

Emma shifts slightly and stops suckling. I move her to my shoulder, draped with muslin cloth, and do my best to bring up wind, preferably without milk. A wry smile crosses my face. Yesterday, her feed ended by dripping down my back. I'm getting used to the smell of baby sick and dirty nappies, and the lack of sleep. But her presence soothes my soul and eases the agony of remorse.

Why the remorse? Dominic made my life unbearable for over half a year. He killed one of my friends, and tormented another. Why do I care that I killed him?

I believe in God, but not the strange 'Almighty One' that Dominic preached about, and who apparently spoke to him at intervals. I know now that Dominic was ill. His sickness wasn't responsible for his manipulative, sociopathic tendencies. That was separate.

I must stop dwelling on this. I need to focus on Emma and on Mark, my husband of five days. He forgave me; probably because he'd have killed Dominic himself given the chance. That was another motive – I couldn't let Mark become a murderer. He would have gone to prison, and it would have been my fault.

We're safe now. A verdict of suicide was brought in regarding Dominic's death. Other than myself, only two people know the truth: Mark, and my friend Jimmy. Neither of them would betray me.

The door opens and Mark comes in, a smile lighting up his face. He's carrying a mug of tea and a plate with buttered toast. The smell wafts towards me. So lovely, and so different from Brotherhood days.

"Thanks, Mark. How's everything going?"

"I'll tell you, but first and most important, how's my beautiful little girl?"

"Just windy; she's not been sick this morning, thank goodness."

"And how are you, Mel?" He looks at me with anxious eyes. I've woken him several times in the last week – my nightmares depriving us both of valuable sleep. "Do you think you might be doing too much?"

"I'm okay. The scars are healing a bit now, but I guess I still need to take it easy. I'm popping in to see Paul Griffiths shortly, and he'll examine me."

"That's one of the things I wanted to tell you about, actually." Mark sits next to me on the sofa, and pops the tea and toast on a nearby coffee table. "We're leasing out the Infirmary to a private healthcare group. They're going to take it on as a private hospital. No more trials; just rich or insured people coming for treatments or diagnosis. I think it will be better. The building will get proper use, and we'll get income to support the thirty-three people left in the Abbey."

"Only thirty-three? Why did so many people leave? There were over a hundred, weren't there?"

"Loads left when Dominic died. They didn't want to live here if the Messiah wasn't around to lead them." Mark's voice is dry. The so-called Messiah was mentally ill.

"Going back to the Infirmary, what happens to the staff who worked there?"

"Paul Griffiths is staying with us. He's moving his things from his rooms above the Infirmary to that room at the top of the stairs near the front entrance of the Abbey. It's got a bathroom next door, so is almost ensuite. Most of the others who were resident have already left. There were a few staff who were visiting, including Emily. I saw her yesterday. She popped in while you were asleep."

"How is she? What's she going to do?" Emily means a huge amount to me – partly because she returned my baby to me, but she helped me in lots of ways even before that.

"She already had another job, so she's not doing anything differently really. She lives a couple of miles away with her parents, and she plans to be a regular visitor here whenever she can."

"She'll always be welcome." I give Mark a curious look. I get the feeling he has some big news, but he seems hesitant. "What else have you got to tell me?"

"I've been speaking to Paul, and he's got some news, but he wouldn't tell me what it was. If you've finished feeding Emma, shall we go and see him now?"

I nod, and sort myself out, settling Emma into her pram. It's easier to cart her around the Abbey that way. I still get very tired, and it's only just six weeks since my Caesarean.

We walk down the corridor to the Infirmary – a much more modern building than the Abbey – and take the lift up to Paul's room. His door is open, and we see him packing his clothes into a cardboard box. I knock on the open door, and he stops the packing and comes forward to greet me.

"Mel, my dear, how are you?" He clasps my hand in both of his, and then turns to Mark with a smile. "Thank you for bringing her this morning."

"I'm not too bad, thank you. Almost healed now, I think."

"I'll examine you shortly, but I wanted to talk to you first.

How about you both come into my office?" He gestures around the poky bedroom, which contains only a bed, small bedside cupboard and a wardrobe. "There's nowhere to sit in here." He leads the way into an office, a few doors down the corridor. "This used to be Dr Harper's, or should I say Benedict Bishop's?"

"Call him Dr Harper," I suggest. "It's probably easier, and we know who you mean. I still think of him as Harper."

"Have a seat, both of you. There's space for the pram over there." The office is quite spacious, and I park Emma in the corner indicated. As soon as the pram is still, Emma wakens and starts crying. I pick her up and cuddle her to my chest while I take a seat in the chair opposite the doctor.

"I wanted to tell you about your operation. I hope you don't mind me raising it with you?" Paul gives me an anxious look.

"Of course not. Please go ahead."

"The surgeons were both visiting Consultants; they didn't live here. That police Inspector, Greg Matthews, found them and questioned them both, separately. It appears they've been less than open with both the Inland Revenue and their employers about this source of income, so Greg's been able to lean on them for information in return for a certain amount of discretion."

"Greg's good like that." I have reason to know.

"Yes, he is. He asked them about your operation. As you know, I accepted at the time that Harper was doing his best, and would have had no reason to lie to me. I apologise for that. I was very wrong."

Shivers run down my spine. When I came round from the anaesthetic I was told that I'd had a tumour; that I'd never been pregnant, and that my operation had been a hysterectomy. Knowing I can't have any more children has been another source of guilt. Instead of risking giving birth alone in a cellar, I'd fallen into a trap and ended up in the operating theatre.

I take a deep breath. "What did the surgeons say?"

"Harper told them to do a total hysterectomy after the C-section, on the grounds of malignant disease. But when the senior surgeon, Mr Curtis, opened you up, all he could see was a perfectly healthy baby, and healthy organs. He decided to use his professional judgement and experience, and defied Harper."

"You mean...?" I can't finish the sentence, so allow Paul to continue.

"Mr Curtis assumed that some scans had been mixed up, or that some other error had occurred. It never crossed his mind he'd been deliberately lied to. As we all know, Harper was very plausible. Apparently, when he explained what had happened, Harper seemed angry, but the surgeon put it down to annoyance at the mix-up."

"So they didn't remove anything? I've still got my uterus and ovaries and everything?"

Paul nods, smiling broadly.

"It sounds like it." Mark says with a grin. "How many kids do you want, Mel?"

I'm unable to answer. My throat is choked up with impending sobs, and tears fill my eyes. I try not to cry, not wanting to wake up Emma who I suspect has fallen asleep on my shoulder. The effort results in hiccups, and I end up laughing, crying and hiccupping at the same time. My baby wakes up with the movement and noise and joins in with wails of her own. As the pandemonium reaches its peak, my friend Brie pops her head around the door.

"Sorry to interrupt. It took me ages to find you here. Greg's been on the phone. Mel, he's found your sister."

Chapter Two

Jess - three weeks earlier

The light! It's burning my eyes, and I can't see a damn thing.

I've not seen full sunlight for nine years.

Run. Escape. Concentrate. Force those eyelids apart, just a tiny bit. Come on, Jess. Pull yourself together, or you'll be back inside in less than a heartbeat.

Squinting, I glance around to see a tidy garden with a neat wooden gate leading into the road. This is my way out. There are no people nearby, and apart from the blazing sun, there's no indication of the time.

I must find people. I'll be safe in a crowd. Where is everyone? My head is pounding. I banged it on the way out. It's not important now though. There's a yell from inside, and my feet suddenly find their impetus. I run, flinging open the waist-high gate, and propelling my thin, weak body through it as fast as I can.

Turn left, away from the sun. The awful burning sun with its agonising, intense light. There's another shout from inside the house. I risk a glance back, and see an ordinary-looking detached house – my prison – hidden away on this normal road. A smart black car occupies most of the drive. I can't see Him, but perhaps He wouldn't risk showing me his face; or letting his neighbours see the version of him I know.

Why have I stopped running? I'm not safe. I need to get as far away from here as I can. Fast. But I mustn't draw attention to myself. I try a quick walk, but another glance at the house shows a face at the window. A masked face. Goosebumps rise on my arms, despite the heat, and I shiver. Forget about attention. I pick up speed and sprint, managing somehow to keep going until I get to the main road, panting and gasping. A stitch in my side forces me to stop, but I'm next to a busy road now. Cars and lorries speed past. As I catch my breath, I notice there are still no people. The traffic is moving too fast for anyone to stop. I'm still not safe. The roar of the traffic here is terrifying. After being kept inside a building for so long, I can't process the loud noises out here, but I mustn't let them distract me.

I jog along a path next to the main road, ignoring the pain in my bare feet as I run over stones and gravel. In places the path disappears and I run on grass, mixed with nettles and dock leaves. I can't keep the speed up for long. There's a gentle but never-ending hill to climb. I slow to a walk, the stitch too painful even for jogging. Eventually I reach a signpost that announces I've arrived in Macclesfield.

I'm in a residential area now. The green fields have given way to lots of stone terraced houses in neat rows by the roadside. I'm getting strange looks from the few passers-by: mostly older people with dogs, or mums with prams. I glance down at myself. Shit. I'm wearing the clothes I escaped in – the ones I was wearing when he came in and removed Kylie's drug-ravaged body. The shorts barely cover my backside, and the crop top fitted me a couple of years ago, but I've developed since then. My boobs are sore from bouncing up and down – another reason to just keep walking. Maybe I'll attract less attention that way. But I need some clothes. I'm aware I've got no money. Tears threaten, but I grit my teeth. I've endured worse than this.

A stone, sharper than the rest, cuts into my left foot. It hurts. I've dreamt of escape so many times over the years, but it never involved blistering heat, cut feet and insufficient clothing. It's not going to plan right now, but at least I'm outside. *Must keep going.*

My walking deteriorates as the pain in my foot becomes intense, and I limp slowly and agonisingly up the hill into Macclesfield town centre. I try to ignore the strange looks, and look for a police officer. Shoppers in brightly coloured t-shirts and shorts bustle past laden with bags; children cry in their buggies; a mother scolds a girl of about ten – the same age I was when He took me from my home. The tears fill my eyes now. I haven't cried for years, not even when Kylie died only a week ago, but now a yearning for my parents and sister burns a hole in my chest. I lean against a brick wall – the side of a charity shop – and sink to the ground, wrapping my arms around my bare knees. Sobs wrack me for a moment, but I don't know if I have time for all this emotion. I'm not safe yet. He's out there somewhere. Even if only back at the house, He'll be planning how to take me back. I know how his mind works.

My limbs have stiffened with the few minutes rest, and standing up again is an effort. Over the years, I've been through phases of running on the spot every day, but watching Kylie fade away deprived me of energy and care, so now I'm unfit.

A scruffy boy in his late teens shouts over to me, "Oy, slut! Why don't you get some clothes on? Skinny arse!"

"I've not got any money." Years of obedience compel me to reply.

"Wanna make some?" His eyes light up in a leer, and it's easy to work out what he means. I turn without answering and enter the charity shop.

A tall woman with dark hair and a mobile phone attached to her ear pauses in her gossip. She stares at me down her nose and sniffs as though something smelly has plonked itself in her precious airspace. My desperation for clothes evaporates for a moment. What a cow. I manage a disdainful look back at her. She looks a bit startled, but carries on talking on the phone as I leave.

There's another charity shop over the road. It's worth a try. I open the door and walk in.

A woman with grey hair in an untidy bob is sorting out clothes at the back near the tills. I rub my nose. She'd better be nicer than the other one.

"Excuse me, I hate to ask, but do you have any clothes you don't think would sell? I really need to cover up a bit, and I've not got any money."

She looks me up and down, but not with the harsh

judgmental expression I expected.

"You look about a size 8, love. I think I've got something in the back. Give me a minute."

I glance outside, still afraid that He might show up. But the only person there is the lad. He's eyeing me covetously through the window. The sooner I get some more clothes on, the better.

The shop assistant returns a minute later carrying a pair of grey, misshapen leggings and a navy crew neck t-shirt that might have been fashionable once, probably before I was born. But they're clean, and not provocative.

"Thank you. You're so kind." I nod my head towards the door and the waiting youth. She purses her pale lips, and then looks at my feet.

"Come with me, love. How come you've not got any shoes?"

"It's a long story. Is there a police station near here? I need to tell the police as well, and I'm so tired. I ran part of the way here."

The kind lady guides me towards the room at the back and a small cubicle with a toilet inside. "Get yourself changed, and I'll give them a call. There's an officer who pops in here every now and again. We get a lot of break-ins. Ridiculous really. We sell things for charity. But then there's people that are after drug money, and this seems like an easy target. Anyway, you don't want to know my troubles. I'll give Polly a call and see if she's got a few minutes to pop in and get you. Then while she's on the way, I'll dig you out some shoes."

Polly, when she arrives, is a comfortable-looking, slightly overweight constable of around the same age as the shopkeeper. The women appear of a similar type, both kindly and caring. I hope they'll stay that way when they hear my story.

After introducing herself as PC Legg, she turns to the shopkeeper.

"Jane, can we go upstairs, and have a chat up there? It's a

bit more private."

Jane looks disappointed. I guess she wants to hear my story at the same time as the police officer, but she delves into a drawer under the till and extracts a key.

"Go on then. There's a kettle and some teabags up there, if you want to make a cup of tea for our young friend. Sorry, love," she says to me, "I've not asked your name? That's very rude of me."

"I'm Jessica, and if you want to see rude, you should meet the woman in the shop opposite."

Jane purses her lips again. "She is not a good example of a charity shop worker. Most of us are not like that."

"You're not, anyway. Thank you so much for what you've done for me. I don't know what I'd have done otherwise." I glance at the door, but the youth has disappeared – probably scared off by the appearance of the police.

I follow Polly upstairs, and sit on a grubby beige armchair while she makes tea. I've not had a cup of tea since I was ten, and didn't like it very much then. My abductor only provided water to drink. Polly puts in two spoonsful of sugar without asking, but says, "You look as though you need the sugar. Sorry if it's too sweet for you, but pretend it's medicine."

I take a sip. It's hot, sweet and quite pleasant.

"It's great, thanks."

"Pleasure. There are some biscuits here as well. I'm sure Jane won't mind if we raid the biscuit tin." She hands me a saucer with three chocolate digestives on. I used to love these when I was little, but needless to say, they weren't on the shopping list for captives. I bite into it, and savour the taste for a brief moment, before scoffing them down quickly. I didn't realise how hungry I was until faced with real food. I've survived the last nine years on cheese or ham sandwiches, with lettuce when He could be bothered to add it.

The thin man in the hostel kitchen introduces himself as a police officer.

"Jess?" He smiles at me, and the tension in my shoulders

eases.

I've seen all sorts of officers in the last three weeks since Polly brought me to this hostel for homeless women. Some of them have been friendly, others snotty and arrogant – refusing to believe my history. The police are marginally better than the journalists, but I would prefer not to speak to either. I give a tired smile and get a nod back in reply. It's hard to sleep in this place, and I'm exhausted. I just want to find my family.

"I'm Greg Matthews, and I'm here to take you to your sister. I spoke to her on the phone half an hour ago, and she's extremely excited about seeing you."

"You've found her? How did you manage? No one else seems to have had a clue. Is there any news of Mum and Dad?"

"Why don't we sit down for a few minutes, and I'll explain?" He indicates some orange and blue fabric chairs around a low table on the opposite side of the kitchen. I take my weak coffee over to the chairs and sit down facing him.

"Sorry to have to tell you this, but your parents died in a plane crash over a year ago. When they died, your sister joined a religious group called The Brotherhood, and went to live in an Abbey not far from here." He pauses, and a grim expression crosses his face. "She had a bad time, Jess. The leader imprisoned her and abused her—"

"Well, I know how that feels," I interrupt. A numb cold creeps into my chest, but I force myself to keep calm. I've learnt a lot over the years about not revealing emotion. "Sorry, carry on. Just a bit shocked. Can't believe Mum and Dad are dead." My voice sounds expressionless. This officer must think I'm a callous cow.

"I apologise. I should have given you time to assimilate that. Do you want a few minutes alone?"

"No. Carry on telling me about Melissa." A vein of excitement tugs at me, until I remember a fact that has haunted me for nine years: my sister had left me alone in the house while she went out to see a friend – leaving me an easy victim for abduction.

13

Greg smiles again. "She's known as Mel now. She has a husband, Mark, and a six-week-old baby, Emma. My god-daughter." His face is a mixture of pride and something else I can't read. Guilt? Maybe, but that doesn't make a lot of sense.

"When can I see them? Do they have anywhere to live? Do they have a spare room?" Anything to get out of this place.

"They're still living in the Abbey. When the owner, Mel's abuser, committed suicide, the Abbey passed to his half-brother, a man named Benedict. He's on the run for various offences, but he sent a letter via a solicitor confirming that Mel and Mark are to have the Abbey and use it as they see fit. It legally belongs to them. They've allowed any members of the former Brotherhood to remain, and are trying to modernise it and run it more as a communal house rather than a sect. Mark told me he wanted to emulate the kibbutz model. Apparently he lived in one for a while before his degree."

"So, they've got a whole Abbey? Will they let me stay?"

"Mel can't wait to see you. They missed all the media coverage about you as they've only just started to introduce technology, and hadn't got around to turning on the new TVs until after I told them the news. Just be gentle with her. She had Emma by C-section, and is still a bit fragile."

So am I.

"Great. I'll get my stuff. Give me two minutes." When Greg nods, I turn and head to the six-bedded room I've been sharing in the hostel. Two of the residents are lying on their beds, one playing on the phone she came in with – her only possession when she arrived. The other is staring into space. They both ignore me. I tried to be friendly, but these girls think they're the only ones who've had a bad time, and don't care about anything or anyone else.

I grab the carrier bag of clothes and toiletries given to me by Jane, and head back down the corridor to the kitchen. Greg is gazing out of the window, where all he'll be able to see are the overgrown weeds creeping through the paving

14

stones in the back yard.

"I'm ready when you are."

He turns at the sound of my voice, and smiles.

"Okay then. Let's go and see your sister, your brother-in-law and your niece."

"I've not had much to do with babies," I confess, as I follow him to a black Audi parked outside the hostel.

"No? I suppose you wouldn't have done. I've read your file. Then we checked the DNA against some that we already held for your sister. I suspected it was you because of things she'd told me, but we needed the confirmation." He takes my bag and puts it in the boot. "Anyway, let's get you to the Abbey."

I wait until we're sitting in the car and he's turned on the engine, before asking, "Is it just called the Abbey?"

"At the moment. Mark has set up a committee to help run the community, and they're discussing new names for the building as one of the minor details. I think it's secondary to the logistics, though. Your brother-in-law seems to be an effective organiser, and he's doing a good job. They mostly like him anyway."

"Will I like him?"

"I don't know. He's kind, caring, and he adores Mel and Emma. If that's the most important thing to you, then yes, you'll like him." He drives off, and the car starts to cool down a bit as the aircon kicks in.

"Thanks. Maybe the bigger question is 'Will he like me?'"

"Can I give you some advice? From someone who knows the situation on both sides?" He's not looking at me at all, focusing on the open road ahead.

I stare at the countryside rushing past for a few moments before replying.

"Sure."

"Be open. You're very defensive just now. I totally understand why, but they've had a bad time too, and everything will be a lot easier if you let them in. They're ready to welcome you with open arms, so let them."

"Thanks. I'll try." I see his quick sceptical glance at me,

and realise my response doesn't leave much hope. "Sorry, I really will try. It's kind of hard for me to trust. Three weeks ago, the only person I trusted died in agony while I watched. I don't want to go through that pain again. Even now, the only people I've met who I've felt the faintest inclination to trust have been Polly, Jane, and now perhaps you. I'm reserving judgement."

"Thank you." He parks the car in front of an impressively huge, old building, with a more modern annexe a short distance away towards the back. "This is the Abbey, Jess. Are you ready to go in and meet them?"

Chapter Three

Mel

"Sit down, Mel, you'll do yourself an injury pacing like that." Mark is in an armchair pretending to read a book, but I haven't seen him turn a single page. He might not be as excited as I am, but he's not calm either.

"Surely she should be here by now." I go over to where Emma is sleeping peacefully in her basket, then force myself to sit on a nearby sofa.

The door opens. I jump from my seat, and feel the faint pull of my stitches. My hand goes to the scar on my abdomen, but of course there's no blood there. It's six weeks and two days since the section; two days since I discovered the fantastic news that my sister has been found.

The young woman standing in the doorway bears minimal resemblance to the girl that was taken so many years ago. A slight blonde with short hair, Jess reminds me of a pixie – a rather diffident, reserved pixie. I hold out my arms and she responds in kind, hesitantly joining me for a hug.

I hold her tight, and tears cascade down my face. She's tense, hugging me back, but without confidence. I don't care. I never want to let her go. Jess breaks the hug after a moment, pulling back with a brittle laugh.

"It's good to see you." Her voice sounds choked.

"You too." The words are barely audible due to the sobs shaking my body.

"Jess, I'm Mark, Mel's husband of a week, and father of our beautiful daughter, your niece, Emma." He holds out a hand for Jess and she shakes it, clearly more ready for a handshake than a hug. My sobs subside with the interest of the meeting between my sister and my husband.

"And this is Emma. She's asleep at the moment, so cuddles will have to wait, but you can have a peek." He moves to the crib, and gently tweaks back enough of the blanket to reveal Emma's pretty face. Jess gets as close as she can, and when she sees her niece, her face breaks into a huge smile.

"She's beautiful. I'm looking forward to that cuddle with her." She steps back, her expression returning to that awkwardness it had when she arrived. "Will I be able to stay here?" she asks abruptly.

"Of course you can," says Mark, at the same time as I say, "You'd better be staying. You're not going anywhere else."

She smiles again. "Thanks. I'll try not to be difficult."

I go over and put my hands on her shoulders, noticing that she's a few inches taller than I am.

"This is your home, Jess. You can just be yourself. Can I show you your room, and then Mark will give you a tour of the Abbey?"

Jess nods, and I lead her out into the corridor.

Greg is standing inside the main entrance, talking to Jimmy.

"Everything alright, Jess? Mel?" Greg hands my sister a plastic bag with some things in.

"Hey," I turn to her, smiling. "We can go shopping together. I need to get some more clothes for Emma. You've never seen anyone grow so fast, honestly."

"I don't know if I'm ready for shopping yet. Can we get clothes from a catalogue or something, like Mum used to do when we were small?"

"We can buy stuff online now. Mark got computers set up in all the common rooms, so we can have a look later if you like, and get you a whole new wardrobe."

"Maybe later. I've got a few things that Jane gave me. She's my friend that first helped me out. I've got her number. She said she'd visit me, but I need to tell her where I am now. I saw her yesterday when I was in the hostel, but thought I'd be there a bit longer."

"I'll let her know, Jess. And I'm sure she'll come and see you." Greg puts a hand on her shoulder briefly. She wriggles away, then rubs her nose.

"Thank you, and sorry," she says.

"It's fine. Don't worry about it. I'll try to remember." He gives her a reassuring smile, but without the physical contact.

Having my sister back in my life may be more complicated than I thought.

Greg takes his leave a moment later. Jimmy smiles, but says nothing and returns to the dormitory, which he's been helping some of the others to divide into separate bedroom areas.

"Would you prefer to be in a room by yourself, or with other people?" I lean against the panelled wall. I feel suddenly drained of energy.

Jess doesn't answer for a moment, but a series of emotions cross her face. Finally, she blurts out, "Not alone, please. But I might wake people up. The girls in the hostel complained because I cried out in my sleep while I was there."

"Come and meet my friend Tina. She's had a difficult time as well, and is only a year or two older than you. I think you'll get on well."

I lead her up the stairs to a door. Within is a two-bedded room above a common room.

"This used to be the bedroom of one of the group leaders. We were divided into dorms, but the leaders each had their own large room. There are twelve of these, and we've managed to allocate most of them now, although the rest of the residents are dotted around in various places. We're trying to renovate inside so that everyone can have their own space, but it will take a while to get that organised." I knock on the door.

"Hello? Come in." My friend Tina is sitting in an armchair, reading a book. The room is sparsely decorated so far, with just two armchairs, two divan beds and a wardrobe and chest of drawers. The white walls are bare, and the curtains are grey.

"Tina, sorry to interrupt you. This is my sister, Jess."

"Oh my God. Jess, it's lovely to meet you at last. I've heard so much about you." Despite the exuberance of the verbal welcome, Tina remains in her chair, her legs curled underneath her, and her hands resting on the book in her lap.

"Thank you. I hope you don't mind me sharing with you. I don't want to intrude."

"It's not an intrusion. I only moved in here this morning, and I was hoping you'd join me."

"Where were you before?" asks Jess.

"I was in the dorm, but they're splitting it into separate rooms. Some of the men are at work moving the furniture out of the way, and then the builders are coming in tomorrow." Tina looks at me. "Mark promised me they'd all be security checked. Do you know if he's done it yet?"

"He was having some difficulty with the checks, so until they're done, they'll be under constant supervision from our security team. Don't worry, Tina. It'll be fine. I'm not great with strange men being around either, but Mark's recruited some proper security staff, recommended by the police, and fully vetted." I look at Jess. "We used to have a group of wardens policing the Abbey, to make sure rules were kept. Some of them were violent criminals and they've been handed over to Greg. I believe they're awaiting trial, but you can both stay out of their way for now. There's no need for you to meet any outsiders if you don't want to."

Jess points to the bed furthest from the armchairs and the door.

"Is that one mine?"

"Yes, if that's okay," says Tina. She gives me an anxious look; obviously keen to please my younger sister. I smile back as Jess goes over and sits on the assigned divan.

"This'll be great, thanks."

I think they should have some time to get to know each other in private, so revise plans slightly.

"Why don't you have some time here chilling out for a while?" I look at my watch. "Lunch will be in half an hour in the dining hall, so come down then. Mark's tour can wait until after lunch."

Both girls nod and look pleased, so I must have made the right decision.

Chapter Four

Jess

Alone with my new room-mate, there's a moment's silence. Tina is quite like me in appearance: pale and thin with long blonde hair. Except mine is short; hacked off with scissors in the hostel because I didn't want to stand out.

She seems almost as scared as I am, which is strange given she's been living here for a while. That was the impression I got from Mel anyway. Being with frightened young girls is something I'm used to. My abductor used to bring them back for a while, as entertainment when He got bored of me. But when He'd had enough of them, He'd drug them and take them away. I asked once what He did with them. It was one day when He was in an okay mood. He told me He'd driven them a long way away and left them in a forest to be found. There were six other girls in total: all in their teens, blonde, thin and pretty. Five were taken away alive. I don't know if they ever made it home. Tina would have been just his type.

I don't know why I'm thinking in past tense. He's still out there. Probably looking for me, and definitely dangerous.

"Tina?" I break the silence suddenly, wanting to warn her, but I don't really know what to say. "Erm, you know I was abducted, right?"

"Yeah, Mel told me. You don't have to talk about it if you don't want."

"I don't want to talk about it now. Possibly not ever. But you need to know. I escaped, but he might come and get me. Or look for a replacement." Guilt pierces me as her face contorts in fear, but I have to make sure she's safe. "Promise me you won't go out of the Abbey alone. Please."

She's even paler now.

"I don't go out anyway, but now? No chance. We've got TV and the internet now, and Mark's bought loads of books. He's creating a library in one of the old common rooms, so we can read whatever we want." Speaking more naturally as she tells me about the changes to the Abbey, she describes a lot of the privations they used to endure. It sounds awful. Not as bad as I've been through, but still grim.

"Why did you stay?"

"I didn't have anywhere else to go. Dominic rescued me from... It was horrible... Far worse than conditions here, even though I had some of the mod cons there. There was lots of stuff I didn't even tell your sister. Mel's lovely, but she's always seemed kind of innocent. She isn't now. I know she had a horrendous time up until a few weeks ago, but I never felt I could tell her any details about what I went through."

I get what she means. Although there's a darkness in Mel's eyes, I don't think I could describe to her what happened to me. It might break her. But Tina seems just as vulnerable. Perhaps we all are.

She carries on explaining. "Anyway, the Abbey was a haven, for a while, and then everything got awful, and then Dominic died. Now Mark is organising everything, but he has a committee, and he offered to run elections for leader, but everyone was just really happy to let him carry on. I like Mark. I think most people do. He gets things done, but he's friendly and approachable, and he wouldn't harm a fly."

"That's good to know. I found him a bit intimidating, but I guess he's protective of Mel. I hope he is." I glance at my new friend in search of reassurance.

"You don't need to worry, Jess. He adores her. It's obvious, and kind of sweet."

The door opens and a grey-haired woman pops her head around.

"Hello. You must be Jess. I'm Brie. I've come to get you for lunch. It's very exciting. We've got ourselves a chef."

Tina and I follow Brie out of the room, as Tina asks her, "Does that mean we don't need to cook any more?"

"Just breakfast and Saturdays. Hugo, the chef, will do lunch and dinner six days a week. Mark's going to work out a rota for when we have to cook, but he did say Hugo might leave us stuff to heat up."

I'm listening avidly, curious about the evidence of change, but a bit bewildered. When that policeman had said I would be going to live with my sister in an Abbey, I didn't know what to expect. But this is still a shock.

The narrow stairs are at the opposite end of the hallway from where I came up, and lead into new territory for me. The place is huge, and it could take me weeks to find my way round. At the bottom of the stairs is a door, which opens out onto another passageway with beautiful oak panelling. Halfway along, past several of the panels, is a set of arched double doors with metal scrollwork attached to the wood. Brie pushes the left side open and leads us into a huge hall. It looks big enough to seat hundreds, but there are three wooden trestle tables laid out, with benches for people to sit on. Faces turn towards us as we edge in, and Brie steers us to the far end of the table on the left, where my sister and her husband await. Mel has a welcoming smile, but Mark's expression is neutral. In a crib at the end of the table, my niece sleeps peacefully.

"She's had her feed while you were upstairs," Mel says. "We thought you should have some time to settle in. There'll be loads of opportunities to cuddle Emma later."

After a tasty lunch of quiche and salad, Mark leans towards where I'm sitting between Tina and Brie.

"Are you ready for a tour of the Abbey, Jess? I've only got about twenty minutes spare, but I can help you to get your bearings in that time."

"Thank you. That will be useful." I glance around the hall. The other two tables are now empty, and the only people remaining are the few I already know. Brie helps me to stand up and turn around. It's tricky without kicking my neighbours, but I manage, and join Mark, who is now standing at the door looking a bit impatient.

He leads me further down the same corridor. Opening a single arched door, he indicates for me to go inside and follows me through. This room seems a bit out of place for an Abbey. To my left, the desk and cabinet are oak, but modern. A black swivel chair behind the desk faces a desktop computer, with the monitor set at an angle so visitors are made welcome. To the right of the door is a long oak table, surrounded by six smart dining chairs.

"Grab one of those chairs, Jess, and we'll have a chat." Mark waits as I pull the nearest chair over to the desk and sit down. "To be honest, I'd rather let Tina show you round, and use this time to explain a few things."

"Okay."

"Mel and I only got married last week. I don't know how much Greg told you, but Dominic, who used to be in charge here, was a nasty piece of work. He was ill, but that didn't excuse his behaviour." Mark rubs his hand on the back of his neck, extracts a tissue from a drawer, and rubs the sweat on to the tissue before dropping it neatly into a waste bin. "Christ! I'm not sure if I'm the right person to tell you about this."

"Don't then."

"Perhaps I should just tell you this used to be a religious sect. It's been disbanded. We're running it by committee now, but more as a community of people who want somewhere safe and comfortable to live. I'm sorting everything out with lawyers. Lots of us had money before we came here. Some of it was signed over to Dominic, but we're managing to get some back – anything that wasn't already spent, anyway. For many members, there were large sums of money, and I've done my best to make sure those people have the means of returning to life outside if they choose. A few people came here with nothing. I want everyone to have a chance at a normal life, but not everyone has that option yet. Meanwhile, this is a safe and free place to live. I want it to be a democracy, with decent living conditions. I'm leasing out the Infirmary, and that's going to bring in a lot of money for things like paying a chef, and providing food, security and clean clothes for everyone. Other than that, everyone will have to do their bit."

"Where do I fit in?" I can see Mark's doing his best, but his thoughts are obviously with the running of the Abbey, and the logistics, and it doesn't seem very relevant to me at the moment.

"I'm sure we'll find ways for you to help out." He seems embarrassed. "Sorry. Look. Greg told us you've been locked up somewhere for the last nine years. Obviously they're trying to find out where, and I'm sure you'll be interviewed by them to get as many clues as possible for them to find your abductor."

I wince. As I said to Tina, He's probably looking for me. I hope the police find Him first, but I don't hold out much hope. I don't know why I didn't take note of the street name when I left, but apart from the sign saying Macclesfield, I've been unable to provide any clues as to location. I've no idea how long I walked before reaching the town. Anger at my own stupidity gnaws at me, but it's too late now.

"I hate to ask this, but have you had any sort of education since you were taken from home?"

I cringe. My lack of education from the age of ten is a sore point.

"After I'd been locked up a couple of years, I asked for something to read. I'd worked out his moods by then, and knew when it was okay to ask for stuff, and when not to. I'd learned by bitter and painful experience. Not all scars are visible though."

"They rarely are," says Mark with a shrug.

"That's true. Anyway, he brought me in the first volume of Encyclopaedia Britannica. It was quite hard going for a twelve-year-old who hadn't read a word for two years, but it gradually came back to me, and I waded through it. In the next seven years, I read through the whole lot, twice. But that's the extent of my education. And the volumes were dated 1985. So I know nothing more recent, and I suppose I'm pretty clueless about the last nine years except what I've learnt since I escaped."

"So maybe that's what you should do for the next few weeks at least. We've got the internet now, and newspapers, and we can work out a programme of education in a slightly more ordered fashion. Perhaps when you've settled down, we can arrange for you to go to college. It's June now; we could enrol you for some courses in September if you like?"

What are the chances of Him being caught by then? If He's not, I'm not going anywhere.

"Let's wait and see. For now, I'll have a look at the internet, and see what I can learn by myself. Thanks."

A head pops round the door without knocking. It's the guy who was talking to Greg earlier, and who was introduced at lunch as Jimmy. For some strange reason, he makes me nervous, but not in a horrible way. Just a peculiar tingling in my gut, particularly when he grins. He does it now. That lopsided grin with the dimple in the right cheek. The tingle spreads to my back, and I feel my cheeks getting pink, but I try to smile back. He transfers his gaze to Mark.

"That builder's here, laddie. I told him you'd be along shortly, and left him in the hall with that security guy, Euan."

"Thanks Jimmy. Can you take Jess back to Tina, and maybe give her the grand tour on the way?"

"Aye. My pleasure." He grins at me, and my insides do a funny little dance.

Chapter Five

Mel - five weeks later

"Mark, is there any news?" I barge into his office, with Emma in a papoose at my chest. He's alone, staring with a frown at the computer. "Is everything okay?"

"What sort of news?" The cleft in his forehead remains. It's been there for weeks now, and I'm getting worried about him.

"Are they letting us have the Abbey as a refuge?" It's a mission of mine to turn our home into a place where abused women and children can come for safety, but there are all sorts of regulations and legal stuff to deal with, and it's been taking ages.

"Oh yeah. I meant to tell you yesterday. We just need a visit from Health and Safety, and if that goes well we can open straight away. They're coming tomorrow at three." He runs a hand through his hair, and I notice a couple of silver strands showing up.

"Is this a mistake, Mark? You seem really stressed. Everything is going well with the Abbey, isn't it?"

"Yes, it's fine. I couldn't do without Jimmy and Keith and Brie. They do most of the organising, to be honest. But we've had to do so much rearranging to isolate a section for your refuge women." He gives me an anxious look, and a lead weight settles in my chest. This feels serious. "Sit down, Mel. You should be taking it easy still."

"I'm fine. It's eleven weeks since the birth. Everything has healed okay. I just need a bit more sleep. Emma's permanently hungry at the moment. What's the problem?"

"It's Jess. She seems to have palled up with Karen – that tall dark girl that used to be in the Benedictines. She stayed

27

on due to home troubles. Didn't get on with her parents, apparently. I can see why."

"You've been really good, taking the time to get to know everyone that's stayed. But why is she a problem? She's not upsetting Jess, is she?"

"Not upsetting her, as such, but I think she's a bad influence. After breakfast, both girls came to see me to ask if they could go into the village this evening to a pub."

I lean back in the chair opposite Mark, shuffling Emma round so she has her head on my shoulder. She's awake but content for once – probably because I fed her right before I came to see her dad.

Jess seemed to be settling in well. A few nightmares, but she's been eating and putting on weight. The new chef is determined to feed everyone up, and the food is lovely. But any suggestions that she go out of the grounds have been met with horror, and I can't believe anyone would persuade her to go out.

"Isn't that a good thing, Mark, if she's getting enough confidence to go out?"

"If it was with you or me or one of the people I trust, I'd say, yes, great, but Karen is tough. She lived on the streets for a few months before Dom... before she was found and brought here. She can probably look after herself and Jess, but I'm worried about what she'd drag her into."

As I consider Mark's comments, I also begin to worry. I've seen Karen around, but not being particularly interested in her, I haven't taken the time to get to know her. I have my own group of friends, and have been too busy with Emma and all the new arrangements to have been bothered with someone who doesn't appeal.

To be completely truthful, after the betrayal by Dominic (and I notice Mark avoiding his name – sweet but unnecessary; I think about what happened all the time), I've been scared to make new friends. I don't trust my judgement any more.

"If you're not convinced, then I'm not either. But I wonder if we should give them some freedom, then maybe send

Jimmy out to keep an eye on them?"

"They'd notice him."

"Well, how about that new warden? What's his name? Gavin? He seems nice."

"They're not wardens any more, Mel, just security guards. But that's not a bad idea. They wouldn't necessarily recognise him, and if they did, he could just say it's his night off, and it's a favourite pub of his."

"Can you give them one of the phones? Give it to Jess. Then if she panics or if Karen goes off without her, she can give you a call."

"Ok. Do you want to go and chat to her? She's your sister, and it might come better from you. I think she sees me as a pain in the backside. I'm always having to tell her off about something."

"I didn't know that. Like what?"

"Oh, like the other day, she was supposed to be doing laundry – she's integrating with the others for chores now – and I found her reading in the common room. I hated telling her off, and I made sure she knew there was lots of free time after lunch, but she gave me this really mutinous look. I'm only eight years older than her, but I felt like a dad telling off a difficult teenager."

"Ok. I'll have a chat with her. Where's she likely to be just now? Is she on duty somewhere?"

Mark consults a chart and shakes his head. "She's free at the moment, so she could be anywhere."

"I'll try her bedroom, then work my way round the common rooms. Thanks." I wait while he digs around in his drawer and extracts a mobile phone and a charger.

"This is one that Brie uses when she goes into town," he says. "It's got a bit of charge, and about ten pounds worth of credit, but it's probably sensible to charge it up before Jess goes out."

I take the phone, and start my search, eventually running my sister to ground in what used to be the Benedictine common room. She's sitting in an armchair with her feet curled under her, chatting to Tina and a dark-haired girl, who

I assume must be Karen. I watch from the door for a moment. Jess has put on a few pounds since she arrived, and looks a bit healthier, although still too thin. They don't seem to notice me immediately, and I listen to the conversation, waiting for a suitable point to interrupt.

"Come with us, Tina," Jess says. "We'll look after you, I promise."

"For Christ's sake, Tina, stop being so bloody wet. You'll be fine. What do you think could happen to you?" Karen's aggressive tone makes my stomach contract.

"Last time I was out there, I got raped, and would have been murdered if Dominic hadn't rescued me. So, no: I really don't want to go." Tina turns to Jess with an apologetic frown. "Sorry Jess," she says, then stands up and notices me at the door. "Hi Mel, is everything okay?"

"I was going to ask you the same thing, actually." I glance round at the three of them. "Is there a problem?"

Jess looks sheepish and doesn't reply. Karen sneers at me. It's left to Tina to respond.

"Karen and Jess want to explore a bit. They've asked me to join them, but I prefer it here. I was hoping maybe you and I could watch a nice movie together once Emma settles down to sleep. Where is she, by the way?"

"I left her with Mark. She's sleeping sweetly in her crib in his office. A movie sounds lovely." I'm very happy for Tina to keep me company this evening. It's occurred to me that sending Mark, Jimmy and Keith round on a pub crawl might be a good way for them to 'accidentally' bump into Karen and Jess, and bring them home safely. I turn casually to Jess as Tina smiles and leaves the room.

"So where are you off to this evening?"

"Karen said she'll take me to a pub. I gather there's one in the village."

"I think there are three in the village, but the nearest is about a mile from here. Are you going to walk?" It's late June, so at least it will be light – even at around ten, it's not quite pitch black.

"Me and Jess will do a little tour of the pubs," Karen says.

"It'll be nice to get out of here for a bit, and it'll do Jess good to get out. She needs to meet some normal people."

I raise my eyebrows. "Normal?"

"For fuck's sake, Melissa. Get real. Half the people here are screwed up; the other half are crackers." She's lounging back against the cushions on a sofa, staring at me down her nose.

"How dare you? If you don't like it here, get the hell out. And don't call me Melissa. I'm Mel now."

"Hey, back off, you bitch. Get away from me."

I'm standing right in front of the sofa, crowding her. My fists are clenched, but it's totally against my nature and conditioning to physically attack. I settle for those few words, but find myself ludicrously close to tears.

"Mel, it's okay. Come on, calm down. She didn't mean it like that." Jess puts an arm around my shoulders and pulls me backwards, sitting me on the armchair she's just vacated.

I slump in the chair, resting my head in my hands.

"You're a fucking crazy bitch. Keep away from me." I hear Karen's voice, then the door slamming behind her.

I'm left alone with my sister.

"I'm sorry, Jess." I glance up, and throw her an apologetic smile.

"Are you okay? You looked like you were about to lose it." She sits down in the seat previously occupied by Tina. "I know Karen can be a bit rude, but she's not normally that… nasty. I'm sorry too. Did you come to have a little chat with me? I guess Mark sent you."

The sarcasm in her voice makes me wince. I'm still shaking from my temper, and have to take a few deep breaths before I can speak calmly.

"Mark is concerned about you, and so am I. We're happy for you to go out, but we want you to be safe." I take the phone and charger from my pocket. "It's got some charge, but you might want to top it up before you go out." I hold it out to her, but she sits still looking mutinous.

"Why would I need it?"

"All sorts of reasons. You might get lost. You might decide

31

you want a lift back here after you've had a few drinks." I don't want to say the next bit, but force myself. "Or you might see someone while you're out who you don't like the look of."

Jess shudders and reaches out her hand for the phone.

Chapter Six

Jess

The walk to the pub seems to take forever. I wish we hadn't bothered. My palms are sweaty and bile keeps rising in my throat. I force it back down, and focus on walking in these ridiculous heels that Karen bullied me into wearing.

"How much longer 'til we're there?" I can't keep the irritation from my voice. A light rain is wrecking my hair, and the country lane is muddy from a recent deluge. Typical English summer apparently. I wouldn't know. The seasons always merged into one in the cellar, and with no windows, I could never tell what the weather was doing. The Abbey occupants are obsessed with the weather. They're always talking about it. Bloody boring!

Karen's tottering ahead of me. We have to walk single file as there's no pavement, and a fairly steady stream of traffic. I get what Mel meant about wanting a ride home. I'm not walking back along this road when it's dark. I've nearly been run over twice and it's still daylight, even though it's gone seven.

"Kaz, are we nearly there?" I shout. She obviously didn't hear me ask first time.

"Christ, Jess. Give it a break will you? We'll be there in a bit."

I stick my tongue out at her. It's childish, I know, but she doesn't see it anyway. She didn't even bother turning round to answer me.

A smart black car speeds past in the opposite direction, just inches from where I'm walking. All of a sudden I'm sweating and my heart's pounding. I'm not sure why, but I don't think it has anything to do with the proximity of the car as it passed. Grey dims the edge of my vision, and I rest back against the hedge for a minute.

"Karen," I call out, but I can barely hear my own voice. I'm going to faint. Heat is rushing through my veins and sounds are fading in and out. There are cars speeding close by. THERE ARE CARS RUSHING PAST. I must not faint.

For God's sake, Jess, pull yourself together girl.

The cars are scary, but they somehow pull me back from the brink. I take several deep breaths, forcing myself to breathe slowly, trying to get air to my lungs and my brain. My stomach reacts to the fear, and I vomit on the roadside. Karen's way ahead now. I don't have the energy to call her, but I can't catch her up either. My legs feel as though they've been de-boned, and all that's supporting me is wobbly tissue.

I remember the phone. Surely I can't phone this early. We only left about half an hour ago, even if it's seemed like hours. But my so-called friend is almost out of sight, and a big black car has given me the heebie-jeebies. I type in the password Mel gave me. It's my birthday, nice and easy for me to remember, even in a state. Just as I search for the Abbey number, there's a hand on my shoulder. I start to scream. I can't help it.

"Jess? Are you okay, lass?" Jimmy's rich accent interrupts the scream before it's roused the village.

I turn to him. Relief triggers a deluge of tears, and he offers me a broad chest for soaking. Pulling me close, he puts his arms around me, and holds tight. I relax into him, unable to believe I've been rescued, let alone by this particular man.

"Are you okay to walk a bit?" he says. "If we go back about a hundred yards there's a passing place, and we can wait safely for Mark to bring the car. He won't be long. I phoned him as soon as I caught sight of you, and I could see that bitch wasn't waiting for you."

I try to stand upright, but my wobbly legs are refusing to help, and I stumble. Jimmy's a big guy. Over six foot, and broad. He takes one look at me, raises his eyebrows in a question, and in response to my weary nod, picks me up and carries me. I'm in much the same position as Emma, when

34

she's being winded. With my head and arms over Jimmy's shoulder, he's holding my back and legs. It's all very platonic and couldn't be misconstrued, but despite my distress there's a little bit of me that wishes he wasn't being quite so clinical about it. It was much nicer when he was hugging me at the roadside.

I push the thought to the back of my mind. It's not a good plan to get a crush on Jimmy, even if he does always make me fluttery inside. He's thirteen years older than me – even older than Mark – and probably sees me like a child. He's been pleasant and friendly whenever we've been in the same room in the Abbey, but I've always been conscious of the age gap, and that he's more of a friend to Mel and Mark than he could ever be to me. It's a shame, though.

More to the point is where Karen has got to. I wait until Jimmy lowers me to the ground at the specified wide part of the road.

"What should we do about Karen?" I ask tentatively.

"Let her go to the pub?" Jimmy wipes his face. It's raining properly now, and water is dripping from a stray lock of hair and falling into his eyes. "You know what, Jess? I don't care what she does, but that lassie is in my black books at the moment. Did she not bother to check you were following?"

"Not really." I hesitate. "I kind of stopped following her. A car went past. Lots of cars went past, but that one freaked me out. I thought I was going to faint."

"Is that why you screamed when I tapped you on the shoulder?"

"Yeah, I guess so." I swallow hard. Even the thought of that car seems to bring me out in a sweat. I didn't see the driver, although I got the impression it was a man. There's a sudden flashback to the day of my escape. I last saw that car, or maybe just a similar one, on the drive of my prison.

Jimmy's watching me, and when I shiver, he pulls me close again.

"I don't know if you're cold or just a bit freaked still, lass, but either way, a hug won't do any harm." His arms stay round me until Mark pulls over in the car a few minutes later.

35

"Get in." My brother-in-law seems furious, but I'm not sure if I'm the object of his fury. Now I'm in the relative safety, dryness and warmth of the car, tiredness washes over me in a tidal wave, and I want to curl up and go to sleep. Jimmy follows me into the back seat.

"Jess isn't feeling well. She had a bit of a shock, and seems to have lost Karen." His voice is dry, but he's resting his arm around my shoulders, and I'm enjoying the novel sensation of feeling protected and safe. I'm now too exhausted to care what's happened to Karen, but apparently Mark isn't.

"We'd better go and get her. Much as she's been a pain this evening, I'm still responsible for her while she's living in the Abbey. Maybe not legally, but morally. She should at least be offered the choice of a lift home." Mark releases the handbrake and sets off in pursuit of Karen.

We catch up with her at the edge of the village. She's looking around, and seems annoyed. Mark pulls the car over, and shouts to her.

"Hey, Karen! Are you looking for Jess?"

"Yeah, she got lost."

I shake my head. I don't think she's spotted me yet.

"What are you planning to do about it?" asks Mark.

"I dunno. Suppose I ought to go back and look for her really." Her sullen tone sets my teeth on edge.

"Don't bother, Karen. I've got her in the car. Are you coming back to the Abbey as well? I think enough is enough, and the rain is getting heavier by the minute. You're drenched. Come back and get dry." He sounds almost as tired as I feel, and it dawns on me that his sense of responsibility is causing him a lot of stress.

Karen hesitates. I know her well enough by now to sense she's about to say something rude, so pull myself together enough to call through the window.

"Come on, Kaz. Just get in. Let's get back, okay?"

She pouts, but opens the passenger door, and gets in next to Mark.

The car's occupants are silent for about two minutes. Then

the row erupts between Karen and Mark. After all I've been through this evening, I don't want to listen. I bury my head against Jimmy's chest, and cover my other ear with my hand. Jimmy hugs me tight, and the sound of arguing fades into insignificance.

Chapter Seven

Mel

I'm lying on the bed feeding Emma when Mark returns from his rescue mission. I've been trying not to worry, but ever since Jess walked out of the door over an hour ago, my shoulders have been horribly tense and my stomach filled with the flapping wings of vampire bats. Mark's expression is guarded when he walks in, and he seems reluctant to discuss the issues.

"How's the feed going?"

"Fine. Did you get them both?"

"Eventually, yes."

"Are they both okay?" This is worse than getting blood from a toddler. "Mark. Talk to me. What's happened?"

He sits on the edge of the bed, angled so I can just see his face. His shoulders are rigid.

"Jimmy gave pretty good directions as soon as he spotted Jess. She'd had a bit of a wobble, and lost Karen who was walking ahead. He seems to have calmed her down, and she was a bit pale when I picked her up, but otherwise okay. So then we went to find Karen. We had a huge row in the car on the way back." He relapses into silence, and after a minute stands up and starts pacing round the room, stopping to tidy the dressing table on his way round. He always tidies, but when he's angry, he gets obsessive about bottles facing the same way. He's now silently rearranging all my toiletries bottles. As he adjusts the orientation of my perfume, I lose patience.

"For God's sake, Mark. What was the row about?"

"Oh, just stuff." He's still fiddling with bottles, but he turns his head and glances at me. Perhaps he sees some of my frustration, because he drags himself away from the now perfectly-aligned toiletries, and sits back down on the bed. "I told her off for not waiting for Jess, and she called me out for interfering. She said I was wrapping Jess in cotton wool, and it would be my fault if she ran away from us."

"What? Is Jess thinking about running away?"

"I don't think so. I hope not. You might need to go and talk to her though. Karen was just goading me."

"You seem very goaded."

"It wasn't just that. I saw something before I reached Jess and Jimmy. Something that reminded me why I came here."

"That day you arrived, Dominic said you'd escaped from a bad situation, but whenever I was about to ask we seemed to get distracted, and you never answered. Was that deliberate?" Emma finishes suckling, so I sit up and put her over my shoulder. I rest a tentative hand on Mark's back, and can feel the tension there.

"Dominic was right. And yes, I haven't wanted to tell you, but I think I should now. Without realising the implications, I did a perfectly legal job for a gang boss in Macclesfield. He sent his heavy mob to recruit me to do some more dodgy stuff, and I resisted. I don't know how I escaped, but I got to my car and drove to the first place I could think of. As you may remember, I'd installed some CCTV and listening devices around the Abbey a short time before, and recalled seeing a very pretty girl there. Although I have to admit, that wasn't the key factor in my decision to join The Brotherhood."

"What dodgy things did they want you to do?" I smile at the reference to the pretty girl. I assume he means me, even if I would argue with the description.

"It's not funny, Mel. They wanted me to destroy some police-owned CCTV. I wasn't going to do it, at any cost. They tried to convince me that because I'd worked for them before, that already made me complicit in their crimes. Frankly, I didn't want to risk going to the police, but that didn't mean I was prepared to work for them."

"I wasn't smiling at your situation. I agree that's grim,

although you could speak to Greg about it. I bet they'd offer you some protection."

"Maybe. Saying it aloud sounds quite pathetic really, but to be honest, they scared me shitless."

"Who was it you saw, and where?" I ask. The thought of Mark in danger isn't something I want to have to deal with, but it's better to know the facts.

"Just one of the heavies." A shutter comes down, and Mark reaches over and takes Emma from me. "Come on, I can wind her. Just drape that muslin over my shoulder will you? Thanks. Right. Go and talk to your sister."

I breathe a heavy sigh and stand up. He's deflecting again, but at least he's told me the basics.

"Okay, if you think it will help."

"It has to be done. Oh, and Mel," he calls me back as I'm half way out of the door. "Not a word about my past to anyone."

I raise my eyebrows.

"Seriously, not a soul."

I nod assent, and head down the corridor to find Jess. Checking my watch – a new addition since Brotherhood days – I see it's nearly ten o'clock. Hoping that my sister hasn't gone to sleep, I knock tentatively on her bedroom door.

"Come in," calls Tina. "Oh, hi, Mel. We never did sort out that movie did we?" I give her an apologetic smile from the doorway.

"Another time. The evening didn't quite go to plan – for any of us."

Jess is curled up on her side on the bed, with her back to me and Tina.

"You two need to talk, don't you?" says Tina. "I'll go down and get myself a hot chocolate and sit in the common room for a bit. Come and find me when you're done, Mel."

I smile inwardly. Tina has blossomed over the last few weeks, and has developed an empathy with people that she lacked when her thoughts were turned towards her own sorrows and difficulties. Now safe from the attentions of any predators, she's free to grow into the sort of person that lay hidden for so many years. I know she's still scarred. It shows in her reluctance to leave the Abbey, and her many insecurities, but she's a lot happier than she used to be.

With Tina gone, I stare at my sister's forbidding back for a long moment.

"What happened out there?" It seems easier to get straight to the point.

"I freaked out. I'm pathetic." She sits up on the bed and faces me, her rigid posture indicating her distress. "It turns out I can't even handle a walk in the countryside." She sounds bitter and close to tears.

Her body language is telling me not to come too near. For the moment, I suppress the urge to ignore it and give her the hug she probably needs. I sit down on Tina's bed, keeping a small but significant distance between us.

"You were out at twilight with a girl who isn't exactly trustworthy, and who left you to cope by yourself on a quiet country lane in the middle of nowhere. Sorry, Jess, but I don't think that was a safe place to start. If you're going to face the lions, you need to begin by watching a trained expert, before building up gradually."

"So who are you suggesting as the expert? Wait. Don't tell me… I should be going out with you."

I shudder, but whether it's at the sarcasm, or the thought of me walking down country lanes with just my sister for protection, I'm not quite sure. I take a deep breath and try to keep calm.

"I'm not ready for it either yet, but at least I didn't barge out with no defences in place."

"Neither did I. I had that phone. And it seems like you didn't trust me anyway, as you set Jimmy to follow me." Her voice softens a fraction as she says his name. I hope she's found someone she likes and respects. Jimmy's a great guy.

"It wasn't you that I didn't trust. And quite rightly, as it turned out. Look, we're trying to help you, okay?"

Jess slumps her shoulders and leans back against the wall, bringing her knees to her chest and hugging them.

"Yeah, I know," she says. "I am grateful, even if I don't

41

sound like it. I'm pissed off with Karen, that's all."

"Yeah, me too." I hope my wry grin reassures her that I'm on her side. "Look, next time you want to go out…"

"There won't be a next time. This might be a bigger prison that I was in before. I'm being treated pretty well here, and most people are nice. But I'm trapped here. Even if it's me that's locking me in. I can't bloody escape. And that pisses me off as well."

Her face is red now, infused with anger and self-hatred. Or that's how it seems. I don't think I'm helping any more. Maybe, as she seems to like Jimmy, he might be able to help her. He's been through a lot too.

Chapter Eight

Jess

As soon as Mel's out of the room, I lie face down on the bed and let the tears flow. I wasn't lying when I told her about feeling like I'm in prison, but maybe it was a bit bitchy. She's given me a home. It's not her fault I'm a bloody wreck. Christ, listen to me. I never used to swear. He wouldn't have stood for it, for one thing. No one else round here does it either. It's only Karen. She's infected me with her crappy views on life. Scummy cow. I can't believe I fell for all that 'best friend' shit either. She was just using me. God knows what for. Maybe she didn't think she'd be allowed out by herself. From the row on the way back here, I reckon Mark would be pleased to see the back of her. Be interesting to see what he does.

I don't really hate it here. I just feel a bit shut in. Even more so now, after what I saw tonight. What did I see? A car speeding past, that's all. Not necessarily the same car that was on the drive. And it totally messed with my head. Was it Him? If so, did He see me? Does He know where I am? I can't risk Him seeing me here. If He knows I'm here, He'll find a way of taking me back, and I can't face that.

As I told Mel, apart from Karen, everyone I've met seems pretty nice. Besides, I've got a bed to myself, with no visitors at night or at any other time. Nobody brings me companions and then turns them into drug addicts in front of my eyes.

He never gave me drugs, though. I don't know why. He'd inject Kylie in front of me, making me watch. But then He'd take the stuff away. Then He'd come back...

"You don't deserve them, Jessica. You've been a bad girl. Kylie pleases me at night. She does what I want without a

battle. You're a stubborn little madam. You make me force you. It's so much easier now I have Kylie to indulge me."

I crouched in my corner, watching as Kylie stroked his thigh. Her eyes looked glazed. Whatever He injected had made her brain go all fuzzy. She'd told me it was easier that way.

He pulls his trousers down. I shut my eyes. I've seen it all before. He's made me watch so often, but I think He's enjoying it too much tonight to care what I'm doing.

I pull my thoughts away. I don't have to watch that anymore. And Kylie's dead. If I'd stayed, He would have gone back to using me for sex. Or maybe He would have taken in someone else. He seemed to get bored with me after a couple of years.

The door opens. I turn my face to see who it is. I can't handle another argument, but it's just Tina. Calm, sweet, undemanding Tina.

"How are you doing?" she asks, sitting down in the exact spot Mel vacated a short time ago.

"Don't know. Crap really."

Tina is the easiest to talk to out of all of them. For some reason, I don't feel defensive with her. I know she's been through hell too, and she doesn't judge. Even though I've heard some of Mel's experiences (second–hand, because she'd never tell me herself), somehow, I can't relax with her in the same way. Perhaps I've never forgiven her for abandoning me when I was ten. If she hadn't gone out that evening…

"Do you want to talk about it?"

I turn and face her, resting my head on my crooked elbow. I push away thoughts of my sister's ancient betrayal.

"Maybe. Yeah. Karen's a shit."

"Well, she's never been my idea of a good friend, but different people… I don't know… I guess she must have something going for her," Tina says doubtfully.

"Yeah. She seemed kind of daring and rebellious, and it suited my mood for a few days."

"I know." Tina gives me that sweet smile, and a shot of

guilt flows through me.

"I've been a cow, haven't I?" I say to her.

"It's fine. You need time to work things out. It's no problem. We're friends. I'm not going to hate you for spending time with other people. It wouldn't do either of us any good. Anyway, I've got other friends as well. Why shouldn't you have?"

"You're too nice. I still shouldn't have gone and left you out of stuff."

"You didn't leave me out – you did invite me. If I'd been the sort of friend I'd like to be, I'd have been brave enough to come with you. But I'm such a wimp."

"You and me both. I'm not going anywhere any more. You'll have to put up with me hanging around here."

Tina looks at her watch. I think I've embarrassed her. "Have you any idea what time it is?"

"No, but I'm sure you're going to tell me." I give her a grin, trying not to offend her.

"It's gone eleven. Long past time to be asleep."

Ten minutes later, we're both in nightclothes, and tucked up under our comfortable duvets. I think it will take me ages to get to sleep, but I drop off almost instantly.

I'm thirteen. I've just finished my first period. A naked man appears before me. Naked except for the mask on his face, covering all but his mouth and eyes. It's night time, and he turns on the torch on the floor, giving the dank cellar a warm glow; a refreshing change from the darkness of the last three years.

"So, you're a young woman now. Time to move on to the next phase," He says, and climbs onto the mattress where I'm lying shivering, as the cold seeps up from the concrete floor. I try to curl into a ball, but He forcibly straightens me, his hand brushing against my small breasts. Once I'm lying flat, He lies on top of me. I scream, but He puts his mouth against mine, and muffles the scream. I thrash my arms about, connecting with his bare back, and He pins me to the bed with his body. His hand covers my mouth, and He pulls back slightly.

45

"Shut up, you little slut. You've been asking me to do this for weeks, begging me with your eyes to take you and teach you the wonders of adulthood. I had to wait, though. I couldn't take a child. We've both had to make do with just touching. But I've seen the blood. I know you've spent hours sitting on the bucket, waiting for the bleeding to stop because you had nothing to clean it up with. It's stopped now, so I'm going to give you what you want."

I try to scream again, desperately hoping to make a sound, to scare Him away.

"Jess, wake up! Are you okay? You were crying out, but kind of whimpering." Tina is sitting on the edge of my bed, with her hands resting on my shoulders. "You were having a nightmare, I think."

"More like a flashback. But from a long time ago." I shiver, and sit up. "Are you okay if we turn the light on?"

Tina stands up and goes towards the door where the light switch is located. The room is filled with soft light. I take some deep breaths. It's going to take me a long time to get over the events of tonight.

Chapter Nine

Mel

It's an important day today. Our first lady is coming to us for refuge. We got a call last night from the charity we've affiliated with, and they asked if they can send her to us. They've kept her overnight, but she's probably on the way now as it's gone nine. I could hardly eat breakfast, I was so excited. It's ridiculous really, but this means so much to me. The irony isn't lost on me either. Dominic brought me here and abused me; now he's gone, I'm turning his home into a refuge for victims of domestic abuse.

We've had to go through lots of inspections in the two months since I made the decision. It's taken a while to get all the appropriate measures in place, and bring the Abbey up to acceptable standards, but that's fine.

It's our home too now, and it's good to have mod cons. But I think what the authorities liked most was the security around the place. All guards have been properly vetted, but there are also strict rules. They're not allowed into the special section designated for the refuge guests. Actually, no men are allowed in there at all. It's lockable, and only myself, Brie, and the guests will have keys. We've given them half the upper floor of the Abbey, which includes two common rooms, a newly-installed kitchen, and eight en-suite bedrooms.

The lady coming to us today, Alison, is in her forties, I believe, and is bringing a teenage daughter. The refuge that called last night is based near Brighton, far too close to where they've escaped from, so they're coming here in a car. Hopefully her husband will never find them here.

I've spent the morning going through the paperwork from the charity, and preparing adjacent rooms for them. The rooms are on the same corridor as Jess and Tina's room – at the back of the Abbey – and used to belong to one of the group heads. My sister and friend were delighted to move into the new wing, with all its safety measures and modern facilities. The new bedrooms are now equipped with single beds, a wardrobe, drawers, and some pretty curtains scattered with daffodils. I look around the room designated for Alison. It's as spotless as I could manage. Cleaning isn't my strong point, but Jess offered to play with Emma after her feed, to give me time and space to make a nice welcome for our new occupants.

"Mel?" Brie disturbs my reverie by shouting.

"Hello. Where are you?" I ask.

"I'm here," she says, popping her head around the door. "Your visitors have arrived. I thought you might want to welcome them in person. They're in the hall."

I look at my watch as I follow Brie to the stairs. "They must have started early. It's only eleven-thirty, and that's a long journey."

As we reach the hall, I see a tall thin lady with a badly-cut bob, and a fading bruise on her right cheek. Standing slightly behind her is a young girl in her early teens, wearing baggy jeans, a loose t-shirt, and a terrified expression.

"Hi. I'm Mel. I run the refuge side of the Abbey." I smile at my newbies and hold out a hand to the older lady. "You must be Alison, is that right? And I'm sorry, I was never told your daughter's name?"

Alison takes a deep breath, before giving me a rather limp handshake. The girl moves another step behind her mum.

"This is Dawn. She's fourteen."

"Hi Dawn. Nice to meet you." I make no attempt at physical contact. She looks ready to run. "You've made good time; I wasn't expecting you for another hour or so. Delighted you're here so soon though," I add, in case they worry they're not welcome.

A sturdy woman of around fifty to sixty comes in, carrying a brown holdall and three carrier bags that look to be filled with clothes. Alison follows my gaze.

"We didn't have much time to get out. My husband went out to the off-licence with his brother, and we grabbed all we could and hid it. Then we had to wait until they'd drunk themselves into a stupor."

"When they were asleep we let ourselves out and ran." Dawn speaks for the first time. Her voice holds much of the same defiance I've noticed from Jess and Tina, and I resolve to help her as much as I can. Something about the tone tells me she's suffered the sort of abuse no fourteen-year-old should know about.

"You're safe now, both of you. You can make your home with us for as long as you want." I turn to the older woman and smile warmly. "Did you drive them all this way?"

"Aye, lass." Her accent is even thicker than Jimmy's. He emerges from the office grinning, although he stays by the office door. The new guests look a little alarmed.

"That's not an accent I expected to hear from Brighton."

"I've lived there only about a year. Before that I'd been in Glasgow for all my life." She grimaces. "But escape is sometimes a necessity, and the further away the better. I now drive my ladies to their new homes. I like to help others if I can."

This is one strong-minded survivor. She impresses me hugely, but she's obviously moved on by becoming a saviour to others in the same situation. I'm humbled, and aspire to do the same, but I don't think I'm there yet. I notice Jimmy has slipped away again, and my visitors have relaxed a fraction.

"Brie, please could you take our lovely driver here for a coffee, and make sure she gets some lunch and a chance to rest before heading back?" I turn to Alison and Dawn. "Would you like to come with me and I'll show you to your rooms? Then you can freshen up a bit before lunch." I take the holdall and carrier bags from the driver.

The newcomers follow me upstairs and I lead them to the room I've allocated for Dawn.

"You said you left in a hurry. Please let me know if you need anything. Toiletries, clothes, whatever. We're here to help."

Dawn takes the holdall from me, sits on the bed, and starts rummaging through the contents. "There's hardly any clothes here, Mum. This is ridiculous. What are we supposed to wear?"

Seeing Alison at a loss for our words, I intercede gently. "We've got quite a lot of adult clothes in our store cupboards, Dawn, but you might need to do a bit of online shopping. In a moment, I'll introduce you to my sister, Jess, and our friend, Tina. They've offered to help you both settle in. Jess is only nineteen, and has become quite adept at online shopping."

"I know it's a refuge, but how do we pay our way?" says Alison. "I don't want to accept charity."

"Do you want to sit down, Alison, and I'll explain a bit about the history and aims here?" I indicate the empty bed, and, closing the door, sit myself on the armchair in the corner of the room. With the door shut, I can see them both properly, and it seems like a good time to get their questions answered before they meet anyone else.

I explain briefly about the existence of The Brotherhood, and how I came to be here, but I don't go into details. I'd spent many hours discussing with Mark, Jimmy, Tina and Brie exactly how much our new residents should be told, and we'd finally agreed that it would be best for them to know why so many people live here. Brie had convinced me of the importance of sharing my own history of abuse, albeit in a very edited form.

"Sorry love," she'd said, obviously responding to the distress on my face. "You can't expect women who've been in that situation to trust someone as young as yourself unless you explain why you're doing this. And they need to trust you."

So, here I am, sharing the history of me and The Brotherhood with this anxious pair: the downtrodden mum and her terrified daughter, embarking on a new chapter in their lives, away from everyone and everything they've ever known.

My heart tugs in sympathy for them. I know how hard this is.

Chapter Ten

Jess

I'm reading the fourth *Harry Potter* book when there's a knock on the bedroom door. I've fallen totally in love with this world of wizards and witches. By drawing parallels with my life and Harry's, and between Hogwarts and the Abbey, it seems to make life more bearable. I drag myself reluctantly back to reality as Mel pops her head around the door. I've barely been outside since my disastrous expedition with Karen two weeks ago.

"Jess, I've brought our new residents to meet you. Do you want to come out here?" I see her eyes take in the mess of clothes and books on the floor. She raises her eyebrows.

"Yes, I'll, er, tidy this up later. Sorry, it seems to have got into a bit of a mess." Knowing that raised eyebrows and the occasional nag are the worst punishment I'll get, this seems to grant me the permission to be messy that I never had when I was with HIM. Not tidying up is a symbol to me that I'm safe, and although Tina keeps her half of the room spotless, mine is generally littered with everything I've used for the last few days. I jump up and follow my sister out of the room.

Standing in the hall are a woman and a girl. They both look bloody terrified, and I try to bury my own fears of meeting new people. My heart is racing and mouth is dry, but they don't need to know that. Something about the young girl particularly draws my sympathy.

"This is Alison and her daughter, Dawn," says Mel.

"Hi, I'm Jess. My friend Tina is helping out in the kitchens this morning. She wanted to stay and meet you, but the chef is off with a bad back, so quite a few of us have had to muck in."

"Wow, you've got a chef?" says Dawn.

"Apparently, the food used to be cooked by residents, taking it in turns, but some of them were so bad at it that when my brother-in-law took over the running of the Abbey, he managed to find funds for a visiting chef. It was just before I started, but the food here is usually pretty good. I'm hoping he'll be better soon."

"Mum used to be a sous-chef at a hotel before she met Dad." Dawn's face darkens.

Mel turns to Alison. "You asked earlier what you could do to pay your way. If you'd like to, any help in the kitchen will be most welcome. When Hugo's off, we really struggle, and even when he's here, he's been asking for some help from someone who knows their way around a kitchen."

"That would be good, thanks. What's Hugo like, though? I've had enough of men for the moment."

"Small, French, and gay. He's a sweetheart. Honestly, you'll love him."

"Do you want me to start now?"

"Goodness, not today. Take some time to explore, and find your feet. You must be exhausted after all that's happened, and then the long journey on top. Jess will help you with anything you need and bring you down for lunch. Unless you'd rather eat in your room? We can accommodate that for today if you prefer?"

I watch them, particularly the girl. They seem torn between wanting to conform and fear of meeting everyone.

"Why don't I take Alison and Dawn along to the common room up here, and we can have lunch there? Tina can join us, and maybe you and Mark and Emma if you're free. It's a lot less daunting meeting a few people than the whole Abbey all at once." I smile at Dawn, who is nodding at the idea. "Mel, why don't you go and rest for a bit before lunch? Does Emma need a feed?"

"Mark said he'd call me when she wakes up, but it's getting pretty close on three hours since her last one, so if you're all okay, I'll head down and sort her out. Thanks." Mel smiles round at all of us and heads off to feed her daughter.

"Who's Emma?" says Dawn. Her shoulders relax as Mel leaves the room. I'm intrigued as to why she'd find Mel scary, but now's not the time to find out.

"Emma's my niece. She's nearly three months old now. She's beautiful."

Dawn asks me several questions about having a baby niece as we wander along to the common room. I do my best to answer, but as time spent with Emma involves mostly changing her nappy, burping her, and (if I'm lucky) singing lullabies, there's not much I can tell her. I'm pleased Dawn is interested, though. I was worried about her when she came in. Alison walks behind us until we get to the common room door. I walk in first, followed by Dawn. Alison is standing on the threshold, as white as washing powder. Tears stream down her cheeks. I gesture to Dawn to sit down, and go to her mother's side.

"Hey, what's the matter? Won't you come in and sit down? I'm worried you'll faint, you've gone really pale."

But instead of crossing the threshold, she sits on the floor against the wall opposite the common room door.

Why did I send Mel away? I need her to handle this. I might be okay for sorting out the daughter, but the mum is freaking me out. I take a deep breath and try again, although at least she's on the floor now, so can't fall.

"What's the problem?"

"The wallpaper is the same as we have in the bedroom at home. The room where…" She stops and looks pointedly at Dawn, before shaking her head and refusing to continue.

I'm really confused now, but I don't know what to do.

Dawn stands up from her seat opposite the door, and comes over. "What's up, Mum?"

Alison shakes her head again, and looks mulish.

"Something about wallpaper apparently," I say. The girl pops her head inside the common room again.

"Oh yeah. It's the same as Mum's bedroom at home. Dad chose it. I remember him throwing a wobbly 'cos Mum wanted flowery stuff, and he insisted on these beige and purple stripes." She goes quiet for a moment. "To be honest, he came home one day to find the paper of Mum's choice – daffodils and bluebells – already on the walls. I was studying in my room, but I heard him yelling, and when I got up the courage to go in, the wallpaper was all torn and in fragments on the floor. Mum was sitting on the floor in tears with a bruise coming up under her eye."

"Dawn! You don't have to tell people everything." Alison looks up, a mixture of fury and humiliation on her face. That I understand.

I put my hand on the girl's shoulder. "It's hard having people know what you've been through. Some things you want to share, and some things your mum will want kept hidden. God knows, I've got lots of things I'm not ready to share yet, but if it helps you both to know, I should probably tell you." I lower my hand and turn my head to look out of the window. I freeze.

Like all the upstairs windows along the front of the Abbey, the window is a narrow, arched pane of glass. It looks out on to the drive, the hedge, and into the field beyond. Lurking near the hedge is a man – a man whose thin shape and upright posture are horribly familiar, even though I don't know his face. He's in shadow, so I can't see his face anyway. What's he doing here?

Does He know where I am? It seems probable now.

"Jess, are you alright?" Dawn's hand is at my elbow, and the need for calm pulls me back from the brink of utter panic. I force myself to breathe; shadows play at the edge of my vision.

"I need to speak to my brother-in-law. There's another common room around the corner. It's decorated differently." I try to prevent any dry sarcasm from creeping into my tone, but after what I've just seen, wallpaper seems bloody trivial. "Come on, let's go round there. I'll get you comfortable in the old Franciscan common room, and then I'll get Mark. Maybe Brie can come and sit with you for a bit."

I head along the corridor, forcing myself to check they're following. I really want to speak to Jimmy, but Mark needs to know first if someone is trespassing, particularly given who I think it is.

Fortunately, Tina is coming from the kitchens, and meets us at the top of the stairs, just inside the door to the closed-off section. I do the introductions. I feel a bit guilty; they've only just arrived, and are already being passed from person to person. But Tina is better placed than me to look after them. She's been here longer than I have, and is more stable.

I leave them in Tina's care, after she promises to accompany them to the Franciscan lounge (as it's now supposed to be known). I can see them relaxing in her company. Both Dawn and Alison seem to find her gentleness reassuring. I don't blame them. So do I.

Turning and heading to the stairs, I make my way down to Mark's office. I knock. Sometimes Mark is interviewing important people, and while he tries not to be angry if I interrupt, there's an impatient expression that appears on his face. I prefer to avoid it if possible.

"Come in." He's alone, working on the laptop when I enter. "Are you alright, Jess? I thought you were with our new residents?"

"I passed them on to Tina. I had to see you." At a gesture from Mark I sit in the comfy chair opposite him. "There was a man in the hedge. He looked familiar."

"From here?" My brother-in-law looks confused and a look of fear crosses his face. "Can you describe him?"

"Tall and thin. Very upright. Other than that, no. He dresses formally, though. Suit, waistcoat and tie."

Mark's face seems to relax, although I don't know why. My heart's racing, and having had a few more minutes to think about it hasn't helped my state of panic.

"Mark, I think it's him. It's the right shape, and he used to wear that sort of thing when he'd been out. He'd come back all smart and smarmy. What's he doing here? Do you think he knows I'm here?"

To give him credit, my brother-in-law doesn't seem to have realised until now who I meant. His expression grows concerned.

"Blimey, Jess. I'll get someone to see him off the premises." He picks up the mobile phone on his desk and presses some buttons. "Derek? Hi. Oh good. You're sure he's gone? Great. Thanks, mate." He puts the phone on his desk. "Derek's one of the security guards. He's just escorted a man off the premises. It sounds like he answered your description."

"Your guard wouldn't have told him anything, would he?"

"Thanks to Mel's domestic abuse ladies, we've trained all the guards to keep all information about the residents strictly confidential. They've had to sign Non-Disclosure Agreements, and they've all had security checks themselves. Derek's a good guy. He'll keep an eye out to make sure your abductor doesn't return."

"Thanks." My thoughts turn to tomorrow. "I won't be going outside again, ever."

"I can see why you wouldn't want to be seen, but maybe we can do something to help. Could we get you a wig or something?"

I roll my eyes. He does try. But seriously? A wig?

"I think he would recognise me whatever colour my hair looks. Anyway, I've chopped most of it off since I left, but I still don't think I'd be safe. I don't mind staying in. I didn't leave a cellar for nine years. At least I have the run of the house here." I can't keep the bitterness from my voice. It's not Mark's fault. He's doing everything he can, but I feel so damn shut in. And now I can't even go outside and enjoy the sunshine. I've not been outside for any long periods, but I spent short times in the garden until that awful evening out with Karen, when I thought I saw the car.

The car! Did He see me that night? Has He tracked me down? Will I ever be safe again?

Chapter Eleven

Mel

My new guests are settling in well. Alison has been running the kitchen for the last three days, and Dawn is hanging out with Tina and Jess, although Jess is adamant about not leaving the house. Since Monday, she's even refused to go into the grassy quad.

I finish giving Emma her mid-morning feed and settle her down for a nap. I'm expecting a visitor shortly. Greg phoned yesterday and arranged to call round this morning. I raid Mark's cupboard for chocolate digestives and take them along to the lounge area that used to be the Benedictine common room. This has been assigned as the room to take visitors, and consequently has a newly-installed sink, a kettle and a hospitality tray – but biscuits have to be kept locked away. The committee agreed that biscuits should be available for afternoon tea, but to keep costs down, they're usually bourbons or budget chocolate chip cookies. No one complains. When Dominic was in charge, biscuits were definitely not allowed.

When I get to the room, it's hot and stuffy. It faces South East, to the back of the Abbey, and is being blasted by the morning sun. I open all the windows.

Brie pops her head around the door. "Mel, Greg's here." She leaves as soon as she's ushered him into the room.

"Hi Mel." He sits in the beige fabric armchair near the coffee table and helps himself to a biscuit, while I make tea. "Do you mind if we have the windows shut? I don't want to be overheard."

I swallow hard and take a deep breath. Given my history, that could be ominous.

"Yes, sure. I'll just finish doing this, or you can shut them if you want." My voice sounds gruff, and the ever-observant Greg can't fail to notice. He closes the windows himself, and waits until I'm seated before speaking.

"It's nothing for you to worry about, Mel. Or not in that sense. Dominic's death is in the past, and the case is closed. No, the reason I'm here is… Do you remember when we first met?"

"Yes of course. It was in the Infirmary; you were there for a trial, and I… had concussion."

"Yes. I don't think I ever asked why you were there – probably very rude of me. I'm sorry."

"No need to apologise." I take a sip of sweet tea. I don't usually have sugar, but with Greg asking for closed windows, I suddenly felt the need. "At that time, it was usually better not to ask questions. I never really found out why you were pretending to be a solicitor?"

"It seemed appropriate to conceal my real identity. I was investigating the man we knew then as Len Harper. I don't think I'd have been allowed on the trial if I'd admitted to being a Detective Inspector."

"No. So, you were going to tell me something?"

"Do you remember Frank?"

"Yeah, of course. He was the one who got really ill. Didn't they cart him off to intensive care somewhere?"

"Yes, he ended up at Macclesfield District General, where he remained until last week." Something in Greg's face tells me Frank didn't recover.

"Oh my God, is he…?"

"Yes. Sorry to tell you, but Frank died as a direct result of the events of last autumn. He had the autopsy two days ago, and we got the results yesterday. This is now a murder investigation."

Thoughts race round my head, falling over themselves in trying to grab my attention. I eventually voice the first thing to make its way from my brain to my mouth.

"Who do you think did it?"

Greg smiles gently. "I've got a number of theories, but

what I need to do today is collect the trial documentation. Do you think we'd be allowed into the Infirmary, or will I have to go away and mess about with getting warrants? It's changed hands, hasn't it?"

"We lease it to a private healthcare company, but I'm sure they'd let us have a look. Do you want to finish your tea, and then we can head over?"

He agrees, and we make small talk about the weather for a few minutes.

A short time later, we're at the reception desk of the Infirmary and Greg asks to see the manager.

"What for?" says the skinny middle-aged woman behind the desk. Greg flashes his badge at her.

"I just need to ask a few questions. Nothing to worry about. Could you give him or her a call please?"

She reluctantly picks up the phone, and a few moments later we're greeted by a woman in her late thirties, or maybe a little older.

"Hello. I'm Sophie. I manage this place now. How can I help?" She glances at me, turns towards Greg, and then looks back at me properly. "Isn't it your husband that runs the Abbey? I've seen photos of you in his office."

"Yes, sort of. He heads the committee that runs it. It's not a dictatorship." I'm very protective of Mark. The last thing I want is for people to think he's another Dominic. Apart from anything else, the Abbey is now totally secular. Residents are free to attend the local parish church if they want, but the chapel is now kept for anyone who wants to pray privately. I realise my attention has wandered, and rein it in. Greg is explaining his mission.

"… if you have any paperwork left from the trials?"

"All documents and files were taken over to the Abbey when we signed the lease. It wasn't our responsibility, and frankly, we wanted nothing to do with it. Trials are not our remit."

I see Greg wince at the word *frankly*; a poor choice of words, but this lady clearly has no way of knowing that a man named Frank had died as a result of a trial here.

59

"Well, thank you," says Greg. "We'd better head back to the Abbey and see what we can find."

I smile and wave to Sophie, and Greg and I leave. Once we're out of earshot, I turn to him.

"Why weren't all the documents taken away by the police when Frank got ill?"

"I was in a delicate position, and couldn't reveal what I knew. The Infirmary authorities played down the whole situation, telling the trial company that Frank's symptoms were caused by a medication error. From the lack of reaction, they obviously believed it." Greg rubs his nose, and flashes a wry grin in my direction. "I joined The Brotherhood myself as soon as the trial was closed down, falsely citing a marriage breakdown as my need to get away. I hoped to get my hands on the documentation after leaving the Infirmary, but Dominic kept an eye on me. I don't think he ever trusted me. Then after... er... his death, there were too many other things to sort out. Frank slipped to the bottom of the pile until he died."

By now, we're back on Abbey premises, so I lead Greg to Mark's office.

"I guess Mark's most likely to know where we'll find everything." I knock on the door in case Mark's in a meeting. He usually keeps the door open when he's free.

"Come in," he calls. "Oh. It's you. Everything alright?"

"Hope we're not interrupting anything?" Greg looks round the otherwise empty office. Mark's computer is off, and his phone is on the desk. The desk drawer is slightly open. Mark looks pale, and his voice is a bit too casual.

"No. No, everything's fine. What can I do for you?" He avoids my gaze, and I say nothing. Has he seen one of those people again?

Greg explains his mission to Mark.

"How come I've never heard about this?" Mark finally looks at me, but with so much accusation in his gaze, I'd have preferred him not to bother. "You never mentioned anyone called Frank, or a trial that went wrong."

"I didn't see you between that time and Emma's birth. A

lot happened in between, and we had other things to discuss. By then it didn't really seem important. Anyway, do you know where those documents would be?" I struggle to keep emotion from my voice. I don't want to cry, but Mark's tone hurts, and it's been a stressful morning.

"They're all in the room next door to Paul Griffiths. It seemed appropriate somehow, as he's the only one left from the medical staff, but I'm sure he had nothing to do with this trial thing. He's always been a very straightforward, decent chap. I can't imagine him having anything to do with dodgy stuff. Let me take you up, Greg." He comes round the desk and puts a hand on my shoulder. "Why don't you go up and have a lie down for a bit? You had a disturbed night with Em feeding, and she'll be ready for another one soon. Get a break while you can."

Soothed by his tone and action, I leave them to it, and manage to rest for almost ten minutes before Emma starts crying for her next feed. This mother business is exhausting. Wonderful, but exhausting.

An hour later, my daughter has been fed, burped and handed over to Auntie Brie for playtime. Brie loves to spend time with Emma, and it gives me time to get things done. On this occasion, I grab a quick sandwich from Alison in the kitchen, and head up to the room Mark described.

The door is unlocked. When I first go in, I just see an empty room. The lurid green curtains over the narrow window indicate it could one day be used as a small bedroom, but there's no furniture in it.

Assessing it for future use, I notice sliding doors on the wall opposite the window. It would need carpet, and those curtains will have to go. Wondering about hanging space, I slide open the cupboard door. There are a few shelves, and some dusty curtains shroud much of the bottom shelf. I pull them aside to get a better look, hoping they might be prettier than the current window dressings. Hidden underneath are two boxes.

Why were these hidden? Was it deliberate? And who

covered them up?

I wipe a finger along the upper shelves. They're all dusty, so the boxes that Greg took must have been on the floor outside the cupboard. A closer inspection of the hardwood floor shows a faint dust line around where the boxes had been. I pull the hidden boxes out of the cupboard and place them on the floor at the edge. Kneeling next to them, I open the first box.

Inside are several black ring binders and a couple of A4 notebooks. I'm about to inspect them, when the phone in my pocket rings.

"Mel, can you come down please? Emma's being sick and has a temperature."

Chapter Twelve

Jess

My eyes jerk open. I'm drenched in sweat. My heart's pounding hard enough to wake the whole Abbey.

I sit up and try to put the nightmare behind me. It's just a long line of memories returning to haunt my nights, as fear of my abductor haunts my days. A faint light streams through the curtains. I'm properly awake now, but my pulse is still racing. I try to slow down my breathing, knowing from experience that this will help to calm me. Tina's still asleep, snoring gently. She's been so much happier lately. Safety suits her. Despite trying not to get close to anyone, I seem to have failed spectacularly with certain people. Tina has become my best friend, and I'm fiercely protective of her.

She stirs and turns over. I hold my breath, not wanting to wake her up. The snores resume, and I breathe again.

Checking the watch on my bedside table, I see it's nearly six. I don't want to turn the light on, but the thought of going back to sleep… It's not happening. I can't return to that cellar again tonight. I've been revisiting the worst days since I saw the man outside. It's only three days ago, but since then the nightmares have been relentless.

I slip out of bed and grab my dressing gown from the armchair where I dumped it last night. It takes me a minute to find my slippers in the dim light. They're further under the bed than I expect, but I don't want to go out of the room without them. The corridors still have wooden floors, and they're cold underfoot. Finally, with dressing gown and slippers on, I collect my book from the bedside table and quietly make my escape from the room without disturbing my friend.

Along the hall is the common room where I first took Alison and Dawn. It's as good a place as any for an early morning read, and I curl up in the armchair and lose myself in the world of Hogwarts, Harry, Hermione and Ron – the only place where I can forget.

A couple of hours later, I'm interrupted by Tina. "Jess, are you okay? I woke up ages ago, and you weren't there."

I rest the book in my lap. "Yeah, I guess. I was awake, and didn't feel like going back to sleep." It's kind of the truth.

"Come down and have some breakfast. Hugo's back, and he and Alison have made some bread. I'm sure I could smell it baking as I came past the stairs."

"I'm not hungry." I pick up my novel again, but Tina comes and takes it out of my hands.

"I don't care," she says, with surprising firmness. I look at her in shock, but she grabs my hand and yanks me out of the chair. "Come on. You're coming down anyway. Even if you only have one slice, you need to eat something. Don't think I've not noticed, Jess. You've not been yourself the last couple of days."

"Fine, I'll come down. You can't force me to eat, though."

Tina pulls me to the door, and doesn't let go of my hand until we're in the dining room. Dawn calls us over to her table, and I follow Jess there. The lack of sleep is beginning to hit me now, and a sluggishness overtakes me. By the time we reach the table, I just want to lie down on the floor and go to sleep. But that's not an option. I take a seat next to Jess and opposite Dawn and Alison. There's a steaming loaf of granary bread on the table, with pats of butter and a jar of strawberry jam. The bread looks and smells lovely, but the heavy rock sitting in my stomach precludes the intake of even fresh bread and jam.

"It's freshly-baked this morning, Jess. Can I persuade you?" asks Alison.

"It looks lovely, but I don't really feel very hungry. I didn't sleep well."

"Please try some. It's my special recipe. I managed to

convince Hugo it would work in bulk, and he'll think I've failed if you don't eat any. Come on. For me."

Alison's wheedling doesn't make me any more hungry, but I haven't the heart to upset her, so I take a slice, with a small scrape of butter. I really can't face the jam. As I take a bite, a flash of memory hits me...

He wakes me up. There's a loaded plate in his hand.

"I picked up a fresh loaf from the baker today, especially for you. After what you did for me last night. I do know it can be difficult for you. You're still young. And I'm well grown. I can imagine it must hurt sometimes. So, I thought you might like a treat today."

I come back to the present with a jerk. I force myself to chew the bread, but it's like chewing cardboard. Not Alison's fault – it smelled beautiful, but He's spoiled the taste of fresh bread for ever.

Five long minutes later, I excuse myself and return to my chair and book upstairs. The window reveals a bright summer's day. Perfect to sit on the lawn and read, but I don't dare to go outside. He's spoilt everything for me – summer, bread, my friends – I hate Him! The common room is empty apart from me, and I wallow in misery.

After a moment of realising I'm too angry to read, I stand up and start pacing around the room. I go to the window, and force myself to glance outside. My breath catches as I see a movement near the trees, but it's just Derek doing his rounds. My eyes scan the room, searching for something I noticed yesterday – Dawn had been cutting out recipes for her mum. Where are the scissors? Unable to find them, I return to my pacing. The lethargy that overtook me in the dining room has been replaced by this restless fury, for all that He's deprived me of. The list is endless, but I start chanting to myself: *Nine years of my life, my innocence, education, spending time with Mum and Dad... Oh God. Mum and Dad. I'll never see them again.*

I sink to the floor, and wrap my arms around my knees, trying to stem the pain – that sharp spike in my chest that's threatening to fill my whole body. I'm never going to see my parents again. How can I bear it? A sob finds its way to my throat and escapes; then another, and another. My whole body is shaking with them by the time the door opens. My eyes are full of bitter, stinging tears and I can barely see who's come in. I dash my hand across my face, trying to brush them away, but it makes the sting even worse.

Arms surround me. I recognise Tina's soft touch, and allow myself to rest my aching head on her thin shoulder.

"Oh, my poor Jess. What are we going to do with you?" she whispers as she strokes my back. The rhythm and her presence begin to soothe me, and the sobs subside.

"Should we fetch Mel, do you think?" I recognise Dawn's voice.

"No, I'm fine. Don't disturb her. I think she's busy this morning." I sit up a bit straighter and allow Tina to loosen her grasp, although she still keeps an arm round my back.

"Why don't we pop along to our room? Then you can have a lie down, Jess, and me and Dawn will stay with you and chat a bit. That way you can join in or not, as you like, but you won't be alone. What do you think?"

I nod. Tina's grown since I met her. She's acquired this innate sense of what I need most: an ideal best friend. God knows what I saw in Karen. She's the complete opposite, and hasn't spoken to me for over two weeks now, except to mutter 'Bitch' whenever she's near me.

Dawn helps me to my feet, and the three of us return to my bedroom. I lie on top of the bed and shut my eyes, listening to Tina and Dawn chatter about innocent things like food and online learning. Gradually, though, the talk drifts to Dawn's past, and suddenly I'm listening hard, with my eyes wide open.

"… argued a lot. Dad got a bit aggressive, especially after a few drinks, but it wasn't aimed at me. I felt sorry for Mum, but somehow Dad always seemed to make out it was her fault. I know better now, of course."

"That's usually what happens, Dawn. My dad abused me for eight years. I didn't tell anyone for such a long time, because he always made out like I was turning him on deliberately. Then when I finally got up my courage and told my mum, she sided with Dad. Like it was my fault. To be honest, I think she couldn't face the thought of all the adverse publicity. He's a politician. So I ran away, and found myself here. It took a long, long time before I realised it wasn't my fault."

Remorse washes over me. I knew Tina had been abused, as she'd mentioned it when we first met, but I hadn't realised it had been so prolonged. I've been so focussed on my own troubles. But it explains why Tina's so understanding. I turn over to face my friends, resting my head on my crooked elbow.

"Yeah, well it wasn't until Uncle Thomas turned up, that everything went downhill really fast."

Tina blanches at the name. "When did he turn up?" she asks faintly.

"The middle of May. He said he needed somewhere to stay for a while, as he'd fallen out with his pals that he was living with before."

Tina's face becomes even paler.

I've not heard of Thomas before today, so have to ask, "What's up? Who's Thomas? Apart from Dawn's uncle, obviously."

"If it's the same one, and the timings do seem to work out, he used to live here. He made my life hell, then left when Dominic died. Too many police floating around, I think. I testified to what he'd done to me, so he's wanted by the police for rape and causing actual bodily harm. I was relieved when he ran, as I didn't think I could face a court case. Now, I wish he'd been locked up."

"It sounds like too much of a coincidence, but it could be the same Thomas. My uncle tried it on with me. I mean, he came into my bedroom and started touching me. Then when I screamed, he made out like it had been a joke." Dawn's face is clouded over as she falls quiet, apparently lost in unpleasant memories.

"Oh God. That sounds just like him, Dawn. What does he look like?" Tina seems to hold her breath as she waits for the answer, and I find myself doing the same.

Dawn wrinkles her nose. "Short and fat. He's a bit thin on top, and he always stinks of cheap aftershave and sweat."

Tina's shaking now, and I drag myself off my bed to sit on hers, and put an arm round her shoulders.

"Does that sound like him, Tina?" I ask, and hand her the tissue that Dawn has thoughtfully passed to me.

She nods and sniffs, before taking the paper hankie and blowing her nose. The noise resembles an elephant trumpeting, and is startling for someone so slight.

Dawn giggles, and the tension breaks for a moment.

"Sorry," says Tina, sniffing again. "I shouldn't be crying, but I was so terrified of him. He used to come in to the dorm at night and touch me. Your sister rescued me once or twice, Jess, but then… Oh, it just got too awful. Everything was so horrible for ages and ages. It was such a relief when Thomas left. I'm sorry he went to your house, Dawn, but I don't ever want to see him again."

If Thomas is wanted for rape, then he obviously went a lot further than just touching. I give Tina's shoulders another squeeze.

"I think we should tell Mark. We have to tell someone, and he can decide if it's appropriate to mention it to the police."

"Why not Mel?" asks Dawn.

I'm trying to think of a good reason other than 'it doesn't seem right', when Tina answers for me.

"Lots of reasons really, but mostly because I don't want to worry her. She's had a lot to deal with lately, and she's still feeding Emma, so lots of raging hormones. Mark's a good idea, although even he's been looking a bit haggard lately."

"I know, but he'll have to cope. Unless we mention it to Jimmy?" I'm not sure I like the brief speculative glint in Tina's eyes, and wish I hadn't said anything. "No, forget I mentioned it. Mark's got the authority really. That's probably why he looks so tired."

"I expect so, and he'll probably be getting woken up in the night by Emma as well. Either way, I think he's the best man for the job." Tina starts to look anxious again, her moments of decisiveness clearly at an end. She starts chewing her fingernails.

I think I know what's coming. Dawn's face shows that she's clocked it too. Who's going to be the one to tell Mark about Thomas?

Chapter Thirteen

Mel

It's taken me nearly two hours to settle Emma, and I'm going to have to resort to Calpol. She's two days short of the minimum three months age requirement, and she's still quite small, but bathing her head and body with cool water has no effect, so I give in. I'm about to call Mark from my mobile and ask him to get some, but Brie is ahead of me, and has been to the local shop for supplies. She walks in to Emma's bedroom holding the bottle and syringe.

I check the bottle, and it says the medicine can be given at two months after vaccination, so I'm reassured, but it reminds me that I need to get her vaccines sorted out.

We have to endure a frustrating further twenty minutes of grizzling. Thankfully Brie is still with me, and takes turns to rock, cuddle and soothe my poorly baby girl. Eventually, the medicine kicks in and Emma falls asleep. We tuck her up in her cot.

"You must be exhausted, Mel. Go and have a lie down for an hour or two, then you can take over. It'll probably be time for her feed then if she's up to it."

"Okay, phone me if you need me." I leave Brie curled up in the armchair next to the cot. She's got a novel with her. I take a quick glance as I pass.

"Georgette Heyer," Brie says. "I used to love these before I joined The Brotherhood, then I got here and found novels were banned. I very nearly turned round and ran. At least we can read now. When Mark and Jimmy found all our old cases, I was delighted to be reunited with my collection. This is one of my favourites." She holds it up, and I see the title *Arabella*.

"Can I borrow it after you, please?"

"Course you can, love. I'll bring some of the others down to you later. For now, go and get that sleep."

I try to obey, but I have too many things going round my head.

After about ten minutes, I give in to temptation and go to the room with the hidden boxes. Sitting on the hard floor, I open the first box and pick up the A4 notebook. The initial pages are filled with lists of drugs, serial numbers and expiry dates, and I skim through to find this continues for about half the book. Further investigation shows that each page is dedicated to a different drug. Some of them are routine medicines, such as paracetamol and ibuprofen. Other pages contain drugs with strange names or strings of letters and numbers. Finally, I get to the pages of dangerous drugs and anaesthetics.

My heart misses several beats as it alights on the page of potassium chloride. There is nothing obvious to suggest that any of the vials went missing, except my own knowledge; but as I gaze at the page, I realise the final total is three. Equal to the number of vials I took.

I turn to an earlier entry. All packets of ibuprofen are accounted for, either by use, expiry, or sale prior to the lease of the Infirmary. The final total is zero.

Fascinated but fearful, I slowly go through the book. Only two pages don't finish with all items accounted for. The potassium chloride page is one of them.

My phone buzzes in my pocket. I check who's calling, and answer it quickly, the notebook forgotten for a moment.

"Is everything ok?" I ask Brie.

"Yes, fine. Em's woken up, and seems a bit brighter. She's playing with that musical thing in her cot. I just wanted to check you're okay. Mark said you weren't in your room?"

"I'm fine. I couldn't sleep, so I'm just looking at a few papers I found. Nothing important really." I try to keep the tension out of my voice.

"Of course not. You carry on, love. I'll see you later. Your daughter is fine for now. I'll let you know if you're needed."

I know from Brie's tone that she's realised something is

up. She knows me too well.

I return to my perusal of the notebook, and the page of trial drug X5-0311-ALB. The dates tie in with my stay after concussion, and the arrival and treatment of Greg, Frank and Charles, amongst so many others. Letters next to some of the entries seem to relate to initials of the trial subjects. I recognise GM, and there's FC and CL. Then there's a date a few days after Frank was taken away, when fifteen vials were sent back to the provider for analysis. Five vials were unaccounted for, and were left as the final total.

So what does this mean? And why has no one picked up on this? Surely whoever did the final accounting would have spotted that some were left over? What if they meant to go back to it, but were stopped? Thousands of theories crowd round my head, but none of them seem very plausible.

And there's a bigger problem. If I show this book to Greg, it contains evidence of the removal of those potassium chloride vials. But if I don't show him, I'm suppressing evidence that could lead to Frank's killer.

I return to the page that incriminates me. One of the entries shows that five vials were destroyed. How easy it would be to change that five to an eight... but then I would have to change that remaining three to a zero – much more of a challenge.

My nurse training, whilst now in the distant past, rebels against the idea of forging documents anyway. There must be another way.

I wade through the rest of the box. Most of the contents are loose documents relating to various of the drugs that were kept in the Infirmary pharmacy. It seems strange that trial activities and routine work are all jumbled together, but I realised when I was being shown around that it was not a very professional or well-organised operation.

Underneath a sheaf of patient information leaflets for routine prescription medicines, I find a batch of leaflets about the trial drugs. I leaf through until I find one for the trial that Frank was on, and start reading:

Side effects:

As suggested by pre-clinical trials, the following effects may be observed: -

Common: >1 in 10 – nausea, vomiting, headache…

There are several more side effects noted, then,

Extremely rare: <1 in 100,000 – severe immune effects. Swelling, Encephalitis, Risk of cardiac arrest.

A bit further down the leaflet, these same conditions are listed as a potential result of overdose, with suggestion that in severe cases, death may result.

At the bottom of the box is a patient information sheet for the trial. And also, numerous signed consent forms. Amongst others, I find the consent forms for the three men I know of: Greg Matthews, Frank Coombes and Charles Lindon. I hadn't known Frank's or Charles's surnames before, and suspect this is a valuable clue for Greg.

The patient information sheet should list the possible side effects, but doesn't, and I wonder how on earth it got through ethics. There is a vague mention of headache and nausea, but no suggestion of the more frightening effects. How many of those men would have signed on the dotted line if they'd known the risk?

And who stole and administered that lethal dose?

I open the other box while these questions spin around my head, but there's nothing interesting in there, just supplies of syringes, needles, swabs and cotton wool. I delve to the bottom just to make sure and my fingers encounter a folded piece of paper.

I'm about to open it and read the contents, my heart racing again, when the phone rings once more. *Bloody hell, Brie, you choose your moments!*

Checking the screen, though, I see it's Mark. I hit the green *Answer* button.

"Hi, Mark. Is everything okay?"

"Where are you, Mel? Brie's been sitting with Emma for hours and she's starting to whine again. It must be time for a feed."

"Okay, I'm coming. Why didn't Brie ring me?"

"She's exhausted. I sent her for a rest. She's been sitting

with Emma for nearly three hours. And you didn't answer my question. Where are you?" He sounds irritable, and I'm not sure I want to discuss it with him just now.

"I'll tell you later. See you in a minute. Are you still in Em's bedroom?" I wait for him to confirm, then hang up. Slipping the phone into one pocket, and the unread piece of paper into the other, I throw everything back into the boxes, and run through the Abbey to my daughter's room.

Once there, I ignore Mark's rants about negligent mothers, and take a whining Emma from him. She feels a bit warm again, but not as hot as before. I settle on to the armchair and prepare to feed her. There's a stackable chair in the corner, and Mark grabs it, and sits next to me. He takes a deep breath, and I'm not sure whether to expect another rant or if he's trying to calm himself down.

"Okay. I'm sorry I shouted. I can see you're stressed about something. What's going on?"

I decide it might be time for a confession. "I found a book that contains a clue to Frank's death."

"Surely that's good?"

"Yes. Unfortunately, it also contains evidence that incriminates me."

"Shit! That's not good. Where is it, Mel? What am I looking for?"

"You know that room where you took Greg?" He nods, and I continue. "There were a couple of boxes hidden in the cupboard in that room. I found them by accident."

He raises his eyebrows. "I think I'd better go and get them. They'll be safer here anyway. We can't just leave evidence lying around for anyone to find. When I get back, we'll have a think about what to do."

When he's out of the room, and the sound of footsteps has faded, I reach into my pocket, trying not to disturb my feeding baby.

I unfold the paper and read. My eyes open wider with shock as the contents become clear. I'm alerted by the soft thud of shoes outside the room, and stuff the paper back in my pocket. I can't discuss this with anyone.

Chapter Fourteen

Jess

I've been nominated by Tina and Dawn to find Mark and tell him about Thomas. So I've just spent the last hour rushing all over the Abbey, trying to run my brother-in-law to earth.

I've checked everywhere except their private rooms. I don't know what's kept me away from there, but somehow I don't like to intrude on their personal space.

I stand outside the door to Emma's room, deciding whether to knock, when Mark himself emerges.

"Jess? What are you doing here?" He doesn't sound angry exactly, but there are lines of stress etched in his face, and his tone is impatient.

"I was looking for you, actually. Is there somewhere we can talk?"

"You'd better come to my office. Are you okay?"

"I guess. This isn't about me, though. I'll tell you in a minute." I follow him into the office and take a seat opposite him at the desk. He looks expectantly at me, so I take a deep breath. "It's kind of complicated. Tina and Dawn were talking upstairs while I was... resting. The conversation turned somehow to Dawn's uncle, who happens to be called Thomas."

I pause, and watch Mark's face for a reaction. I don't expect much – Mark's reserve tends to make him wary of giving much away. I don't know if that's an after-effect of what he's been through here (and I've guessed, from bits and pieces people have said, that he's had a tough time), or if it's natural reserve. Either way, I manage to evoke the mild response of a raised eyebrow.

"Anyway, Dawn's uncle happens to be the same Thomas

that left here after…" My voice trails off. There's now more than enough expression on Mark's face. His cheeks are scarlet, and he looks as if he might hit someone. I hope it's not going to be me.

I remind myself that Mark doesn't go round hitting people, but I shut up just in case.

"How the hell did you come to that conclusion?"

"Dawn's uncle visited her in the night, and touched her in the same way that Thomas here used to touch Tina."

Mark's face darkens even further.

"And the physical description sounds the same, even if it could apply to a lot of horrible, short fat men, who wear cheap nasty aftershave." I watch in consternation as Mark's fists clench, but then he takes a deep breath, and his expression returns to normal: serious but kind.

"Alright, Jess. Sorry I shouted. I know you mean well, and you were right to tell me. Even if it's not the same one, it's a clue that might lead the police to Thomas's whereabouts. To be honest, I'll be really surprised if it's the same one. It's too much of a coincidence. But either way, your sister needs to speak to Greg today anyway, or maybe tomorrow – it's getting late – so I'll tell Greg then. He might want to speak to you."

"That's fine. I like Greg. He's friendly but not in a creepy way. Just like, I dunno, someone I can trust I suppose. Outside of here. Obviously I trust you and Mel, and a few other people."

"Talking of trust, what's going on with you?"

"How do you mean?" I can't stop a wary note creeping into my voice. I might trust Mark, but I reckon he's got enough on his plate at the moment. He doesn't need my troubles added on.

"I've heard you're not eating properly, and you look pale. Have you seen that guy again? The intruder?"

"I, er, I'm not sure. It was just a movement in the shadows. I shouldn't get so freaked out. It was probably nothing." I watch as Mark comes round the desk and perches on the desk right in front of me.

"Jess, you're my sister now. I admit I get a bit distracted now and again, and I'm sorry if I seem distant at times, but I'm here to protect you. We've managed to keep the reporters away, and Greg has done his best to reduce the number of police interviews since you got here. You're part of my family, and I will not let you come to any harm. That bastard is never going to get near you again. I swear it."

I sniff. My eyes fill up, and next minute, I'm sobbing my heart out. Mark pats me on the shoulder. He's very sweet, but it's all his bloody fault. His talk of family and protection completely knocked through my defences.

There's a knock on the door, but instead of waiting, Jimmy comes straight in.

"Och. Sorry for barging in. Is everything okay? Are you okay, lass?" He sounds genuinely concerned, and I can't help but be pleased to see him.

"Well, she's clearly not, but I don't seem to be able to help much." Mark turns to me. "Jess, do you want to chat to Jimmy for a bit? I've noticed you two seem to get on."

Bloody hell. Has the whole world noticed I've got a crush on Jimmy?

"Yes, thanks. If Jimmy's got time?" I sniff, and the object of my crush hands me a crumpled but clean hankie. I blow my nose. This is not a great way to attract a man. I must look a wreck.

Mark pats me on the shoulder again, and then leaves.

"Come on Jess. Mark's bloody useless, leaving you sitting on that hard chair when there's a comfy sofa over here." Jimmy holds out his hand. I take it, ignoring the spark that flows.

Once on the sofa, he puts his arm round me. Unlike Mark's pats, this makes me feel properly protected, and I relax against him for a moment, dabbing at my eyes, with the cleaner bit of the hankie.

"You have a good cry if you need to, lass, then you can tell me all about it if you want."

I keep the summary of events brief, focussing on a quick description of the Thomas situation, but Jimmy isn't satisfied.

"Aye, well that's all very interesting, and I can see why Tina and Dawn would be freaked out, even though it's a bit unlikely, but it doesn't explain why you're in a state. Come on, Jess. We're friends, aren't we? What's the matter?"

His arm is still around me, and he gives me a squeeze. My stomach flaps inside, but that might be because I've not eaten properly. I discard any other explanation.

"I'm scared, Jimmy."

"Not of me, I hope?" There's a laugh in his voice that reassures me; together with his earlier assertion about us being friends.

"No, obviously. I wouldn't be here if I was." I turn to him, and see the concern in his face.

"Come on then, lass. Tell me what's wrong." His arm has fallen from my shoulder, but he takes my hands in his.

"I've seen him. Twice I think now, since you rescued me in the lane."

"Who? Your kidnapper?"

"I don't know if he qualifies as a kidnapper. He didn't exactly hold me for a ransom. Abductor really. The man who held me prisoner for nine years, and who I never want to see again."

"Are you sure it's him?"

"I don't know why anyone else would be watching the Abbey. He's the same shape and size, and every time I see him, I freak out." I shiver. "I feel like a prisoner in here now. Obviously no one is mistreating me here, and everyone is lovely, except Karen, and she's not important."

"Shh." Jimmy puts his finger to his lips, and I look at him curiously. The door is shut. No one could be listening. "There are a couple of secret passages around here," he says in a low voice. "I don't know who else knows about them, but best not slag anyone off too loudly."

"Shit. What if she heard?"

"As you just said, she's not important, so don't worry about her. But maybe be careful about what you say and when, and how loudly."

"Okay. Anyway, what do I do about him?"

He looks closely at me.

"Do you trust me, Jess?"

"Yes." I don't even have to think about it. I can feel it in my whole being.

"Well then, believe me when I say he's never going to get near you again. Not if I have anything to do with it. And if I ever see him, he won't survive long enough to draw another breath." His expression becomes grim. "I've killed before. It's not something I like to do, but if I have to..."

Chapter Fifteen

Mel

Mark decided I should get a good night's sleep before tackling Greg. He came back about an hour after leaving me and told me about his meeting with my sister. I don't know quite how he expected me to sleep, with Emma poorly, Jess fretting and Tina and Dawn worried about Thomas. As he doesn't know the main reason for my terror, he probably figured everything else could be pushed to the background.

I managed to get a few snatches of sleep between Emma's cries, Calpol doses and the tossing and turning that accompanies a night of stress and fear.

I'm now sitting bleary-eyed at the breakfast table with a slice of toast in front of me. Emma's been fed. Her temperature seems to have settled down; the fever broke early this morning, and she's now sleeping like a young baby should.

Trying to distract my thoughts from the inevitable, I survey my family and friends around me. Jess is sitting between Jimmy and Tina, looking a bit more relaxed than yesterday, although she keeps glancing at Jimmy. His expression is one of concern, but there's a light in his eyes which worries me. I've never asked his actual age, but he must be well into his thirties. He's had a troubled past. My sister is nineteen.

Tina and Dawn both look troubled. I wish I could set their minds at rest, but I'll be speaking to Greg shortly, and hopefully he'll be able to provide some reassurance.

At the other end of the table, Alison is talking to Derek. She looks more animated than I've ever seen her. I think the cooking job is suiting her, and she seems happy here. I hope she and Dawn will stay. They're lovely people, and a positive addition to our little community.

On nearby tables, other Abbey occupants chat amongst themselves. They all seem oblivious of the heavy atmosphere that seems to hang over a few of us. The thought is helpful in itself. In a way, the Abbey is thriving. We've had no new additions since Alison and Dawn, but we're still open to the refuge charities, and all are welcome.

I have to do something useful. In addition to all my other concerns, guilt still rages within me, filling my nights with tortured images. These are not only from my own experiences, but the sins of Dominic also fill my head. Whilst he was alive, he had an opportunity for redemption and remorse. I've now deprived him of that option. Have I condemned him to a life in hell? Perhaps he deserves that, given what he's done, but it shouldn't have been me that did it.

With threat of exposure hanging over my head, the enormity of my crime has come home to me. Should I confess to Greg? He's been very kind so far, and has ignored his obvious suspicions. He wouldn't be able to ignore a direct confession, and perhaps it would get him into trouble. I can't do that to him. But if this letter comes to light…

"Mel!" The sound of my name penetrates my thoughts, and I glance at Mark, who's standing next to me and frowning.

"What?" I frown back.

"Just had a call from Greg. He's on his way, and bringing a colleague. They'll be here in five minutes. Go and tidy yourself up a bit."

"Thanks." I don't bother keeping the sarcasm from my voice, but stand up and head back to our room. Once there, a quick look in the mirror has me mentally apologising to Mark. I look horrendous. The bags under my eyes would hold all the Abbey laundry for a week, and I'm almost as white as the bed sheets. Probably not a lot I can do about either of those, but in the cupboard is my case from when I first arrived at the Abbey. I've extracted the clothes, but the make-up is still there.

I delve in the case for a minute, and find my old make-up bag in a compartment in the lid. There's some foundation and some pale pink lipstick that would help a bit. The foundation makes me look a bit less pasty and disguises the black laundry bags, but I discard the lipstick. It doesn't seem appropriate. Another examination in the mirror: my face looks better, but my baggy t-shirt is stained with old baby sick, and my jeans have similar stains. I would like to make a reasonable impression on Greg and his friend, even if the friendly detective has seen me in quite a state.

I open the wardrobe. Mark's been tidying again, and all the clothes are hung neatly in organised sections. I select a white blouse that doesn't actually have any marks on it, and a pair of clean navy trousers. These were bought for me by Mark, selected online with the help of Brie, to augment my meagre clothing supply.

Once changed, I look smartly professional, and only a bit tired. The eyes reflected in the mirror don't appear to be hiding guilty secrets, so hopefully this meeting will go smoothly.

Downstairs in the entrance hall, Greg and an older woman are sitting in the new fabric-covered chairs. They stand up as I arrive.

"Mel, this is DI Michelle Anderson." Greg indicates his colleague, and we shake hands.

"Just call me Shelley, dear," she says, with a kind smile that makes me wonder what Greg's said about me.

"Thank you. Has anyone offered you a coffee or tea?" When they shake their heads, I catch a passing resident and ask for the required drinks in Mark's office as soon as possible. Assured of refreshments, I take my visitors along to the office, and get them settled around the table.

"You've done some work here, haven't you?" asks Greg, indicating the space with a sweep of his hand.

Mark joins us at the table. "Yes, we joined the office and what used to be Dominic's bedroom, and combined them to make this multi-purpose space. It allows us to have meetings in here and for the whole committee to feel as though there's a private area for them. My desk can be screened off if needed. We had to do something with Dominic's room – it was a waste of space as it was."

Mark glances at me, and I frown at him. There's no need for him to let Shelley know what I went through. We should keep things as brief as possible. She might not feel the same way as Greg does, so I don't want to chance anything.

Drinks and biscuits arrive at that moment on a trolley. I thank the young woman who's brought it, whose name I can't remember.

Mark brings the meeting to order as soon as everyone is seated with a full cup and biscuits. "Thanks for coming, Greg and Shelley. As I told you on the phone, Greg, we've found another box that might be relevant to your investigations."

"You know I used to be a nurse?" I ask Greg.

He nods.

"During my training I worked with a Sister who was doing a clinical trial in addition to her routine work. She taught me quite a bit about it, so I was very interested when I saw what was going on in the Infirmary. Anyway, yesterday, I was tidying up and came across that box. I had a look through, and found some drug records from the trial."

I go over to the box and pick up the book containing the inventory logs. Following private instructions from Mark, I turn to the now bookmarked page that shows the clinical trial drugs.

"Okay, so this book has records of all the drugs used in the hospital, and this one here shows the trial that Greg, Charles and Frank were all on. If you have a look at the totals at the bottom, you'll see that there are vials that couldn't be accounted for." I pass the book to Greg, who pores over it with Shelley.

"So, you're saying these, er, vials went missing somewhere along the line?" Shelley looks at me keenly.

I swallow.

"Yes, that's what it looks like." I point across the table to the entry in the book where the unused bottles were sent back. "There's no reason why someone would send some vials back, and leave a few, unless they were missing. I just thought it looked a bit... Of course, it's possible that the Infirmary staff were careless and didn't check properly. They're not the best kept records ever." I'm digging myself a huge pit. I stop talking abruptly.

"We've seen from when Dominic died that he managed to take items from the Infirmary without logging them," says Greg, "so I assume other people could get in to the drugs cupboard or fridge or whatever, and also extract things they weren't entitled to."

Shelley nods, and looks grim. The earlier smiles have disappeared.

Greg glances at her, and shifts in his seat. My throat constricts, despite Greg's comments.

"Perhaps I should explain," he says. "As I was a patient on that ward, and involved in the trial, I could technically be a suspect."

I stare at him. He's absolutely right, but it hadn't occurred to me before. I wait for him to continue.

"So Shelley is taking over the investigation of Frank's death. But I'll still be involved with the investigations and follow-up with crimes inside the Abbey from that time. For instance, I'm still looking for Thomas."

"Funny you should mention that," says Mark, giving me a quick sideways glance. He explains about the possible coincidence of Dawn's uncle. "I was just waiting for you to finish talking about the Frank issue, so I could bring it up, but you kind of beat me to it."

"Thanks, Mark. We'll definitely look into that. It's probably someone completely different, but could I have a chat with Dawn and her mum?"

"I don't see why not, Greg. Mark, why don't you see if you can find them?" I rub my nose. I suddenly want to speak privately to Greg and Shelley. It feels like the right moment to bring up something that's been worrying me, and I don't want my husband to hear.

Chapter Sixteen

Jess

After a restless night pondering Jimmy's confession, and a tense breakfast, I finally get him alone in the common room opposite Mark's office.

"Who did you kill?" I shut the door firmly behind me.

Jimmy slumps on the sofa.

"A man I liked and trusted. It was a choice between him and me." He sits forward, his head against his bunched fists.

"You mean, like, self-defence?"

"Not exactly, Jess. I was given the choice: if I didn't kill this man, I'd be tortured and killed myself. He had a quick and painless death, but it eats me up that I had to do it."

I put a tentative hand on his shoulder. Silence fills the room, becoming oppressive.

"Can we get out of here, Jess?"

"What do you mean?"

"This room. Where I'm sitting now is within a few feet of where I was when I was given the instructions. I hate this place sometimes. It's only marginally better than the office."

"We could go to one of the other common rooms if that's better?" I stand up and hold out my hand. "Come on."

He accepts the hand with a half-smile, and using it to help himself out of the chair, pulls me into a brief but very welcome hug.

"You're a sweet lass. Far too nice to be hanging out with a rough old sod like me." He lets go of me, and opens the door leading out to the hallway. I follow him along the passage until we get to another door. This one leads to an inner courtyard with a pretty garden.

"Is this okay? I know you don't like going outside much

now."

"I can handle just about handle this place. I come here when I'm desperate for a bit of air." But I've not forgotten his last statement. "How old are you, Jimmy?"

"Thirty-two in years, and about a hundred in experience. Too old for you, lassie."

I turn away as my eyes fill with tears. "Don't you want to be friends?" My voice sounds strange and thick. I want him to hug me again, but there's no touch this time.

"Aye, of course I do. But maybe we shouldn't be. Look, there's a bench over there. Another of Mark's little additions to improve this place. Let's sit down."

The quad is deserted except for us. I rub my eyes on my shirt-sleeve, and follow him to the bench. Once seated, I force down the lump in my throat and manage to speak.

"Why shouldn't we be friends?"

"Before I came to the Abbey, I was in prison in Scotland."

"What for?"

"Drink-driving. I killed a child. A little lass. She'd be about your age now if she'd lived. She must have been about nine or ten at the time. Ran out into the road out of nowhere. I found out later she was going to the ice-cream van, but I was too loaded to even notice the van at the time."

"Why were you drunk at the time of day when ice-cream vans go round?" I can sense his guilt. That's two people he's killed, and neither of them because he wanted to.

"I was twenty-two. It's what young, unemployed louts did in Glasgow. Drank. Got stoned. Nicked cars."

"It wasn't even your car?"

"I couldn't afford a car, lass." He laughs bitterly. "That added another two years to my sentence; the nicked car. I was in for six years, then Dominic came." He's stopped laughing, but the bitter expression remains. I can see real hatred in his face now, but whether it's for himself or Dominic, I can't be sure.

I take a deep breath. Does Jimmy trust me enough to keep on talking about this? The silence stretches out, and a lump of lead settles in my gut. Unable to stand the tension, I screw up the courage to ask, "What happened when Dominic arrived?"

He glances at me and shakes his head. "D'you really want to know?"

"Please. If you don't mind telling me." I watch as he breathes out heavily.

"Ok. You ought to know what kind of a man I am before you decide if you want to be friends with me."

For Christ's sake! Does he really think I'll stop wanting to be friends with him? He's killed two people. How much worse can it get? All the same, I nod my head. Anything to get him to tell me now. Enough of the bloody suspense.

"By the time Dominic arrived, I was deeply in debt in the prison. I owed money for protection, drugs, drink, gambling – just about every shitty thing I could have got involved with. Dominic came to the prison and asked to see me. He'd had a letter from me ma. She was dying, and she wanted me out of there so's she could say goodbye. I never found out how she got Dominic's details, but he turned up, paid all my debts, and got me out. I remember him telling me on the way to see Ma that he'd bribed the parole board. He didn't put it like that, of course. He mentioned 'easing the path to freedom' or some such crap. He stayed while I waited with me ma. She died an hour after I got there – like she was waiting or something."

"Maybe she was."

"Aye, maybe. Anyhow, then Dominic drove me all the way back here, and then he dried me out. I'm not talking gentle rehab, Jess. He nearly killed me. Then I was supposed to be grateful for everything. He was such a slimy bastard. I had to do all sorts of stuff that I hated. Some things I never even confessed to your sister."

"How did he make you? What did he threaten you with?" I'm scared in case I know the answer, because I know what I was threatened with by Him.

"He'd have sent me back to prison. The bastard said he would send me back with a message that would make every inmate want eternal revenge. He knew damn well why I'd been paying protection money – and it wasn't out of choice."

Awful though it sounds, I'm relieved, and can't help sighing.

"What're you sighing for?"

"Because I thought he was going to have threatened you with drug addiction."

"That might have been easier."

"No, it wouldn't have been. I put up with a lot when I was abducted, Jimmy. I was raped and beaten at times. But nothing terrified me more than what he threatened with the drugs." I stare at the ground for a moment, unable to speak. Then finding the courage and with it, my voice, I continue. "And he made me watch while he got another girl addicted to heroin. I had to watch her die. Believe me. That was worse than anything else in the world."

"Fuck! I'm sorry, Jess. That's horrendous. You're far too young to have gone through anything like that."

"Will you stop bloody saying I'm too young? I've been through more than almost anyone else in the Abbey, and there are a lot of people here who've been through shit. In experience, you're not the only one who feels about a hundred." I turn away as I finish, to stop Jimmy from seeing the tears filming over my eyes.

"You're right, lass. Of course you are. I knew you'd had a bad time, but… This isn't coming out right. I should just shut up, else I'll say something to offend you. Again." The strain comes across in his voice, and I turn back to him.

"Don't worry about it. You don't have to apologise. Just stop telling me I'm too young to be friends with you. We've both had a pretty crap time. It should bring us closer, not force us apart."

Jimmy's brow creases and there's a moment of tension as I wait for a response. I have no idea of what's going through his mind.

"Jess?" A call from across the courtyard breaks the tension, and I look around to see Brie coming towards me with a letter in her hand. "Oh, good. You're here, love. I've been looking for you for ages. There was a letter for you in the post this morning."

Who would send me a letter? I slowly reach out to take it, but fear churns in my stomach. Jimmy and Brie are both watching me, as I open the envelope and extract a single sheet of paper.

Dear Jessica

Do not get too comfortable in your new home. You will not be there for long. I know where you are now, and what you are doing. Know that I am watching you, and I will be coming to get you back. You belong with me, and I have many plans for you for when you return. Remember Kylie?

See you soon...

The letter slips from my hand and the courtyard begins to spin. A large hand on the back of my neck pushes my head down between my knees, and the blood slowly returns to my head. As soon as I'm reasonably sure I won't faint, I sit up. Brie and Jimmy are sitting on either side of me on the bench, looking at me with quiet concern.

"Did you read it?" I ask in a hoarse whisper. My voice seems to have deserted me. They both nod.

"He's lying, lass. He can't be watching you. Mark's removed all the CCTV from the Abbey, and there's no other way he could see you," says Jimmy.

"What about a telescope?"

"You're not near a window for long enough for anyone to watch you. All anyone could see would be a brief glimpse of you scurrying past." Jimmy grins at me, and a tiny seed of hope settles in amongst the dark anxiety.

"I think you should tell Mark and Mel about this, love," says Brie, waving the letter that she must have taken from me when I nearly fainted.

"Fine. Give it to Mark. He can add it to the long list of things that are worrying him." A recollection of the stress lines on my brother-in-law's face adds to my guilt and tips the balance. "No, forget it. Look. He doesn't really need to know. Neither does Mel. What could they do about it anyway? If I can catch Greg, I'll show him. I'm not sure what he could do either, but perhaps the police could patrol the area looking for someone with a telescope or binoculars or something." My voice is growing stronger as the decision is reached.

I stand up, and head back inside, just as a sudden rainstorm hits. I leave Jimmy and Brie, and, keeping away from the exterior windows, return to my room. If He's out there, He's getting very wet. I allow myself a bitter grin before curling up on my bed to think.

Chapter Seventeen

Mel

With Mark out of the room, I'm suddenly tongue-tied. He asked me not to tell anyone, but this doesn't feel like a safe secret to keep, and perhaps the police can provide some protection. I cast anxious glances at both Shelley and Greg, but am still unable to speak.

"Would you excuse me, love? I just need to use the ladies. Where is it?" Shelley stands up and goes to the door. Grateful for her tact, or maybe just her bladder, I give her directions to the nearest loo.

Alone with Greg, it's easier to raise the subject and as soon as the door closes behind his colleague, I begin to speak.

"I'm worried about Mark. He had some very legal and above-board dealings with some dodgy people before he came here, and I think they're now trying to pressure him into some less... er... savoury activities." Footsteps on the corridor alert me, and I whisper, "He didn't want me to tell you anything though."

Greg nods, and makes a comment on the rain which is now battering the small window. When Mark appears with Dawn and Alison, to all intents and purposes we're discussing the vagaries of British summer.

I get a call to attend to Emma before Greg begins to question them, so have to leave the room, but I cast him an anxious look before I leave. He smiles and nods, and I have to be satisfied with that.

When I return to the room half an hour later, Mark is alone at his desk, reading a letter. He's frowning, but as I approach, he folds it up and stows it away in the desk drawer.

"Anything interesting?" I sit in the chair opposite. I know Mark well enough now to realise he's in a *Don't-come-near-me* mood.

"Nothing for you to worry about. Is Emma alright?"

"Yes, she's fine. Did you find anything else out about Thomas?"

"We got the address from Alison and a more complete description, so we know where he was – if it was him." Mark runs his hand through his hair, making it stand on end. "I think it might have been him. Greg might trot down there himself to check if he's still there, and maybe have a chat with the local police down there. He said he'll phone if he finds anything, but meanwhile, to stay safe, and look after ourselves and each other. Wise words."

I ignore the sarcasm. It's easy to say 'Stay safe', but if Thomas is out there somewhere, he could be a direct threat. My thoughts are crowded by memories of his bullying, but in between, there are flashes of his kindness to me at a time when his was the only face I saw. But then, he was well paid for it. I feel my face flush in embarrassment and shame.

"Are you alright, Mel?" Mark disturbs my reverie, and I grow even hotter. This is not a secret I can share with him. I know he still hasn't entirely forgiven me for letting myself be seduced by Dominic.

"Just unpleasant memories of Thomas."

"Don't worry. Greg will catch him. That's his main priority now, and Shelley will track down Charles and the other trial guys."

A bell rings. We still use the bells for communal meal times – lunch and dinner – although they're not compulsory to attend. Residents are allowed to go out for meals in town, or wherever they choose, as long as they let us know in advance. This is purely for economic reasons, so we're not paying for meals that won't get eaten. Conversely, residents are also allowed to invite guests, within reason and on request. The request includes submission of the guests' names and addresses, and these must be provided at least two weeks in advance. Guests are confined to the dining room and are not allowed to be left unsupervised.

Although it sounds regimented, we need to make sure that our refuge ladies and girls are protected. Even though we only have Alison and Dawn so far, it is my responsibility to keep them safe, and I will defend those seemingly ridiculous rules to anyone who challenges them.

So far, I have only turned down one request. Karen asked if her boyfriend could join us for dinner. On discovering that her boyfriend is the ex-warden, Geoff, I had to decline her application. Geoff is a very unsalubrious character who lives in the nearby village, and who was responsible for various bruises and other injuries in Brotherhood days. I'm not letting him within the grounds, as I don't trust him with my ladies.

The dining room is full for lunch today, or as full it gets these days. Thirty-five people are already tucking into either a delicious veggie lasagne or pizza and salad. Our chef, Hugo, ably assisted by Alison, has done a great job at improving the catering, and I think most of us have gained a little weight as a result.

I'm about to sit down, when I notice an empty space next to Jimmy. I go round and tap him on the shoulder.

"Where's my sister? Brie said she was with you earlier."

"She went up to her room." Jimmy sounds fed up.

"Have you argued?" Perhaps not a very tactful question, but I'm worried about Jess. She's missed too many meals lately, and has lost the little weight she gained when she first arrived.

I receive a depressed-looking grimace in response. "Not exactly. Look, this isn't the time or place to discuss it. Let's chat after lunch, okay?"

I nod, and collect two empty plates from the sideboard. Piling on lasagne and salad, I pop them on to a tray with a couple of glasses of orange juice. Jimmy jumps up and holds the door open for me.

Outside Jess's room, I call her name and wait. There's no reply. I call again. Maybe she's asleep. Putting the tray on the floor for a moment, I open the door... and scream.

"Help! Please someone come and help!" My voice is weak and I can't seem to get enough sound out. I try again. "Help! Please!"

My pulse is racing and I can't catch my breath. I go over to the bed, where my sister is lying on the blood-stained duvet. I need to find a pulse, but my hands are shaking so much.

"Oh, Jess, honey, what have you done?" My eyes take in the razor on the bed, and the erratically-spaced incisions on her arms. My hand fumbles around her neck, trying frantically to find a pulse.

Suddenly, flailing arms cause me to move backwards. Jess is alive. Thank God. I move out of reach of the violent action.

"Jess, calm down, honey. It's okay."

I manage to get her attention, and she focusses her gaze on me. It's full of confusion and fear, but she seems to gradually take in that I'm no threat, and her bloody arms relax at her sides.

"I think you've lost quite a bit of blood, Jess. I'm going to get our doctor to have a look at you. Is that okay?"

Jess nods, then shuts her eyes, and I reach in my pocket for my phone – forgotten in my panic a few moments earlier.

While I wait for the doctor, I go to the cupboard and grab one of the clean sheets from the pile. My hands are still shaking, and I don't trust myself to use the razor from the bed – now safely on her bedside table, out of the way of accidents. With no scissors around, I decide to use the sheet to mop up and stem the flow of blood. Bandages will have to wait.

With a word of reassurance to Jess, whose eyes are still closed, I gently dab at the bleeding wounds on each arm. She winces, and I'm reluctant to apply more pressure, even though it's needed.

A moment later, Paul Griffiths is in the room. He looked after me so many times during my pregnancy, and is the only doctor I really trust. He's also resident, which makes life a lot easier. He smiles at me, and goes round to the other side of the bed.

"Jess, my dear, how are you feeling?"

Her eyes flicker open, and she smiles weakly. "Lousy, I guess. I don't really know."

"Your sister needs to clean those wounds properly. Mel, my dear, why don't you go to my office and get the first aid kit from my desk? Jess will be alright with me for a few minutes."

I send a questioning glance to Jess, and she nods.

Along the corridor in Paul's office, I find the kit quickly, and am about to leave when a letter, lying open on the desk, catches my eye. Curious as ever, I skim through it, and catch my breath.

But I don't have much time. I put the box down for a minute, and find the photo function on my phone. Taking a couple of snaps to make sure I've got the whole page in – there's only one sheet of paper – I put the phone back in my pocket, and grab the first aid box again, before running back to Jess's room.

Paul is sitting on the bed next to Jess, talking quietly to her, but holding her arms together tightly wrapped in the sheet from the cupboard.

"Ah, Mel, my dear. Pleased to see you found it." Is there a glimmer of sarcasm in his voice? It's not like him, but then after reading that letter, I realise perhaps I never really knew him at all.

The next few minutes are spent bandaging Jess's wounds properly. But now the immediate danger is over, I'm more concerned with why they were there at all. I'm about to ask her, but the doctor interrupts me.

"I think Jess should sleep now, don't you, Mel? Why not call Tina to come and sit with her? I think you and I should have a chat."

Leaving Tina with my drowsy sister a few moments later, with strict instructions not to leave her alone, I follow Paul down the corridor back to his office. Vampire bats dance in my stomach. Has he guessed that I've seen the letter? While I sit down in the grey plastic chair on the visitor side of his desk, I notice him folding the letter and putting it in a drawer.

My stomach lurches, but I make no comment. Instead, I get settled and wait for him to speak.

"Why would your sister be self-harming, Mel?" He looks at me with real concern in his eyes. I search my memory, but can't remember discussing her history with him.

"You know she was missing for years, don't you?" I wait for him to nod, then continue. "She was abducted and held hostage for nine years. I can't believe I haven't already told you this."

"Everyone's been very busy. And as you probably know, I've been doing shifts at the village practice. I feel as if we've hardly seen each other since the Infirmary closed. But we'll come to that in a few moments. So, yes, my dear, I can see why being abducted could have an effect on Jess, but she's been here for several weeks now, and seemed to be settling in well. Why would she begin to self-harm today?"

Good question. And one to which I don't have the answer. Jimmy's depressed expression pops into my head. Any idiot could see that they've bonded. Perhaps if they've argued... But even that wouldn't be sufficient to cause her to cut her arms until she passed out. Would it?

"Mel?"

I realise I haven't replied. "I don't know. But we need to find out. Should I try to talk to her? Could I do more damage?"

"You could try, my dear. I don't suppose it would do any harm. The next step is to get a professional counsellor. All the residents here are registered with the local practice now, and this is considered a satellite centre, so I can refer Jess for help from here. I'll do that today, but these things can take weeks to sort out, so you see what you can do in the meantime." He takes a deep breath, and my insides squirm again. He's going to ask me about the letter.

"So I wanted to ask about you and Emma?"

My shoulders relax slightly, and I suddenly realise how tense I've been.

"What did you want to know? I left her in the dining room with Brie when I went up to Jess. My little girl is learning to sleep through all sorts of noises, but when she's awake, she likes to be looking around, so we use the car seat and pop her on the table so she can watch everyone. Brie has adopted her as a kind of niece really, and does most of the baby-minding when I'm busy. She and Emma seems to like each other." I'm rambling, but nerves are getting the better of me.

"That's lovely. How's your scar?"

"Pretty much healed now, thanks. It's a relief to know that I should be able to have more kids."

Paul smiles grimly. "I've been thinking about that. I'm so sorry, Mel. Harper told me you'd had a tumour, and I just accepted it. It never occurred to me to question him. I don't think anyone was more shocked than I was when I saw the truth of his identity."

"Have they ever caught him?"

"They found his clothes and identity information in a neat pile at the top of a cliff – Beachy Head on the South Coast. The police believe he was filled with remorse and killed himself. You do know they favour the theory that he killed his brother?"

"I hadn't realised. Thank you. That's helpful to know." That is more than helpful – it's a huge weight from my shoulders – I can feel some of the tension releasing as I digest the information. Harper (for that's how I still think of him), has gone out of his way to take the blame for my crimes. Perhaps he feels guilty for what he did to me. Or for what Dominic did to me, and which he failed to prevent, even though he must have known. Either way, there's some perverse justice. My fears for myself can be at an end.

My thoughts return to my daughter.

"Emma seems fine now. She's had a bit of a tummy bug and temperature, but it's settled down. I think she's due for her vaccinations as well."

"I'll have a look at her later. I have to go the surgery in half an hour, but I'll send you a message when I get back and you can bring her to see me."

"Thanks. That will be great. I'll feel much better if you can look her over. I don't know why I didn't think to bring her to you straight away."

"It's not a problem, my dear. Don't worry. As I said, it's been a while since we've bumped into each other. Now, about the letter you saw on my desk…"

Chapter Eighteen

Jess

The room is in total darkness. Kylie's shallow breathing is punctuated by coughs and dry retching. There's nothing to be actually sick with. Neither of us have eaten for three days. We have the water from the sink tap in the cellar, but that's all. Starvation is nothing new, but I've never before had to watch a friend deal with heroin withdrawal. Her last injection was the day He left; Monday, I think. According to the chalk marks on the wall, it's now Friday. Kylie's so ill; I can hardly bear to watch. It's a relief now it's dark, but she's shivering. All I can do is hold her. I try to share my meagre body heat. We have one blanket between us, and she has it. He said we didn't need blankets – it's summer. He said He would be back in a day or two. I don't know why we have no food.

Kylie retches, and shivers again. She's burning, though. Her fever is dangerously high, but I can do nothing. I've spent hours sponging her down, but she complains so much of the cold, it seems cruel. I don't know what to do next. We lie next to each other on the narrow mattress. I shut my eyes. I don't know how much I can bear, but I know she's in more physical pain than I am. The agony of withdrawal. If only there was something I could do to help.

I wake after a brief doze. Pale dawn light filters through the tiny grate. I tried to scream once, a long time ago. I tried to get attention. He made me regret it. I still have the scars years later. Cigarette burns are just the physical scars. The mental scars are worse. Flesh heals to some extent. And the grate is now covered by a soundproofed greenhouse. He told me that with glee; smug that He'd defeated me in yet another way.

The room is in silence. I can't hear Kylie's breathing any more. I reach out to touch her. She's deathly cold. I try to scream, but no sound comes out…

"Jess, are you okay?" Hands on my shoulders shake me gently. I open my eyes and see Tina's sweet but terrified expression. I'm in the Abbey. Safe, for the moment.

Kylie's been dead for three months now. Nothing I can do will bring her back, and I couldn't save her. That guilt never goes away, but telling Jimmy about it earlier, even in such abbreviated form, brought it all back. After fifteen minutes on my bed, I went to the bathroom, and found a new razor. I glance at my arms. They're covered in bandages now. Paul Griffiths did a good job of dressing them, but they sting like crazy. Somehow, the physicality of the wounds takes my mind off the worst of the guilt.

I look into Tina's scared eyes. "I'm sorry. I didn't mean to upset you."

"God, Jess. You don't have to apologise." Tina sits on the edge of my bed, her left hand holding my partly-bandaged right one. "I don't know where to start. You probably don't want to talk at all. Do you?"

"I don't know." I squeeze her hand as well as I can. The bandage is tight across my palm. "Talking to Jimmy earlier brought back memories that I've tried to bury. I couldn't handle them." I stop at the sight of tears falling down my friend's cheeks.

"Killing yourself won't help. Well, maybe it will help you, but please don't, Jess." She sniffs, and dashes her sleeve across her nose. "Sorry. That's gross. I didn't mean to do that. But you mustn't do it. I couldn't bear to lose you. I love your sister, but you and I really understand each other. I've never had a friend like you. Please promise me you'll never try to kill yourself again."

Can I promise her? I'd like to. I wasn't even trying to do away with myself. I just wanted to detract from the emotional pain. The cutting helps for a while. It's not the first time, but I've not done it since I arrived here. A habit of wearing long sleeves has kept all the old scars hidden.

Would I do it again? Maybe not, but I've tried to give up before. And I feel so messed up, and so scared – of everything. I can't promise.

"I wasn't trying to kill myself. Just to cut, but I guess I went too deep. Then I fainted."

"Would you…" Tina hesitates, her expression anxious. She takes a deep breath. "Can you bear to tell me why you did it?"

I want to tell her. She's so kind, and is the one person I really believe would understand.

"I…" Words desert me. I bite the already stubby nail of my left forefinger. Tears sting my eyes. "I'm so sorry, Tina. I can't say it. It's like there's a huge block, and the words won't come through."

"Hey, don't worry. Maybe another day. You've had a tough time. I'd be too freaked out to talk if it was me."

A flash of lightning draws my attention to the window, and I remember the letter. I don't want to scare my friend, but she's blonde too, and He might try to get at her to get at me.

"Tina, there's a letter on the desk. Would you read it?"

She picks up the envelope and extracts the sheet of paper. Her eyes widen as she reads it.

"Crikey, Jess! This explains plenty. But you can't manage the burden of this by yourself. What are you going to do?"

"I showed it to Jimmy and Brie. They wanted me to tell Mark and Mel, but I didn't want to worry them any further. They've got enough to be concerned about."

Tina gives me an incredulous stare and shakes her head.

Shit! She's right. I've caused far more anguish, with what I've done, than the letter alone could possibly have managed. I hope my expression conveys sufficient embarrassment at my stupidity.

Before either of us can speak again, there's a knock on the door. Tina glances at me with raised eyebrows. I nod, and she calls out, "Come in."

The door opens enough for Mark to pop his head in. The rest of him follows, carrying a bundle in a green blanket. My heart lifts at the sight.

"I thought seeing Emma might cheer you up a bit. Are you well enough to sit up and hold her?"

Tina helps me into a sitting position. My arms feel very weak.

"I'm not sure if I should hold her, but maybe she can rest on my knee?" Between the three of us, we manage to find a position where my niece is safe and secure, and I get to give her cuddles without fear of dropping her. The love for this beautiful, innocent little girl eases my pain for a while, but also makes me angry with myself. I never want to do anything to hurt her. I vow to myself that I will do anything I must to do to keep her safe.

The first step is to tell her dad about that letter. I ask Tina to pass it to him as soon as we're settled and comfortable. Mark takes it and sits in the armchair between my bed and Tina's. My friend sits cross-legged on the end of my bed, watching Mark anxiously.

He finishes reading the brief note, then looks first at my bandaged arms, then at my face.

"Is this related, Jess?"

I shrug. "Probably. I'm sorry, Mark. It was stupid."

He nods. I hold my breath for a few seconds, waiting for the burst of anger that shows in his expression.

It doesn't come. Instead, he sighs.

"I don't know what to say, girls. Tina, I know this isn't in any way your fault, but I'm going to say it to you both, because I think we've got some challenges ahead. The Abbey is your home, as it's also ours. You're part of my family, and as I'm older than the pair of you, I take responsibility for your safety. If anything – and I mean anything – occurs to make you scared, or worried, you need to come and tell me. Nothing is more important. I don't care if I've got visitors; come and tell me, whatever the circumstances. A letter like this needs to be dealt with. That's what we have security for. But if I don't know about it, I can't do anything."

"I didn't want to worry you," I mumble, and then regret it as my brother-in-law's expression darkens again. Unable to meet his gaze, I look down at Emma.

"Seriously?" He shakes his head.

"I know. I'm sorry. I was stupid."

"You've had a bad enough day. I won't bang on about it, but next time anything weird happens, or if you're scared, come and tell me, okay?"

"Mark, what did Greg say about Thomas?" asks Tina.

"He's gone looking for him, but that's exactly why I'm worried about you too. He always had a thing for you." Mark glances over at Tina and sees how pale she's become. "Oh God, sorry. I shouldn't have said that."

"It's fine." She brushes a stray hair back from her face with a defiant gesture. "It's not like I didn't know. Honestly, Mark. I'll be okay. Jess and I are going to look after each other, aren't we?"

Tina smiles at me, and I nod. Keeping Tina and Emma safe is the only thing that's going to keep me grounded, and I won't let them down.

Chapter Nineteen

Mel

I stare at Paul in horror. He's just told me the background to his letter, and I can't quite believe it.

"So, tell me if I've understood this correctly. Your boss at your old job enticed you into a relationship with him, and then blackmailed you into keeping quiet about it. Dominic 'rescued' you and brought you here, and everything was fine for a while?"

"Yes, that sums it up fairly well. Unfortunately, after Dominic died, and I had to get a job in the village, Simon heard that I was back in circulation, so to speak."

"And now he's threatening you with exposure, and with the possibility of losing your job, if you don't… What does he actually want you to do? The letter just said '*Do what you have to, or else!*' Really not very specific."

"Hmm, well, my dear, you didn't see the letter that preceded it. Would you like to?"

Of course I would, but something tells me that the doctor wouldn't really appreciate the invasion of privacy.

I compromise. "How about you tell me the gist?"

"Thank you." He smiles wryly. "Simon has got himself involved in some rather unpleasant dealings at a senior level. There are letters that could be sent to extricate him, but they would require me to perjure myself, as they could end up in court. I don't want to take the risk, but neither do I wish to lose my job or livelihood, which I enjoy."

"You're always welcome to live here, even if you weren't paying for board with money from your work at the surgery. There are plenty of ways you can support life in the Abbey. It doesn't have to be financial. Now that Mark and I have been able to get Dominic's dubious arrangements reversed, we've both been able to access quite large sums of money. Between these walls, he and I could afford to buy a house a long way from here, and forget everything. But we care too much about our friends here, and we'd rather use the money to make the Abbey work as a community."

"Thank you, my dear. That's lovely to hear. But my work makes me feel valued, and I love being a GP. I don't want to lose that, but I don't know what to do. It's a relief to be able to unburden myself. I wasn't sure how you'd take the knowledge of my preferences."

"So you're gay. Why does it matter? It makes no difference to me, and I'm sure it won't make a difference to anyone else here either. If they don't like it, they can go away. We're not forcing anyone to stay. Anyway, you might have noticed our chef is that way inclined too."

"Yes, true. That's kind of you, and again, no more than I'd expect of you or Mark, but there are some prejudiced people about. Sometimes a community that calls (or in this case called) itself 'religious' can contain some of the most bigoted people. And Hugo doesn't live here. He spends most of his working hours in the kitchen. I only met him at all because he hurt his back."

"We don't have to make this public if you don't want. I mean, obviously, I'm not going to tell anyone about the letter, although I'd like to tell Mark if you'll let me. But it's entirely up to you whether you come out about being gay. Maybe give it some more time for everyone to settle down. It's only just over three months since The Brotherhood dissolved; I think we still have a few affiliated members who just haven't found anywhere else to go yet. Wait until they're gone, and hopefully we'll all be able to be one big family."

"That's sound advice, thank you again. But we haven't solved the real problem yet. Discuss it with Mark, please, but no one else. Perhaps between the three of us, we could come to a solution."

"How about Greg?"

"What do you mean?"

"Would you trust Greg enough to tell him what's been threatened? I mean, it's basically blackmail. You haven't done anything illegal, but Simon has: he's blackmailing you. I can understand why you wouldn't want to just go to the police as such, but Greg's different."

"I agree, he is." Paul looks away, gazing out of the window. He seems troubled, even more so than warranted by these letters. "I didn't tell you the whole story. I'm extremely embarrassed about it, to be truthful, but there was some criminal activity. None of it instigated by me, but I participated, even willingly at times. It was during the period that I was infatuated; I thought I was in love, and I believed, mistakenly, that he felt the same way."

"Greg would understand. He's very human, and weighs things up fairly. He would find a way to help you, I'm sure."

"Alright. I'll think about it and let you know. Meanwhile, discuss it with Mark, and see if you can come to a solution that doesn't involve the police. I think that would be preferable."

What on earth has Paul done that he doesn't want the police involved? It's hard to equate this pleasant, grey-haired, moustached doctor, with the usually twinkling eyes and kind smile, with the depraved criminal he apparently believes himself to be.

For now, though, I smile and agree. Taking my leave, I head back to see how my sister is getting on.

Two weeks later, no solution has been reached. Greg is still away searching for Thomas. Jess's dressings have been removed and her scars are healing, although they still look red and angry, and Paul looks anxious whenever I see him. He is spending a lot of time at the surgery; he seems to have increased his hours, and despite my latest worry, it's hard to get time with him.

Over the last few days, Emma has begun to lose weight. She appears to have stopped thriving so well, seeming a little thinner in her cheeks, and she's always hungry. I've been feeding her until my breasts are sore, but she's still not getting enough. I left a note under Paul's door asking for advice, but he sent a polite note back early this morning, recommending me to take her to the surgery.

The note contains the phone number for the surgery, so I type the number into my mobile and wait anxiously for a reply. The ringing tone seems to go on for ages, and during that time, Emma seems to be getting increasingly listless. Eventually, a voice arrives on the end of the phone, and I'm able to make an appointment with the health visitor for after lunch. Apparently there are no doctors available today. I stay in my room most of the morning, observing Emma in her cot and pacing the floor intermittently. After I've taken her temperature for the twentieth time, Mark pops his head around the door.

"Everything okay?"

"No!" I snap, frustrated that he's only just thought to check now, and I've been going frantic for over an hour.

"What's up? I didn't know there was a problem until Brie said she hadn't seen you or Em all morning."

"She's poorly. I don't know what's wrong. Paul Griffiths is tied up at his blasted surgery, and I can't even get an appointment with any of the doctors there. The best I can do is a visit to the Health Visitor at 2pm." By the end of this speech, tears are filling my eyes, and I can't keep my voice from thickening.

"Hey," he says, putting his arms around me. "It'll be fine. She'll be okay." He rubs my back, and I reluctantly return the hug. It's the first time he's held me for about two weeks. Even though we're living and working in the same building, and sharing a bed, we seem to have stopped sharing thoughts and feelings. We're both wrapped up in our own worries, and keeping them bottled inside.

The hug feels good, but the tears flow even faster. Since telling him about Paul, we've not had a proper conversation, and he's becoming a stranger.

Emma begins to cry and I pull away. This is not the time to worry about my marriage.

"I need to sort her out," I say, picking her up and cuddling her. She has no fever, despite my regular checks, and her breathing is okay; she's just not like herself, and is not eating well.

Mark sits down on the bed. "How are you getting there?" His voice is flat, but there's an undertone that puts me on the alert.

"I've not thought about it. I suppose I could ask Jimmy to drive me. Unless you want to come?"

"I wish I could. But if you're going out, you need to not be associated with me."

"What? What are you talking about, Mark?"

"I don't want you to go. I'll phone Paul and see if he can assess Emma when he gets back."

"He doesn't seem to want to talk to me at the moment."

"That's no excuse, Mel. He has a responsibility here to be our doctor, and he can't just back out of that because he's embarrassed, or frightened, or whatever his reason is. It's not safe for you to go outside, and there's no excuse for you to put yourself and our daughter in danger just because of his whims."

As he finishes speaking, his phone rings. He answers, and a moment later, his anger fills the room.

"He can't just walk out. Not now. Where's he gone?" There's a pause while the person on the end of the phone speaks. Mark stands up and starts pacing. "Bloody hell. We need him to see Emma, she's not well... No, I don't suppose... Mel's made her an appointment at the surgery, but I don't want them to go. There's a lot going on, and I don't think it's safe for them to be out and about at the moment... Would you mind, Brie? I'll send you all in the car with Derek. You'll need to go straight there and come straight back – no side trips. Yeah, okay. I'm trusting you to look after them. Report anything strange back to me, okay? You promise? Okay, thanks. See you in a bit." He turns the phone off and looks back at me. "You can go, but I don't like it."

"Who's gone? Is it Paul? What did Brie say?"

"He told her he had some business to attend to, and would be away for a few days. We're to pack a few things in an overnight case for him, and Brie will take it to the surgery when she goes with you this afternoon." He hesitates, and then touches me briefly on the shoulder. "You all need to be careful when you're out. It's not safe out there."

Chapter Twenty

Jess

The scars itch, but each day the urge to inflict more grows stronger. It freaks me out that I want to hurt myself, but I've promised so many people that I won't do it. Now that Emma's poorly, both the urge and the arguments against are even stronger.

Tina and I are sitting in the common room, supposedly reading. With all the *Harry Potter* books finished, I've lost interest in anything else on the shelves, and the mass-produced romance that I drew at random is so pathetic that I can't bear it. My eyes are drawn again to my bare arms. I would have liked to cover them up, but the friction of fabric against them is more of a distraction than the damned scars.

"Jess, stop looking at them. They won't heal any faster," says Tina, glancing up from her novel. "It's really stuffy today. Shall we go into the courtyard for some air?"

Neither of us have been outside since I hurt myself. Each of us is too scared of the consequences, but the confinement is beginning to pall. I should be used to it really. After nine years in a cellar, the size and range of the Abbey is massive, and Tina and I spend an hour or so each morning exploring. Apart from the occasional dirty look from Karen when we bump into her, there's no hint of the dangers lurking outside.

"Do you reckon he'll have stopped hanging around outside?" I ask abruptly as we sit on the bench in the courtyard. It's cloudy but hot; the air heavy with the possibility of an impending storm.

"I don't know. If he's not there, Thomas might be. Greg still hasn't found him, or if he has, he's not mentioned it in his calls."

"How do you know?" I shift my bottom on the bench, and gaze again at my left arm, which is slightly worse than the right. I guess I slashed at it with more strength.

"I asked Mark yesterday. He said they speak to Greg most days on the phone, and he's still searching. Apparently Thomas left Dawn's house two days after they did, and hasn't been seen or heard from since."

"Oh. Where is Dawn anyway? I've not seen her since lunch."

"Derek's driven them in to Macclesfield to get some clothes. Mel told me he was going to drop her, Brie and Em at the surgery, then take Alison and Dawn to Macc."

I think about this for a minute.

"That doesn't sound sensible. I heard Mark going mad at Mel earlier, saying that they had to go straight there and back, with no side trips. How's that supposed to work?"

"I don't know, Jess. Perhaps we'd better trust to a bit of luck. I'm not sure Mark can take much more stress."

We sit in a reasonably companionable silence for a long while, both of us playing with the weeds that grow up the side of the bench. I look at Tina, and see she's also making posies of the rushes. We both laugh. It's nice to spend time with her – apart from being a sweetie, in some ways she's almost as screwed up as I am.

A moment later, a flash of lightning and almost immediate crash of thunder send us diving back inside.

"Back to the common room?" asks Tina.

I shake my head. I'm sick of the sight of the place. "Let's see if Mel's back with Emma."

Tina agrees and we go and knock on their bedroom door. Mel answers. She looks very slightly less stressed than when I saw her this morning.

"Oh, it's you," she says. "I thought it might be Alison."

"What happened at the doctors?" I ask. "How's Emma?"

"They've given me some formula milk to supplement her feeds. They think some of the stress here might be affecting my milk supply. The health visitor wants me to go back again next week so they can weigh her. Mark's not happy about it."

My sister glances over at the cot, where Emma's sleeping, and looking more settled than I've seen her for a few days. "I fed her as soon as we got back and it does seem to be helping a bit, so we'll see." She looks at her watch. "It's nearly four o'clock, they should be back by now."

Another crash of thunder draws us to the window. It's an outward-facing window, looking onto the driveway. There's no sign of Derek's car. It's still not raining, but the sky looks grim and dark – more like ten o'clock at night than four on an August afternoon. My eyes scan the bushes, but it's too dark to see if any intruders lurk. I shiver. Strange when it's so hot, but the atmosphere is giving me the creeps. "When did you last see them, Mel?" asks Tina.

"Derek dropped me and Brie at the surgery with Emma, and went on from there. It should have only been about a ten-minute drive from the village to Macclesfield, but he came back for us after dropping them off, and he was waiting for us when we finished. We had to wait a while. I didn't think to check times particularly." Mel sounds defensive, as if she feels guilty, but we don't know if there's a problem yet.

"What time was your appointment?" Tina's gaze, like mine, remains on the outside view.

Mel retreats to the cot and checks on Emma. "Two o'clock. I think we must have been back for three; I've had time to feed Em and get her down to sleep before you showed up."

Another lightning fork brightens the sky for a moment. The thunder is simultaneous. It sparks a flashback.

"The storm can't hurt you in here, Jessica. Perhaps if you're afraid, I should take you outside to get the full benefit of it. It's a shame I can't trust you not to scream. I will have to teach you instead that there are worse things than thunder and lightning…"

"Jess, are you okay? You've gone very pale." Mel's voice brings me back to the current reality, but my stomach contracts and I dive into her ensuite to throw up.

That storm had been five years ago, but I remember vividly. Fourteen is too young for such a violent attack from

112

behind, but it didn't get easier as I got older, and that time was the first of many. My arms itch, and I glance at the razor on the bathroom shelf.

"Jess?" Tina's at the door. She takes my hand – the right one, that was reaching towards the sharpness, desperate to overwhelm the emotional pain. "Come on. We'll talk about it later if you want, but I think for now we need to focus on Alison and Dawn. They've not answered their mobiles."

She leads me back to the bedroom. I take a deep breath, and try to swim up from the depths. Another crack of thunder sends me to the bedroom floor, to curl up on my bottom, hugging my knees.

I repeat to myself, "Alison, Dawn, Alison, Dawn, Alison, Dawn…" until the cellar recedes; until He recedes. I force myself to remember the faces of my friends. Tina is right in front of me, and Mel is sitting on the bed, looking anxiously at me. They need to focus on finding Alison and Dawn, not on me throwing wobblies about the past. I'm safe here. I know that, really. While I stay inside the fortress. The Abbey, and its grounds, is kind of like a fortress. It's my refuge, and I need to remember that, and not lose it whilst others might be in danger.

Tina sits down beside me and clasps my hand. It's reassuring and helps to anchor me.

"Right," she says, throwing me a quick smile, "we need to work out what we're going to do."

I have myself under control now and I focus on a solution. A face swims before me.

"Should we send Jimmy out looking for them? Has Derek got his phone? Maybe they could sort something out between them?"

"I'll give Jimmy a call, but, I've not been able to get hold of Derek." Mel taps the numbers into her phone. After a brief conversation, she goes to the window and glances out. "Jimmy's coming up, but he doesn't know what he'll be able to do."

Bats flap around my gut. I've not seen Jimmy to speak to since before the cutting. He's avoided me at meals, and been completely elusive the rest of the time. Maybe he's disgusted with me. He obviously doesn't want to be friends with me. I don't know why I suggested him, except for the Jimmy-sized hole that seems to occupy my chest.

A moment later, he's in the room. He nods at Tina and Mel and avoids my gaze. Insanely, though, I feel reassured by his presence. It feels as though he might be able to help.

"I'm going to drive into Macclesfield and see if I can see those lasses. Maybe when I get closer, I might be able to get into contact with Derek as well. I don't know if the storm is affecting the phones, but it's no' impossible. They're lasses. They've gone shopping. Chances are they're fine and they've just lost track of time." He looks directly at me then. "Jess, walk down to the front door with me."

I get up and throw Tina a weak but hopefully reassuring grin. My legs feel wobbly. Once we're out of the room, Jimmy turns to me.

"How are you, lass? I've been a shit friend. I should have asked ages ago."

"Yeah you should. I might consider forgiving you, though."

"You've no' answered my question."

"How the bloody hell do you think I am?" The frustration of him not bothering to check on me for two weeks boils over, and I lash out, hitting him on the arm with my fist. His arm feels rock-solid. "Jesus Christ! What have you been doing?" I nurse my now sore hand against my chest.

"What? Oh, sorry. I've been working out. Mark put some gym equipment in one of the cellars, and I've been using it. Replaces some of the crap memories I have of that place." He rests his hand on my shoulder for a second, and I have to forgive him. There are more pressing matters than his biceps and my hitting abilities. We keep walking.

"What are you going to do about Alison and Dawn?"

"I told you in Mel's room. I wish I could ask you to come with me. I'd love the company, but I won't risk your safety. Not for my own enjoyment. It wouldn't be fair."

"Thanks, Jimmy. If things were different…"

114

"Aye, I know." We've reached the front door by now, and he pulls me into a hug. I rest my head against his chest. I've missed this. I allow myself to savour it for one minute.

"You'd better go. Let us know how you're getting on, and as soon as you have information, please?" I pull away and look up at him.

"Aye, of course."

A second later he's gone, and I return to Mel's room upstairs to find that Brie has joined the party to worry with us.

Chapter Twenty-One

Mel

Jess opens the door, and tension leaves me. I know she was safe with Jimmy, but they've obviously argued at some point, and I was terrified she would do a detour to some other bathroom or somewhere else with sharp objects. Ten minutes ago, Tina told me what she'd just stopped Jess from doing.

I get up and pull my sister into a wordless hug. She returns the pressure briefly before pulling away and giving me a strange look. We aren't in the habit of physical contact after all these years, and only the relief at seeing her whole and safe could have sparked that impromptu embrace.

"I thought I'd come and see how you were all doing." Bless Brie! At her words, the atmosphere returns to nearly normal. At least, as normal as it could be while we wait anxiously for our friends to return.

"Okay, thanks. Jimmy said he'll phone us as soon as he has any news." Jess glances at me, defying me to say anything about Jimmy. But I wouldn't intrude. She'll tell me what's going on when she's ready. She has enough problems without me prying. Anyway, I can check in with Jimmy later. Not that he would tell me much, but his reaction might give me a clue. We've been friends ever since I arrived at the Abbey.

We sit quietly for a while: Jess and Tina on the floor, Brie in the armchair, and me on the bed. Emma stirs, and I pick her up for a cuddle. She seems a lot happier since she had the bottle.

Thunder rolls in the distance. The storm is passing, and the lightning is a lot further away now. Tina counts seconds out loud between the next flash and subsequent thunder.

"Three miles away. I'm not sure which direction, though – isn't that over towards Macclesfield?"

Brie looks out of the window. It's raining heavily now.

"Yeah, I think so. Don't fret. They'll all be okay. They're probably sheltering in one of the big stores, and they'll have run out of charge on their phones. Jimmy's the one who'll get wettest, running around looking for them."

Derek should have been doing that, and he should have been keeping us updated with what's going on, not disappearing off the planet with no contact of any kind. I shiver, but I don't want to share my thoughts and worry the others even more. I trusted Derek. What if he's hurt them?

"Stop it, Mel," says Brie. "I know what you're thinking, and he wouldn't harm a hair on their heads. Derek's in love with Alison. It's obvious to anyone who's seen them together. He'll be tearing the town apart looking for them, and has probably run out of his own phone battery trying to contact them."

"So why the hell hasn't he found them yet?" Jess bursts out. "Something's wrong. I can feel it."

I feel it too, and can't bring myself to say anything reassuring. I turn away, not wanting them to see my own anxiety. I try to put Emma back in her cot, but she's had enough sleep now, and wants attention.

"Give her to me, Mel, and grab her bouncy chair from the nursery," says Brie. "We can play with her while we wait."

I nod, and go to the room two doors down which is serving as a nursery and playroom for my little girl. I return a moment later with the low chair and a contraption that sits over it, with lots of dangly toys and rattles hanging down. Brie settles Emma in, and sits down to play with her. Jess and Tina are still both silent; probably unable to distract their thoughts from our missing friends. I join Brie on the floor, and force myself to act as if nothing is wrong. I can see Jess casting me irritable glances, but a screaming baby wouldn't help the situation at all.

We somehow manage to get through the next hour and a half. Eventually Jess and Tina pull themselves together and

117

take a turn at playing with Emma, and Jess is singing nursery rhymes in a soft voice when the door opens.

We all jump. Even though we've been waiting anxiously for news, it's been so long that none of us were expecting anything.

Mark comes in, holding three huge pizza boxes. "I figured you girls will have forgotten about food, but it's nearly six, and starving yourselves won't help Alison and Dawn."

"Is there any news?" I find my voice first, but it comes out strange and shaky.

Mark comes and sits on the bed and puts his arm round my shoulders. I'm still feeling lonely after a couple of weeks with no physical contact. I suppress the sob that comes to my throat and twist my head to see his expression. He's not quite smiling, but he looks less stressed than any of us.

"They've been found. They haven't had a good time, but they're okay."

"What the hell does that mean, Mark?" Jess is on her feet now, glaring at my husband. I don't blame her. I can't bring myself to remove from that contact otherwise I would be doing the same. But I feel weak, and the guilt I've felt all afternoon has released the tears. How could I have allowed Derek to leave them in town to bring me home?

"Jimmy found Derek first, and then spotted Dawn's ribbon at the edge of the road, half hidden in a bush. Obviously, I don't know the details yet, but they did some hunting in the local area, and found them locked in a deserted shed. Jimmy phoned a couple of minutes before I came up here, but I'd already ordered the pizza. All the same, I figured you wouldn't eat anything until you knew they were safe."

"I'm going to give Emma another bottle while we wait for them to get back. You all start eating. I don't think I can eat just yet anyway." I force myself to stand up, and feel bereft at the loss of contact. I glance at Mark, and he touches me briefly on the hand. I'm not sure what happened to us over the last few days, but perhaps it's resolved now. I hope so. "Do you know how long they'll be, Mark?"

"Jimmy reckoned about half an hour. They were on the far

side of Macc, and it's still pretty wet out there. He's going to be driving carefully." He smiles at Emma, who's beginning to get restive. It's definitely her dinner time. "You should be fine to get that bottle sorted out. Do you need any help?"

I nod. I don't really, but the opportunity to have Mark to myself for a minute while I heat the milk up is very welcome. Also, I've only made one bottle up so far, and am still not sure what I'm doing. On second thoughts...

"Actually, I should be okay. I need to focus until I'm a bit more used to doing the bottles."

"Of course. Sure, that's fine. I'll wait here then. Do you mind if we tuck in?" I catch his glance at Jess and Tina, both of whom look pale and washed out.

"Get eating. I won't be long."

Half an hour later, Emma's fed, winded and settled down to sleep. The rest of us have adjourned to the old Cistercian common room to wait for our friends. The pizza has barely been touched.

We don't have long left to wait. We're barely settled into the armchairs and sofas when the door opens. Jimmy and Derek come in, but they're alone.

I rush over to them. "Where are Alison and Dawn?"

"They're fine, Mel. They've gone for a bath. They said they would see you later, but would rather not do the Spanish Inquisition thing tonight." Jimmy turns to Jess. "Are you alright, lass?"

She nods. Her tension level has dropped since Jimmy arrived, but she still looks pale and drawn.

"You both look a bit damp, chaps. Don't you think you should get yourselves into dry clothes before you spoil the upholstery?" Brie grins at them, able to joke around now that we know that everyone's safe for the moment.

"Are you sure?" asks Derek. "I know you're keen to hear what's happened, and I think the ladies would rather we told you while they're having their baths. They gave us permission for full disclosure. To you, anyway. Anything we say here is confidential between us."

"Obviously. Brie's right, though. You need to get changed

before you catch cold. We can give you ten minutes to get dry." I wave them back in the direction of the door, and with a sense of relief, reach for a slice of cheese and tomato pizza.

Chapter Twenty-Two

Jess

Jimmy glances at me briefly as he heads out of the door, and flashes me a quick grin. It irritates and reassures me at the same time. I tap my foot on the floor while I wait for them to come back. Mel and Brie are devouring the previously untouched pizza as if they hadn't eaten for years, but I still can't face food – not until I know what happened. Suppose He took them? And if He did, how did they escape?

Tina catches my gaze, and sends me her sweet smile. At least someone understands how I feel. Jimmy and Derek seem to take ages to dry off and return to the common room.

Finally the door opens, and Derek comes in – alone.

"Where's Jimmy?" The words are out before I can stop them.

"He got held up by a phone call. He gestured to me to come along and start without him. Do you mind if I grab a slice of that pizza? I'm starved." He puts two slices on a plate and settles himself in a comfy chair.

My mouth curls. Derek seems like a nice guy, but he wouldn't know starved if it came and hit him in the balls. But I really need to know what happened to Dawn and her mum, so I let him eat in peace, to assuage his 'starvation'.

A moment later, he wipes his mouth on a handkerchief from his pocket, and sits back in his armchair.

"So where should I start?" he asks my sister.

"Why don't you begin from when you dropped us off?" says Mel.

"Okay." He wipes his brow. Sweat is beading on his forehead, and with a sudden and surprising flash of insight, I realise he doesn't like being the centre of attention.

121

Sympathy tugs at my gut. I'd hate to be in his position.

"Just tell my sister," I interject. "Pretend the rest of us aren't here." Maybe that was unhelpful, as he now looks pale as well as sweaty. But it was meant well.

"Okay," he says again. "Mel, I dropped you, Brie and the little one off at the surgery, and then drove into Macclesfield. Alison asked to be taken to the centre of town, so I dropped them in the centre, before heading back to pick you up. I got to you at about two forty-five, and you were just ready, so I brought you all back here, and then headed back to the town to collect Alison and her daughter. I forgot to say, I'd arranged to pick them up outside the railway station, so expected them to be waiting when I got back. I didn't want to have to pay for parking, and the car park was full anyway, so I drove round a few times. It was raining quite hard by then, and I figured they wouldn't want to be waiting round too long in the rain, but each time I passed, there was no sign of them. I found a parking spot eventually, and tried to give them a call, but I had no signal. I don't know if the storm was affecting it, but it was completely dead. It was gone four by that time, and they were supposed to have been meeting me by three-thirty. Alison said they only wanted a few things, but," he stopped and flushed, "I assumed they were being typical shopping-hungry women. I forgot their history for a moment. I guess I was fed up with driving round in the lightning and the rain."

"It's okay. Don't blame yourself," says Mel.

Just then, Jimmy comes in, accompanied by Greg. They both look grim.

"Sorry to interrupt, ladies and gentlemen," says Greg. "It seemed sensible to hear everyone's stories while they're still fresh, and no one is fed up with telling them."

No one asks what Greg is doing here. Last thing we knew he was away hunting Thomas. Has he found him? Is there a connection between what's happened to Dawn and her mum and Thomas's disappearance? I consider asking, but before I get a chance, Greg turns to Derek.

"Please carry on with what you were saying, Derek. You

can fill in the gaps later, but it sounds as though you're just getting to the interesting bit anyway. I'm Inspector Greg Matthews by the way. I don't think we've met before." Greg smiles kindly and holds out his hand to Derek.

Derek shakes hands with him but looks even more intimidated than before. His Adam's apple bobs up and down as he swallows hard a few times. He moves to the edge of his chair, looking as if he wants to make a run for it.

"Er, right, okay. So, I drove round a bit more, in case they'd got lost or something, and kept checking my phone, hoping to find a signal, but it wasn't happening. I didn't get a signal. I didn't find the ladies, and the rain was getting heavier, the storm was getting louder, and the visibility was getting worse by the minute. After about another half an hour, I pulled into another parking spot to consider my options. I was never going to come back to the Abbey without them, but I was fast running out of ideas. Then Jimmy tapped on my window."

"Shall I carry on from here, pal?" says Jimmy, who's also clearly picked up on the other man's nervousness.

Derek nods and sits back in his chair. Jimmy rests back in his own chair and slings one foot over the other knee, looking very chilled out; completely opposite in demeanour to Derek.

"Right, to go back a wee bit, I'd been driving around Macc myself for a bit, and had just decided to get out and look on foot, despite the rain, when I recognised Derek's car. As he said, I tapped on the window, and he lowered it for me.

"'Can I get in?' I asked, as I was already drenched, even though I'd only been outside for about ten minutes. He let me in and we had a wee chat about what to do next. I persuaded him to go a little way on foot, and we spent a while searching the general area. It was bloody awful, to be honest. The rain was coming down in sheets and we couldn't see for the downpour filling our eyes. Then lightning hit a tree on the pavement. We were on that road that leads up to the General Hospital, and the tree just fell down in front of us. The pair of us legged it back to his car, as it was nearer, and took the next phase driving. I reckon the sky must have cleared a bit, or we'd have never seen it, but suddenly Derek gave a yell and pulled over.

"'That's Dawn's ribbon,' he said. We both jumped out of the car, and went over to this bush at the side of the road. Hanging from a branch was a purple ribbon, and Derek remembered seeing Dawn wearing it when he'd dropped them off."

"I commented on it when we left," says Derek, all his nervousness seeming to be gone in the interest of the narrative. "It was very pretty and matched the top she was wearing."

"Aye, just as well you remembered it. There was a path leading past the bush and into the field. We were well into the countryside by now; a good couple of miles from the town. It was still raining, but we could see a lot better by then, and the path took us quite a way before we hit a kind of trail crossroads. We were wondering which way to go, when I saw a barn off to the left. With no other clues, we decided to investigate, and as we got closer, a faint shouting came from inside."

Jimmy stops and looks around. His gaze rests on me for a second or two.

"I'm not sure the girls should hear the rest," he says.

"Jimmy, do you remember what I told you the other week?" I glare at him. "Anyway, I would rather know. Are they okay? Why don't we get them in to tell us themselves? They'll be a lot less squeamish about it, and should be able to fill in the gaps as well, like how they got there, and what happened between Derek dropping them off and you two finding them." For someone supposedly bright, Jimmy can be bloody stupid sometimes. "What do you think, Mel?"

"If they're up to it, I think they should fill in the gaps. I'll run up and see how they are."

Mel leaves the room and we all wait in silence, the air thick with tension.

Chapter Twenty-Three

Mel

I knock on Alison's door in some trepidation. I don't know what to expect, and when Alison opens the door wrapped in a bath towel, I'm relieved to see that at first glance she's looking normal.

"I thought it might be you," she says, "otherwise I probably wouldn't have been so quick to answer the door." She indicates the towel, and I notice her hand is shaking. "Come in for a few minutes, Mel."

"Are you okay? Greg's downstairs with Mark, Jimmy, Derek, Brie, Tina and Jess. We've all been very worried."

"If it's any consolation, so were we. I can't face everyone this evening. But I'll tell you what happened, and you can share it with the others."

"Okay. Let me just phone Mark first and tell him what's happening, or they'll be starting to panic." I wait for her nod, and then call Mark from my mobile. I tell him they'll all have to be patient; I'll go back down when Alison has finished telling me her story. When I end the call, I turn back to my friend. "Do you need anything? Food, coffee, alcohol?"

"All three?" she says with a shaky laugh. "Yes, probably, but let me get this over with first." She slips a nightdress over her head, then removes the towel with a practised gesture. Her arms are covered in fresh bruises, particularly around her wrists. She takes a dressing gown from her wardrobe and wraps it round her, before sitting on the bed, propped up against the pillows. She gestures to the chair next to the bed, and I sit down, shuffling round slightly so I can see her face.

"Are you ready?" I ask.

"As ready as I'm likely to get," she says, rubbing her nose.

"Well, to go back to the beginning, Derek dropped us off in town, and Dawn and I wandered around the shops looking for the couple of items we needed. We didn't find much, to be honest. Everything was either not our style, or horrendously overpriced. We were just about to head into a small mall, when my phone rang. I answered it without thinking, assuming it would be Derek, but it wasn't. I didn't completely recognise the speaker, but it was a young woman, who sounded vaguely familiar. She said you'd been hurt, and needed our help." Alison pauses and looks at me, shame and embarrassment clouding her expression. "I was so stupid, Mel. I didn't stop to think. Dawn and I listened to the woman's instructions to go to the end of the road, and turn right by a certain shop. She said it would be about a mile out of town, and then we'd need to turn off onto a certain road. I can't even remember the name of it now. It was getting dark and grim outside, and just beginning to rain, but we did as we were told, blindly and stupidly. It was only when we got on to the road she'd mentioned, that Dawn tore off her ribbon, and placed it in a hedge at the side of the road.

"'Sorry, Mum,' she said. 'I'm probably being daft, but I don't like this. It doesn't feel right.' I remember trying to reassure her, but that was the last thing I recall. I woke up lying on my side with my hands tied behind my back, my feet roped together and a rotten headache that seemed to be coming from the back of my head.

"'Dawn,' I called out. 'Are you there? Are you alright?'

"'I'm alive, Mum, but we're not alone.' Her voice shook. Then someone helped me to sit up. I don't know who. Dawn was tied up similarly to me, but her t-shirt, jeans and knickers were scattered several feet away, and a strange man was sitting behind her. He said he'd waited for me to wake up. Dawn started screaming."

Alison gulps and seems unable to speak. My imagination leaps forward fifteen years, and the thought of having to watch someone molesting my Emma brings bile to my throat and tears to my eyes.

"Oh God. Dare I ask, what did he do? Don't go into

details, but did he rape her? I'm sorry to be so blunt, but there are no easy ways to ask."

Alison nods. Tears are streaming down her face, and her anguished expression says far more than words could do.

I sit on the bed next to her, and ask gently, "Where is Dawn now?"

"She's in the shower. She said she felt dirty and needed to clean herself," Alison says, between sniffles and sobs.

"Okay. Alison, honey, I don't think Dawn should be left alone. I'm going to call Tina and Jess to help her out. They've both been through it, and can help her like no one else." Dawn shouldn't have been allowed to shower until she'd been examined by the police, but it's too late now.

Alison nods, and I call Mark again, entreating him to urgently send my sister and Tina to Dawn in the bathroom next to her bedroom. After I hang up, I leave Alison for a moment, and go to the bathroom myself. I can't leave Dawn for another minute.

"Dawn?" I call out.

"Yes?" She sounds calm and normal, but I know from my own experience the sense of numbness that can take control after the horror.

"It's time to get out, honey. Tina and Jess are coming up and they want to see you. Can you get out and put your dressing gown on and come to your room?"

I hear sounds of her obeying; the shower going off, and her moving about in the bathroom, and she emerges, just as Jess and Tina reach the top of the stairs, panting for air, their expressions frantic. I don't have time to fill the girls in properly with what's happened, but whisper in Tina's ear, "She's been raped."

An appalled expression crosses Tina's features, but is quickly filled with sympathy, even as Jess, who didn't hear, but who perhaps recognises the numb look on the teenager's face, puts an arm around Dawn's shoulders and guides her next door and to bed. I leave them, and return to Alison, who's still sobbing and shaking.

"God, Mel. It's all my fault. I led her there, and they

127

started by touching her, but then they forced her down, and assaulted her, while they held my head, so I couldn't turn away, but I was tied up and could do nothing to help. And God help me, I was scared they were going to rape me too." She beats her head with her fists.

I sit next to her, and put my arms round her, gently stopping her from hitting herself anymore.

"Alison, listen to me! There was nothing you could have done. If you hadn't followed that path, they would have found another way to get you both there. Why don't you tell me what happened next?"

"Okay," she nods, looking slightly relieved.

"When he finished what he was doing to Dawn," she stops and shudders, "he stood up and pulled up his trousers, leaving my beautiful girl sobbing on the floor. His companion let go of my head, and went to the door. He said something like, 'Let's go. Boss said he'll pop in later to sort them out. He said we could 'ave our fun, then leave 'em to stew for a bit. They'll be more docile by the time he gets 'ere.' Then they left us. There was an electric light in the ceiling. It was some kind of barn, I think, but they turned the light off when they left, and we were in darkness. All I could hear were Dawn's cries and the thunder outside. We must have been alone for about half an hour, maybe longer. Dawn wouldn't speak, and I didn't really know what to say. My guilt at being unable to help her was so intense. It still is. I feel crushed by it. Have you ever known anything like that, Mel?" She speaks in a tone as if she expects the answer to be no. It would be for most people.

"Yes. I was forced to watch while Thomas assaulted Tina." I stop at the horrified expression on Alison's face. She waves her hand for me to continue. "It was a long time ago, but the guilt never leaves me. I've had a lot of other guilt added since then, but that's the worst, and it's the one I really couldn't do anything to prevent." I take a deep breath. "The rest of the guilt is to do with my own actions at other times; other incidents; but it's the enforced inaction that hurts with the most intensity. And yes, it is crushing. I wish I could say it would get better, but I can't. I do understand, though, if that helps at all."

"Maybe. Anyway, to carry on: the next time the door opened, it was accompanied by Derek's voice. He sounded frantic, calling our names. I replied, telling him that we were there and tied up. For a brief moment, in the relief of the rescue, I forgot about Dawn's state, and asked Derek to turn on the light, so when he did, I'm afraid he saw my daughter naked and bleeding on the floor, as did Jimmy, who came in behind him. Derek just stopped dead for a moment, then came slowly to me, seeming afraid to go near Dawn. I can't blame him, though. Jimmy took a pen-knife from his pocket and cut Dawn's ropes first, before helping her to dress. He was very calm and matter-of-fact about it, almost clinical. It helped somehow. Derek was able to take the knife from Jimmy when he'd finished with it, and he cut my ropes, and helped me to stand. My legs would hardly carry me. Dawn was completely unable to stand, and Jimmy picked her up and carried her like a baby. Derek supported me, and we somehow got back to Derek's car, and he brought us all back here. Jimmy's left his car in Macclesfield. He said it would be okay there until tomorrow."

Now the story is complete, Alison rests back against her pillows. She looks pale and exhausted. Emotionally battered, and physically bruised, I know she'll be scarred from today for life. She took Dawn from her home to protect her from something like this, and now... Well, neither of them will ever be the same again. I feel guilty myself. I allowed this to happen, by making Derek return for me and Emma, instead of staying with Alison and Dawn. If he'd done that, they'd have been safe, and Dawn would still be an innocent and unscarred young girl.

My chest grows tight, and I can barely bring myself to look at Alison. My arms drop to my sides.

"I failed you, I'm so sorry," I manage to whisper.

I half-expect Alison to forgive me and say it's not my fault, but she snaps, "Yes, you did." Perhaps she's relieved to have someone else to blame. "You were supposed to protect us. This is no refuge. At least, it is, but it's also a prison. If you can't protect women when they leave the walls of the building, how can you justify offering this as a place of safety?" She looks at me with sudden venom, and I leave the bed and go to the door. Standing in the doorway, I glance back at her.

"As I said, I'm sorry. The circumstances were... Oh, I don't know. So many things lined up for this to happen. So yes, I'm partly at fault, but the guilty people are the ones that actually did this. If you can bring yourself to remember that, perhaps we can all work together to help them get caught and put in prison. Then we can all be safe. I'm not saying you should forgive me, but please, just bury the hatchet for a while."

I close the door behind me. I don't feel I can bear any more of the accusations. I rest my back against the wall, and cover my face as I sink to the floor.

Chapter Twenty-Four

Jess

Dawn lies in her bed, now clad in a nightdress. Her back is turned towards me and Tina, who each occupy one of the chairs near the window. She hasn't said a word since we got her into bed, but Tina mouthed at me that Dawn had been raped, and that's enough for me to want to help her. Drastic action is needed to break this uncanny silence.

Tina speaks first. "I was younger than you are when it first happened to me, Dawn, and Jess was even younger. We've both been there. If there's anyone you can talk to, it's us."

"I know." A muffled voice comes from the depths of the pillows.

"So, talk to us then," I say. "It's like a giant shitty splinter. Dig it out as fast as you can. The scar won't disappear, but the splinter will be gone." I consider. "Well, it's not quite like that, but it does help to talk about it. I had no one to talk to until I met Tina, and she's helped loads. It's good to know that other people understand." I'm waffling, but I really want Dawn to feel like she can talk to us.

She finally turns over, horror in her eyes. It's a strange improvement on the blank calm from before.

"I feel so filthy. And to make it all worse, my mum was there. They made her watch. It's so sick. I'm not her baby anymore."

Tina goes over and sits on Dawn's bed, and clasps her hand. "You know what, Dawn? That's beyond awful, but we're going to get you and your mum some help. Last week, Mel finalised an arrangement with a professional counsellor, and she's going to come in and do some group and individual sessions. Maybe she can work with you and your mum to help you both find a way to cope with this. It'll take time, but it's not impossible." Tina smiles at Dawn and then at me.

I suddenly realise that the counsellor is being brought in to help me too. Shit. My mind is filled with the memory of those bandages, and the scars underneath. They're probably right about me needing help. Even now, I'm filled with the need to reach for a sharp object, and it takes effort to sit still with my friends. Seeing Dawn in such suppressed agony helps in a strange way. I have to stay here. She needs me more than I need the razor. I repeat this inside my head several times, and the urge lessens slightly.

"Jess!" Tina pulls me back to the present. "I think it would help Dawn if you told her about your first time."

Seriously? Tina wants me to share that? I swallow.

"Dawn, would that help?" I ask.

"Maybe. It might take my mind off my own troubles for a bit anyhow."

"It was a long time ago. I was only thirteen. I'd just finished my first period when he decided I was old enough. He'd been touching me there for years, and I hated it, but this was the first time he forced himself into me. I thought I was going to suffocate. He was so much bigger and heavier than me. It hurt so much too. And then I bled loads afterwards. I thought I was going to bleed to death, and the pains that I'd had with my period were nothing in comparison. It was like my whole pelvis went into spasm; like it was protesting against this invasion." I tail off as a thought crosses my mind. "Are you bleeding, Dawn?"

Tears fill her eyes.

"No." She pulls the sheet up over her head. "It wasn't my first time," she says, her voice muffled again.

Tina and I look at each other; her face mirroring my own confusion.

"Have you been... raped before?" I ask in a whisper.

"No." Dawn sounds sheepish now. "It was a teacher at school."

Now the look exchanged between me and Tina is filled with shock.

"That may have been consenting, Dawn, but it's not legal. Technically he raped you as you're underage." Tina explains this gently, still holding Dawn's hand.

A head appears from under the sheet. She's smiling shyly; a huge change from her previous expression.

"So, what happened?" I ask. The question is driven primarily by curiosity, but the benefit of making Dawn feel better is a definite bonus.

She sits up, releases Tina's hand, and moves her pillows to support her. Then she crosses her arms in a defensive gesture.

"He was my maths teacher, but he was dead young. Only just qualified really. I think it was his first job. He was twenty-four. I was not quite fifteen. About six months ago, he suggested I went to him for extra help, as it was only a year until GCSEs and I was struggling a bit. We met several times at lunch break, and gradually found ourselves chatting more about each other than about maths. Then, one time he suggested meeting after school, back at his flat, as we would have more than half an hour, and might manage to fit in a bit more tuition. But as soon as we were inside his flat, we started kissing, and he was touching me." She smiles, a secret, satisfied smile. "We just made out at first. It was lovely. Then we did a bit of maths before I left, so I could tell Mum I'd learnt something. It must have been the fourth time I went round there that we lost control. The kissing and touching went beyond the point of no return, and he was inside me. It did hurt, and I bled a bit, but he was very gentle, and got me some towels and stuff. I told my mum my period had come early, and she didn't give it another thought. He used a condom. Then and the other times. It happened every week for about two months, and then he left the school. He called me on my mobile to cancel our next lesson, and just said he had to go back up North as his Dad was ill and he had to take a job near where he could look after him. I never saw him again. I tried to call him, but I reckon he blocked my number."

Tears fill her eyes, and her face takes on a pained expression again. "So, I miss him horribly, but I guess it

133

made it easier that he wasn't around when we left home. It would have made everything more complicated."

She falls quiet, and it's hard to guess if she's thinking about her teacher or about what happened today. Neither Tina nor I interrupt, but watch as she hugs her knees through the sheet.

"Mum would go ape if she knew, but I don't know if she's freaked out more because she had to watch that foul creep doing what he did, or if it's because she thinks I lost my innocence."

"If you were in your mum's shoes, what would freak you out most, do you think?" asks Tina.

Dawn thinks for a moment, then shudders. "I can't imagine anything worse than having to watch while someone you love is raped. I hated what happened more than anything that's ever happened to me in my life, but in a way I would rather it had been that way round. I couldn't have handled having to watch anyone do that to Mum."

"Maybe you should tell your mum that," I say in an abrupt tone. I do feel sorry for Dawn; no one should have to endure that, but I don't really think she's taken in the full horror yet. Two hours after my first assault, I couldn't have added up two and two, let alone reminisce about an affair with a teacher. Obviously, as I was abducted when I was ten, there hadn't been any affairs with teachers, but I was incapable of thought – except that I wanted to die. It's taken a lot of years to get past that, and perhaps I never have entirely. Sometimes the cutting is more than just symbolic.

"Jess is right in a way, Dawn. Talking to your mum as soon as possible is necessary for you both. Do you want me to take you in there?" Tina waits for Dawn's nod of assent, and then stands up. "Come on. I'll walk you to the door. Do you want us to wait here for you to come back?"

"I don't know. I might stay in my mum's room tonight. I think it would be good for both of us," says Dawn. "I've got my mobile. I'll call you if it doesn't work out, and you can come back."

"Don't go anywhere, Jess. I'll be back in a minute." Tina

flashes a warning glance at me, and they're gone.

I don't know if Dawn talking to Alison so soon is a good idea. Surely it would be better for them to cool down a bit first, but what do I know? I had no one to talk to for years after the first time. Talking doesn't come easily now.

Tina's only gone a couple of minutes, but she's not alone when she comes back in.

"Mel, are you okay?" I jump up. My sister is crying so much she's almost hyperventilating. "Sit!" I force her down on to the chair Tina vacated earlier. "Take slow deep breaths. Slower. On my count. Breathe in…two…three…four…five, and out…" I talk her through breathing until she's calmed down, and the sobs have settled. I used to have to do this with Kylie when she was first taken, and I became a bit of an expert. I learnt quickly what worked and what didn't.

When Mel is quiet, and breathing more normally, I kneel at her side. "Okay, let's go to my room and you can tell me and Tina what's up… No, don't talk yet. Let's get you out of here first."

Mel nods and allows us to guide her along the corridor to our bedroom, which is bigger, and runs less risk of intruders.

As we're walking along the corridor, I realise I have finally forgiven my sister for leaving me that night when I was ten. I'll never forget it perhaps, but the anger has been replaced by love. When I arrived, I'd have been pleased to see her upset, and would have rejoiced that she was 'getting a taste of her own medicine'. But now, I can't bear it.

Once we arrive, I signal to Mel to sit on my bed, and I sit next to her, grabbing her hand, and clasping it, albeit a bit awkwardly. Tina sits on her own bed, facing us with an anxious expression.

"Okay, now tell us, calmly, what happened to get you in such a state? I thought you were with Alison, and she was telling you all about it."

"Yes," Mel sniffs, "but then I made the mistake of apologising for getting Derek to come and pick up me and Em, rather than staying with them."

I unravel this somewhat complicated sentence in silence.

135

"So Alison reckons it was your fault?"

"She does now, although I don't think it had occurred to her before." Mel sniffs again. "The problem is, it kind of is my fault."

"Bollocks!"

"Jess, that's not nice," says Mel.

"Seriously? Come on, Sis. I'm sorry, but I'm not going to let you talk such crap without swearing about it. There wasn't a cat in hell's chance that Mark was going to let you take Em to the doctor without being dropped off and picked up again. It's not your fault that Alison decided to gatecrash the trip." Fury races through my veins and pounds in my head. I won't let anyone make Mel feel like shit just to ease their own guilt.

"Jess, sit down." Tina waves me back to the bed. I don't remember standing up and going to the door. "What are you planning?" she asks.

"To tell Alison the truth. It's her own bloody fault. If she hadn't insisted on going with you today, rather than waiting until tomorrow, she could have had Derek's undivided attention, which is probably what she wanted anyway. She obviously fancies him." I manage to bring a half-smile to my sister's face. I look at her properly, and beneath the blotchy redness she looks exhausted. It's been an emotional day for everyone.

I take a deep breath. I'm not too wrapped up in my own shenanigans to realise I'm probably not helping much. "What time is it?" I ask Tina.

"Just gone eight," she says. "Mel, why don't you go to bed? You're pooped. Jess is right in a way. You absolutely mustn't blame yourself. We'll get this all sorted out calmly and quietly, and Alison will apologise to you tomorrow. Brie and I can sort out Emma's bottle between us. Jess can go and tell Greg to come back in the morning – late morning – to hear everyone's statements. Everyone involved is going to bed early. The Abbey will look after itself for the rest of the night."

Mel and I turn to gaze at Tina with awe. She's such a quiet, reserved girl, but she's showing steel in her nature: a strength of character at dealing with a crisis that I wouldn't have dreamed of when I first met her.

"I mean it," she says, with a determined smile. "Mel, go to bed now, and stop worrying. Jess, go downstairs and tell the men to stop waiting for us. Then you can come back and go to bed too. It's been exhausting for everyone. We'll get everything sorted in the morning. Then Greg can catch those bastards."

Chapter Twenty-Five

Mel

After a night spent battling with guilt in all its forms, I wake
with bleary eyes and a headache. I can't face breakfast, so as
soon as Emma's been fed – ironically, she had a good night's
sleep for the first time in over a week – I put her in her chair
to play in Mark's office and wander along to the chapel. I've
not been in there since Dominic's demise, and I'm curious to
see if it's changed at all. I also have a strange belief that it
might help put some of my demons to rest; even more
bizarre, given the source of some of those demons.

Unlike in Dominic's time, there are new pews laid out in
rows. Flowers decorate the altar, and it's been set out as a
beautiful place for private worship. Before my refuge ladies
began to arrive, I arranged on the phone with the vicar at the
local church that he would visit on request to conduct
services in the chapel here, but so far no one has asked for it.
I wonder who has been keeping the chapel looking so neat
and clean.

Despite the flowers, though, there is a presence. Dominic's
ghost seems to hover: berating Jimmy for killing a wasp,
glowering while Mark proposes to me, avoiding my gaze on
so many occasions. Latterly, of course, I was unable to attend
services, and took to praying silently in my head.

Recently, despite the help given to me at the end, I've all
but stopped praying. Guilt stabs at me again, but a different
kind to the guilt that plagued me all night. This is a religious
guilt – for forsaking the 'Almighty One' despite everything. I
sidle in to a pew and sink to my knees. After a muttered
rendition of The Lord's Prayer, I get to what I really want to
say.

I don't know if God can help me with forgiveness for Dominic's murder, or for my lack of repentance about it; or whether He can get Mark to forgive me for my sin of adultery (if it is adultery, given that it happened before we were actually married). I know Mark tries to forgive, but it's hard for him to forget. My prayers are ardent in that direction. Mark's coldness to me is often justified, but if prayer would help dissolve it, I would be on my knees here night and day.

My guilt for yesterday's actions is also complicated. Part of me knows that Tina and Jess are right. The circumstances conspired against Alison and Dawn yesterday, and no amount of prayer will change that. Unable to pray for God's forgiveness, I shift my focus, and pray for Alison's. Shutting my eyes, I bend my head low over my clasped hands, and beg God to send a forgiving heart to my one-time friend.

"Mel?"

A quiet voice next to me rouses me and I open my eyes, to see Alison herself sitting in the pew next to me. I attempt to get up, but I've been kneeling so long, my knees have seized up. She reaches out her hand and clasps my arm, giving me a bit of gentle support; enough to help me off the floor and to sit back in the pew.

"Thank you," I say, but I can't keep the note of nervousness from my voice. I rub my knees, avoiding eye contact while I don't know if hostilities are about to be resumed.

"A lot happened after you left me yesterday evening. I had visits from Dawn, and from Tina." There's anxiety in Alison's voice too, and I look at her cautiously. "Dawn was distressed by what had happened, but the sweet girl was more concerned that I had to witness it. It made me determined to try to bear it, if it makes her easier in her mind."

I nod, unwilling to say anything to break the flow.

"Dawn stayed with me last night. She said she needed me near, but it worked both ways. I was relieved to have her near me. But before we went to bed, Tina came in." Alison looks over at the stained glass window – Samson and Delilah; in

139

Brotherhood days, the Cistercians used to stand next to it for prayers. Then she looks directly at me. "Tina said firmly that if I'd waited another day to go shopping, Derek could have come with us and stayed with us, and this would never have happened."

I silently bless Tina and thank God. It looks as though He's sent that forgiving heart after all.

"She also said that Mark had reasons for not allowing you and Emma out unaccompanied, and Derek was under strict instructions to bring you both back here as soon as you finished at the surgery. Apparently he was pushing it by leaving you there to take me and Dawn into town, but he wanted to do us a favour if he could. I need to speak to him this morning. He was trying to help us, but I'm afraid I shouted at him in the car yesterday too."

It sounds as if Tina has hammered the point home well, and now it's time for me to respond, and perhaps smooth things over, if it's possible.

"Tina's right. I can't say much about it, but Mark has made some enemies out there, and they've sent threats. He didn't want me to take Emma to the clinic at all, but Paul Griffiths (who would normally have seen her here at the Abbey) has had to go away, and we didn't have any choice. If you and Dawn want some professional help to deal with what happened, I've arranged for a counsellor to come in once a week for a while for a group session to help a number of women who are dealing with rape and its consequences. You're welcome to join the group. Or, if you prefer, I could arrange for you to see her separately at first?"

"Thanks Mel. Maybe the group sessions, but I think we need to see Greg first. If it's possible to catch those evil bastards, that has to be the priority." Her voice and hands shake as she speaks, but her over-riding emotion seems to be anger, and not against me. I send up another silent prayer of thanks.

I look at my watch. "Did Tina say what time Greg would be here?" I ask. "It's nearly ten."

"Ten-thirty, but when have you known Greg to wait until

his appointed time? Let's go and get the kettle on in the common room, and see if we can rustle up some biscuits."

"Good plan. Thanks Alison." I tentatively hold out a hand for her to shake.

"Don't be stupid, Mel. One idiot is enough round here." She ignores the hand and pulls me into a hug.

I hold her tight for a moment. "Thank you," I whisper.

As we break apart, I see I'm not the only one with damp cheeks.

Twenty minutes later, settled in the common room with coffee and biscuits, Alison and Dawn explain to Greg and Shelley the chain of events that led them to the barn yesterday with such awful consequences. I sit in the corner of the room listening quietly, but not interrupting, even when Alison glosses over some of the details of Dawn's assault. I can fill the police officers in privately if they can't get it directly. When Alison finishes speaking, Shelley asks to speak to Dawn privately.

"Why would you want to do that?"

"Mum, it's fine. I don't mind," says Dawn. She gets up to go with Shelley, and smiles reassuringly at her mum. They leave and we sit in silence for a few minutes. Finally Greg shuffles in his seat.

"I'm afraid we didn't precisely find Thomas, but he's been seen in the area, and there's a suggestion that he was in the barn after everyone left."

"What makes you think that?" I ask.

"It's almost too cheesy, and I'm not totally convinced by it, but a handkerchief was dropped with a T monogrammed in the corner."

"That doesn't sound like the sort of thing my brother-in-law would carry. Actually he was more likely to wipe his nose on his sleeve than carry a handkerchief – let alone a monogrammed one."

I nod in agreement. The Thomas I knew was a complete slob.

"T is not an uncommon letter for a name to start with, and

could just as easily be the start of a surname," I say.

"I agree, ladies. We don't even know if it belonged to the man who was expected. It might have been dropped to incriminate someone. The bigger clue is that we've shown his photo around in Macclesfield and some of the villages, and he's been identified, but the last sighting was three days ago, when he checked out of a hotel in the town centre. He didn't give his proper name. He paid cash, and showed an old-style paper driving licence for ID. The name on it was," Greg takes a notebook from his pocket and checks, "Robert Miles."

"That's the name of my husband's boss," Alison says. "I assume they decided to use it for cover. I can't imagine Bob being complicit. He was quite a nice chap."

"Can you describe the man who assaulted your daughter?" asks Greg, sympathetically.

Alison shudders. "He was wearing a balaclava, black t-shirt and black jeans. He had no defining marks – no tattoos or anything on display."

"What was his build?" Greg's voice is calm and patient.

"I don't know really. Muscular I suppose. Quite big, but not flabby; like he worked out regularly."

I refrain from commenting, but she could have described half the men in Macclesfield. Greg's pleasant expression doesn't change, but his brow tightens fractionally. I suspect he's thinking the same thing.

"Okay, well if you remember anything else, just give me a call." He hands Alison a business card.

"Greg, is there any news about the men in the trial?" I ask.

"You're probably best to ask Shelley about that, Mel." He shakes his head. "As you know, I'm technically a suspect, as I was on the ward at the time, and had no more of an alibi than anyone else."

"That's ridiculous. And I assume they don't really think you killed Frank, otherwise you'd have been suspended."

"Maybe," he laughs. "Although we're so short-handed at the moment, I reckon they think it's best I carry on working where they can keep an eye on me."

"Rubbish. They know you." I shiver. I wonder how well they know Greg, and if they recognise that he perhaps assisted in a miscarriage of justice. But I can't afford to dwell on that. He's watching me with too understanding a smile.

"I believe Shelley's tracked down most of the trial patients, but Charles has been elusive. Apparently he gave a false address. The doctor he named didn't have him on their system."

"Wow. That is interesting. Charles had more of a motive than anyone else in the ward." I turn to Alison. "Last year, the Infirmary was the site of a clinical trial with healthy volunteers. One of the volunteers was Greg, two others were called Charles and Frank. Frank was given an overdose, we believe, and it caused a really bad reaction. He died in hospital quite recently, but before the overdose, we found out that Frank had been having an affair with Charles's wife. Charles reacted badly to the information, and tried to beat up Frank in public. The big question is whether he later decided to take more permanent revenge. It's now a murder investigation, I believe. That's right, isn't it, Greg?"

"Absolutely. That's a good summary, Mel." He looks at Alison. "Obviously, as I was one of the trial patients, I could theoretically have killed Frank myself, but I was actually on a job, and it didn't become apparent until Frank's post mortem that his death was anything other than a tragic accident."

I open my mouth, about to ask if my discovery of the drug inventory records had made a difference, but an almost imperceptible shake of the head from Greg deters me.

The door opens, and Shelley comes back in alone.

"Where's my daughter?" Alison demands to know.

"She's gone to get the clothes she was wearing yesterday. Nothing to worry about. We all want to catch the men who did this, and Dawn agrees there might be traces of DNA available from her clothes. She shouldn't have showered really, but it's done now, and hopefully the clothes will give us something."

Alison nods, her anger subsiding.

143

A moment later, Dawn arrives, carrying a plastic bag, presumably filled with the clothes she wore yesterday. She hands it over, and Greg and Shelley take their leave.

"Apparently Derek and Jimmy told their stories last night," says Dawn. She seems subdued, but otherwise okay.

All the same, I resolve to organise the counselling for them. There are some wounds that don't heal without help.

Chapter Twenty-Six

Jess

My bedroom is usually a haven, a place where I can hide from everyone except Tina. I've not bothered with lunch today. The thought of food makes me feel a bit queasy. My latest book, a biography of Eva Peron, is failing to keep my attention. I don't know whether to be relieved or irritated when there's a knock at the door.

Dawn enters without waiting for a reply. "Can I come in?" she asks.

I refrain from pointing out that she already has, and indicate the chair between the beds. After what she's been through, I don't have the heart to be horrible to her, however much a part of me wants to wallow in my own bad mood.

"How are you doing?" I sit up properly on the bed and cross my legs in front of me.

"I gave all the clothes I was wearing yesterday to that policewoman, Shelley. She seemed to think it might help to catch him."

"She's got a point. Is your mum feeling a bit better today? Has she realised that my sister isn't at fault?"

"Yeah, Tina sorted it all out. Mum and Mel seem to be friends again anyway."

"Good." Silence prevails for a moment, a long drawn-out beat in time.

"Will you teach me how to cut myself?"

"Bloody hell, Dawn. Why would you want to do that? Shit. That is so screwed up to even ask."

I put my head in my hands. Shit, shit, shit, shit, shit! I don't even know if she understands what she's just asked, or if she really wants to hurt herself, but I have to find out.

Sodding hell. I can't have that on my conscience.

I take a deep breath and look directly at her. "Look, sorry I shouted just then, but you freaked me out. Let's talk about this calmly." I'm anything but calm. My hands are shaking so much, I sit on them to keep them hidden.

"Okay. Sorry. I didn't mean to freak you out, but I don't know anyone else I could ask."

I try not to roll my eyes. She might have just been raped, but she's an innocent in so many other ways. I take a few more deep breaths, until the shaking subsides. Finally I'm able to move my hands from under my bum, and I roll up my sleeves.

"You don't want scars like this, Dawn. Seriously. This tells the world you're screwed up. It's a sign you're not normal. If you want to make a statement, dye your hair and wear funky clothes. You don't need to scar yourself."

"So why do you do it?"

I stare down at the worst scar, halfway between my wrist and elbow on my left arm. It's still not fully healed. It's the one I pick at when I can't find a razor. How do I tell her? Is there a way to say enough of the truth to put her off, without sounding like a weird survivor-hero type of person?

"It's hard to explain the hell of being raped every day for six years. Even when he brought in other girls to add variety. And that was its own kind of hell, because he forced them into drug addiction." I fall silent again, unable to speak for a moment.

"What happened to those girls? How many of them were there?"

"There were three. I watched one die from heroin withdrawal, when he left us alone for a week. Before that, the other two were taken away. I don't know if they're still alive." I find a voice, but it doesn't sound like my own.

"What hurts most? Is it that you had to watch your friend die, or was it being raped every day?"

Holy crap. This girl gets to the point a lot. It's only because I care about her that I force myself to think about it. I can't let her get to this point.

"Look, Dawn. I don't want to minimise what happened to you. No one should ever have to be in that situation. It's completely shit. But it happened once. They won't be able to get to you again. You're safe here, and you'll stay here until they're caught. I was at his mercy all the time. If he wanted to starve me, he would. If he wanted to tie me up while he took me from every sodding angle he could think of, he would. The more I cried, the more he loved it. Getting those other girls hooked on drugs wasn't about them; it was about me. It was all to do with fear and control. Then one day, he left a razor near the sink in the corner of the cellar. It was before Kylie arrived, but shortly after her predecessor, Anna, disappeared. I think some insanity got hold of me. I had a stupid idea that I could be in control. I could be in charge of when there was pain. The first cut hurt like hell, but it wasn't deep. I just did one at a time to start with. I used tissues to mop up, shredded them and pushed them down the plughole in the sink. It was months before he realised what I was doing. He'd decided to take me during the day, and made me strip for him. He went through phases of whether I had clothes, or if I had to be naked the whole time. I detested the naked times. It was complete degradation. I could hide nothing from him. Anyway, that day, he said he was fed up with me always being covered up. He watched while I took my clothes off. Even in the cellar there was a kind of dim light during the day, filtering through a grate. I'd kind of forgotten that he hadn't seen my scars. I was so used to them by then, that I took them for granted."

"What did he say?" Dawn's voice breaks my reverie. I'd almost forgotten she was there.

"He beat me. He said if I wanted pain, he'd give it to me, and he did. I could hardly sit down for days. The bastard also took the razor away. Looking back, though, I wonder if he originally left it there on purpose. It was another form of manipulation. A way he could get at me, and then destroy me. Anyway, I tried to find other ways of cutting myself. Occasionally he'd leave scissors around, telling me to cut my nails. I always cut more than my nails. I couldn't help it by then. The addiction was unbreakable, even so early on. I found places on my body that he wouldn't easily see, as I was still deprived of clothes at that time. It made it even more painful when he raped me, but it gave me a feeling of power. Even though it hurt, it kind of said that this pain was of my choosing, not his." I give a mocking laugh. "As I said, totally screwed up."

The shakes are back: my whole body this time. I want to control them, to be able to tell Dawn not to start cutting, but even my teeth are chattering now. Dawn looks round, alarmed, and then takes out her phone. I hear her asking someone to come to the room, then she puts the phone in her pocket. "I phoned Tina. I hope you don't mind, but you look ill. Sorry, it's my fault for making you tell me that stuff."

"P-p-p-promise m-m-me y-you w-w-won't s-start."

She nods vigorously, panic in her face. I must really look like shit, but I can't stop this trembling. Cold seeps through my limbs, filling every cell – every space in my body – until I don't know if I'm shaking or shivering.

The door opens and Tina comes in, followed by Brie. Tina comes straight over to me, and takes my hands.

"You're burning up, hun. Lie down." Tina pulls back the covers, and helps me into bed, even though I'm fully clothed, in shirt and jeans. I curl up on my side, still shivering now. I've decided it's definitely shivers, not shakes. Brie is over with Dawn, having a conversation in low tones so I can't make out what they're saying. But they leave after a few seconds, and I'm left with just my room-mate.

"Okay, Jess. Let's get you into your PJs and then I'll go and get some paracetamol or something for you." She helps me undress, taking care not to hurt me in any way. I surge of affection fills me, and I resolve once again to do anything for her. "When did you start feeling like this?"

I want to tell her everything, but a huge lethargy has taken over from the shivers, and although I still feel freezing cold, I'm now too wiped out to talk. Fog fills my brain. I need to tell Tina something. What's it about? Dawn?

Shit. I can't remember.

I wake up to find the room in darkness and a cold draught blowing at me. I sit up, but feel dizzy, so I lie down again. The breeze is coming from an electric fan. Apart from me, the room is empty. I get up and turn the fan off, staggering across the spinning room, and then falling back into bed with relief.

Memories flood back. A long conversation about life before I escaped. Why was I telling Dawn about that? It seems a strange choice of confidante for that sort of conversation. I'm fighting the fog in my head to come up with an answer, when my bedroom door is flung open, and Alison storms in.

"You bloody bitch! How dare you tell my daughter how to cut herself? And then you hide away in here and pretend to be ill? Is it shame at what you've done? Or are you such a heartless cow, that you wanted to give her the ideas and then disappear while she puts them into action?" As she rants at me, she yanks back the bedclothes and grabs my upper arms, hauling me up to face her.

I stare at her in shock, trying to assimilate what she's just told me. The spinning room isn't helping, but I try to ignore it. It gets easier when Alison lets go of my right arm and slaps me round the face. The imprint of her fingers stings on my cheek. I panic. She continues to hit me. It's the first time I've been hit by anyone other than Him, and I don't know what to do, but some sort of survival instinct kicks in.

"What the hell do you think you're doing?" I yell at her. My timing is immaculate, because the room is instantly full of people.

"Alison, stop that now. Leave Jess alone."

Mark's voice fills me with relief. His sense and kindness are invaluable just now. I can't think straight with Alison hovering over me, even though she's stopped slapping me. Someone pulls her away, but I'm not sure who. With her out of the way, I lie back down, and the room settles a bit. I'm able to work out who's here. Mark is standing on my left, between my bed and the wall. Brie is next to Alison, with a firm hand on her shoulder, and they're now near the door.

Jimmy is standing quietly in the corner, on the other side of Tina's bed, and my sister is between the beds, sitting on the chair, but on the edge, as if she's waiting for something.

Perhaps she is, as when all is quiet, she's the first to speak. "Alison, Jess is not well and has nothing to do with Dawn's actions."

"My daughter left here an hour ago, and ten minutes ago, was found bleeding on her bed. Tell me how that isn't Jessica's fault." The fury in Alison's voice would terrify an army. It reduces me to a pulp, even after what I've been through.

"I made her promise not to," I say, the words coming up from the depths of my consciousness. I only barely remember what happened before I fell asleep. I felt so ill.

"You actually discussed it?" Dawn's mum stares at me, her face filled with disgust.

"She asked me about it. I tried to put her off, and to tell her not to start. I told her why I started; trying to show her that her situation wasn't as bad as mine had been, and didn't justify her cutting herself. Maybe I didn't say the right things, but I tried to."

"So why are you hiding in bed now?"

"She's not hiding, Alison. Jess was taken ill just before your daughter left the room." Brie's voice is sharp. Lovely Brie. She's trying to protect me. She lets go of Alison's shoulder, and comes over to me, laying her hand on my forehead. "You're still hot. You need some peace and quiet; not violence and horror." She smiles at me, then looks around. "Who's with Dawn now?"

"Tina," says Mel. She looks pointedly at Alison. "Shouldn't you be with your daughter, trying to find out the truth, instead of jumping to conclusions? I'll come and see you later. Tina should have finished bandaging Dawn's arms by now."

Alison shrugs her shoulders. "I never could stand the sight of blood. Tina sent me out of the room when I went faint."

Mark shakes his head and rolls his eyes. There is some irony in there somewhere, but my brain is too mushed to

150

work it out.

"Come on then. Alison, I'll take you back to Dawn. If you come back in here, you'll be sent to a different refuge before you can blink. So stay away from Jess." Mark holds the door open for Alison, and then follows her out.

Brie takes something out of her pocket, and after a bit of fumbling, hands me two tablets. Mel leaves the room silently, and returns half a minute later with a glass of water. The tablets are in my mouth by now, tasting horrible and going nowhere. I take the water and drown the tablets, leaving them no choice but to go down my throat.

"Thanks," I say, when they're finally gone.

"Do you want to go back to sleep?" asks Mel.

"Not really." I glance over at Jimmy. I don't know why he's here, but there's no one else I want to talk to just now. After such a traumatic day and a half, I feel lost, and the only safe light is Jimmy. If he's still willing to be my friend, and given that he's here I guess he's not unwilling, then I need to talk to him.

Chapter Twenty-Seven

Mel

When I leave Jess, guilt sends me to check on Dawn. I'm not sure why it should be my fault, but perhaps I shouldn't have lost my temper with Alison.

Dawn is sitting on her bed, a bandage around her left arm, and a sulky expression on her face.

Alison glares at me as I walk in. "Why are you here?"

"How are you feeling, Dawn?" I ask. Nothing I can say will ease Alison's aggression, so I don't bother trying.

"I don't know." The sulky look intensifies, but I'm guessing Dawn feels stupid and embarrassed. I would, in her place. I look around and smile across at Tina, who's been relegated to the corner of the room with the arrival of Dawn's mum. Thank goodness for Tina.

"Shall we leave Alison and Dawn to catch up?" Tina nods.

I glance at Alison. There are all sorts of things I want to say to her: *Keep calm*, *Take it easy*, *Don't shout*, *Be patient*, *Try to understand*. Every single one of those statements is guaranteed to inflame her already-volatile temper.

Tina is watching me. When she sees me looking, she shakes her head slightly. I take her silent advice, and opt for a more general parting shot.

"Hopefully we'll see you both later for dinner." I force a pleasant but neutral smile to my face, and follow Tina from the room. Once out of probable earshot, I ask Tina where we should go to chat.

"How about your room? When's Emma due for her next feed?"

"Oh God, yes." I check my watch. "Half an hour ago. Unless Mark's sorted her out, she must be going ballistic."

We hurry along to my room, but all is silent within. By mutual consent, we go down to the office. Mark's in there, with Emma in his arms, managing a bottle as if it were the easiest thing in the world. He's otherwise alone. He looks up and smiles when we enter, and a boulder-sized weight lifts from my gut.

"Is everything alright?" he asks. "When I left Jess, I checked in on Em. She was stirring, so I grabbed one of the bottles you'd prepared, and shoved it in the microwave. I did check it before I gave it to her. On my wrist like you showed me."

"Brilliant. Thanks Mark. You get top Daddy points. Everything is reasonably settled upstairs I think. Jimmy is with Jess, and Alison is with Dawn. I don't know what we're going to do with them though."

"Sit down, both of you." He shifts Emma in his arms and adjusts the angle of the bottle. "Sorry, getting pins and needles. Yeah, Alison and Dawn. Obviously we need to give them time to come to terms with what's happened. And I guess some counselling is needed urgently."

"Tina, what did Dawn tell you?" I ask.

"Not much, really. I got the impression that Jess made her feel inadequate. I'm sure it wasn't intentional. Jess likes Dawn, and would have tried to help, but—"

"I'm trying to get a grip on the chain of events here," Mark interrupts. "Dawn went to see your sister, Mel, and asked her about self-harm, is that right?"

Tina and I both nod.

"So it seems," says Tina. "When I went into the room I share with Jess, she was in a state, barely able to speak, and with a raging temperature. She fell asleep within a couple of minutes, though, and Dawn confessed that Jess had been telling her awful things about her imprisonment. She said it made her rape yesterday afternoon seem trivial. I put an arm round her, and said 'Your experience was dreadful. No rape is trivial, and we will get you help to get through it.' She just shrugged, and to be honest, I was more concerned with Jess's state at that moment. So I let Dawn go, while I rigged up that baby monitor for Jess, so we'd be able to keep an ear out for when she woke up. When I'd sorted that out, I decided to check in on Dawn, and that's when I found her. Thankfully she hadn't had time to do much. Just one cut on her left arm, but it was quite deep."

"Well done, Tina." Mark smiles warmly at her, and I suppress the tiny surge of jealousy. I should know better than to be jealous of Tina. "You've been a star today. I don't know what we'd do without you."

The surge gets bigger.

"It's been an exhausting couple of days. I think Mel needs to take some time for herself." Tina looks at me, and I force myself to meet her gaze. "Mel, you're running around trying to put out fires. I know Emma's settled down a lot with her new diet, but I've noticed you're struggling with the consequences. You must be feeling awful."

"Tina, are you okay to finish giving Emma her bottle? Sorry to dump this on you when you've been so brilliant, but I think maybe I need to take my wife to our room and get her to bed."

"Of course, take your time. I'm always happy for a chance of a cuddle with my adopted niece anyway." She takes Emma and bottle from Mark and sits herself in his empty chair.

Mark comes round and pulls me to my feet. By now, all the emotions of the last two days are fighting for attention, and as Tina so delicately pointed out, my chest has developed overnight in to two large, unyielding melons – full of milk that I can't get rid of. I meant to try to express some of it off, but the lack of free time today has meant it's been impossible to get the opportunity or privacy for such activities. Tears begin to stream down my cheeks. I brush them away impatiently, but allow Mark to guide me to our bedroom.

When we arrive, he sits me on the bed, and sits behind me, rubbing my shoulders gently.

"You know I love you, don't you, Mel?"

"Yes, I think so. I just get jealous sometimes."

"Me too, but there's no need. I know really that you wouldn't go off with Jimmy or Greg or any of the others. You should know that you have nothing to worry about from anyone either."

"You do care about Tina, though, don't you?" I can't help asking.

"Of course I do. In the same way I care about Jess – as if she was my younger sister." His hands still on my shoulders and start to caress my arms. I turn to him, and he wraps his arms around me, touching me gently. A hand rests briefly on my hot, swollen breasts. "Blimey, Mel. That must be really uncomfortable."

"It is. How can you tell?"

"It's hot and feels like it's solid. That's not normal."

"I need to try to express it. Would you bring me some hot damp towels and a bowl please, and I'll try now?" I can't keep the regret from my voice. If things had been different, a tender session of lovemaking might have been imminent. We were heading in that direction. But I couldn't have tolerated it just now, so perhaps it's as well that Mark called a halt.

Five minutes later, Mark's back with the requested items, but his expression is marred by a huge scowl.

"Thanks." I take the towels and bowl, and unbutton my blouse. I'm aware that Mark's eyes are on me, but they're unfocussed as if he's not registering what he's seeing.

"What's up?" I ask.

"I've had another letter. It didn't come through the post, but was handed to Derek by some random kid."

"Have you read it? What does it say?"

Mark sits heavily on the bed, removes the letter from the envelope and reads aloud:

"*Dear Sir,*

"*You appear to have ignored our previous instructions. We have given a hint of what happens to your friends when you disobey. Next time, it will be your family.*

"*Unless, of course, you change your mind and decide to work for us as requested…*

"*Obviously, you are being watched. We are aware that you are colluding with the police on other matters. If there is any suggestion that this letter has come into their hands, you will all be killed.*

"Yours sincerely,

"The Boss"

"They clearly don't know their letter-writing skills. Someone should tell The Boss that you don't sign off as *Yours Sincerely*, if you start with *Dear Sir*. Anyway, why doesn't he address you as Mark? I assume this letter is for you?"

He shows me the envelope, addressed very clearly to Mark Winterton-Jones. I glance up at him, distracted from expressing milk for a moment. He's pale, and a pulse beats visibly below his jaw. He stands up and starts pacing.

"What are you going to do?"

"Sod it, Mel. I don't bloody know. What do you think I should do?"

"The letter says they would know if we've told Greg. How would they know? You're the engineer. What technology could they have that would enable them to know?"

Mark stares at me, perhaps surprised at the logical response. He sits down again, looking thoughtful.

"Phone tap, personal tap, bugs around the Abbey. God knows there have been enough of those around. Okay, good point. I can check around the office and common rooms. I'll check my computer for spyware, now we've thought about it. I'm not sure what I can do about the phone landline or the mobiles, but I think we should take precautions."

"If they tapped the landline, would it be from here, or from the junction box?" I ask.

"Could be either. I'll do a bit of detective work. For now, I guess we'll need to be careful what we say and where. When you've finished doing that, lie down and have a nap. I'll bring you some dinner later. You've got a couple of hours until then." He drops a quick kiss on my forehead before leaving the room.

Left alone, I manage to express quite a bit of milk, but my breasts still feel hot and hard, particularly the right one. My head hurts with all the stress of the day, and I think I might have a bit of a temperature myself. Perhaps there's a bug going round, and I've caught it from my sister. Poor Jess. She tried to help Dawn, but it completely backfired. Dawn did the cutting anyway, and Jess has been left with the trauma of remembering what happened to her.

I would like to go and see her, but when I stand up, a wave of nausea comes over me, and I sit down abruptly. I sit down, and recall that Jimmy is with Jess. He'll look after her. I grab the nightdress from under my pillow, and change slowly, trying not to make myself feel any worse. Then I get into bed. I'm about to drift off to sleep, when I remember the letter.

We're all in danger. If they can do that to Alison and Dawn just for living here, what would they do to me or Emma or Jess or Tina?

Chapter Twenty-Eight

Jess

Left alone with Jimmy, I'm conscious of being a mess. I want to talk to him, to tell him what's been going on, but I don't know where to start. Glancing shyly at him, I manage a half grin. He lowers himself on to the chair next to my bed and reaches out his hand. I take it, and a strange energy flows up my arm. I don't know if it's relief, or comfort, or something altogether different, but it feels good. We sit in silence for a few minutes, just holding hands.

"It's been a crazy couple of days, hasn't it?" he says eventually.

"Yep, sure has. Thanks for staying with me just now."

"Any time, lass, and you know I mean that."

"Yes. Thanks." There's another long pause, while I try to collect my thoughts. "Was it horrible, finding them like that?"

"Aye. In a way, but it was a relief as well. We'd been looking so damn long, and I was imagining all sorts. It's shit what happened to that young lass, but it could have been worse." He looks away. "I know you went through worse, Jess; much worse before you started with…" He makes cutting signs on his arm.

"Maybe it was just lack of opportunity. I didn't start cutting until he left a razor within reach. I don't think it says anything particularly great about me. I feel awful about Dawn, but maybe I said something wrong to her. She promised me she wouldn't, but I felt so poorly by then, I didn't have the energy to make sure she meant it."

"Hey, don't blame yourself. You were trying to help her. No one else did." He frowns, but doesn't seem to be annoyed with me particularly.

"She didn't ask anyone else. I was the only one in a position to help her, and I failed."

"Bullshit, Jess! Her mum should have helped, or at least asked for help. She knew Mel was going to sort something out, but she should have realised it was urgent. She could have called the refuge charity and told them what happened. She could have told Shelley. And Shelley should have done more to help. She talked to Dawn this morning. No way should she have left her in that state."

I squeeze his hand, which is still gripping mine, although it's become almost painfully tight. He relaxes it a bit after my squeeze.

"Dawn seemed really calm when she came in here. If she left Shelley like that, there was no way anyone would have known there was a problem. I wouldn't have known either, if she hadn't asked me about cutting."

Jimmy nods slowly, as if deep in thought. "I guess it's easy to lay blame," he says. "No one wants to have to take responsibility for something like that happening, but perhaps the only blame lies with the bastard that did that to her."

"So you don't blame me for when I do it?"

"I don't know about blame, lass. I just don't want you to ever do it again. Do you need help to stop that happening?" He gets off the chair, and perches on the edge of my bed. I move over to allow him to sit there properly. He's facing me, and looking very serious, but something in his gaze almost stops me breathing.

I try to think clearly. I promised myself I'll always be honest with Jimmy.

"Yeah, I probably do need help. I'm sorry, but I'm constantly fighting it. It's always there."

"Okay. We'll get you some help. I wish I could help you all by myself, but I'm not stupid. You'll not crack an addiction without professional support. Unless you have a git like Dominic forcing you to go cold turkey. And anyway, I don't think it works like that with cutting."

He's holding both my hands now. I want to tell him to hold

me; that he's all I need. But I know I need professional help. Will he support me through it? Maybe. He moves towards me, as if moving in for a kiss, but the door opens, and he quickly returns to the chair.

Mark comes in. He casts Jimmy a quick curious look, but then focusses his gaze on me.

"How are you feeling, Jess?"

Gutted, because you just stopped Jimmy from kissing me, but...

"I'm okay thanks. Paracetamol seem to have kicked in. I feel okay."

"Do you feel up to a wander around the Abbey? I could do with all the help I can get, but I can only ask people I totally trust."

He's got my attention. I glance at Jimmy, who looks as intrigued as I feel. He catches my look and grins at me.

"What do you want us to do, pal?" he says.

Mark closes the door properly and looks around the room intently. He moves curtains out of the way, and checks behind all the furniture while Jimmy and I watch. Eventually, he nods and leans against the wall, facing us.

"Mel and I have deduced that there may be bugs in the Abbey, and I'm not talking of the insect or germ varieties. We need to do a full survey of the buildings, including wires, windows, any corner where a device could be hidden. I have to check all the phone lines and computers. For now, don't say anything to anyone."

"What if someone asks what we're doing?" I say.

"Grab a bottle of multi-purpose cleaner from the store cupboard and carry it with you, and then you can tell anyone who comes in that you're doing a bit of spring cleaning."

"Aye, pal, it's the middle of summer."

"Give me a break, Jimmy, you know what I mean. We need to go through the Abbey thoroughly. We might be looking for something that doesn't exist, but there are people out there who seem to know things that they shouldn't."

"Like what? And who?"

"I can't tell you much, Jess, as I don't know a lot myself,

but I've had letters from someone I once did some work for. They're quite threatening, and they drop hints to suggest they know about our friendship with Greg, for instance. At the moment I don't dare tell Greg about them, as they threaten dire consequences if I do. Until I know for sure that the Abbey is free of devices, I can't risk talking to Greg, or indeed anyone official. Needless to say, I hope, I'm trusting you two with a secret. Don't discuss this with anyone, not even Tina or Brie at this stage. Derek's on patrol outside. He knows about this, and he's surveying the grounds. There's a suggestion that the phone has been tapped, but I'm going to check it out tonight when it's dark. If they have left something there, I can't be seen removing it."

"That sounds crazy, Mark. You could get yourself hurt. If these people are that awful, and they must be to get you in such a panic, then going outside alone at night is insane."

"I never said I'd be alone, Jess. Derek's going to watch my back, and I hope Jimmy will too."

"Aye, I owe you that," says Jimmy. A bitter expression crosses his face, but it doesn't last long.

"Forget it, mate. You did what you had to do. I don't hold grudges and neither does Mel."

"Where is my sister?"

"She's resting. She's had a tough couple of days. Anyway, are you ready to give bug-hunting a go?"

I get gingerly out of bed. There's a brief spell of dizziness when I stand up. "I'm not sure I'm up to this, but I'll follow Jimmy around and stand watch, if that's okay?"

"Maybe you should stay in bed, Jess," says Mark, looking concerned.

I walk slowly around the room, and it's okay. I'm not too wobbly. "The cleaning idea might be a bit mad, but I could just say I needed a bit of exercise, so I'm exploring the Abbey."

"Sounds good, lass, and I can be looking after you, to make sure you don't collapse on the way."

"Whatever works, guys. Anyway, have a look at these." Mark digs in his pockets and extracts a few items. "These are

161

the sort of things you'll be looking for. As you can see, they're pretty tiny."

"But they're black, so I'd have thought they'll be hidden. Wouldn't they either be against something dark, or behind something? I was watching you when you were searching."

"Yes, most likely. But if you see anything that looks a bit odd, note its location and let me know. Don't try to remove anything yourselves."

A short while later and Jimmy and I are strolling down the corridor past Mark's office, and heading, apparently, towards Jimmy's old common room. At his insistence, I'm linking my arm through Jimmy's. It's probably as well, because my legs feel decidedly wobbly.

"Come on, lass, let's have a look in here. I've not been in for a while, although I know your sister uses it to meet with important people, so it'll be interesting to have a shufti."

I nod. It makes perfect sense. Particularly if it's a place where Mel's spoken to Greg in the past. I push the door open, and go in. It's a pretty room now, like a large lounge, with a coffee table, bookshelves and a TV. It has a 'kept-for-best' sort of look.

"I'll lean back against the door, shall I? I need a rest." I'm trying not to say anything too obvious, but the big man next to me takes a hint, and grins at me as I shut the door and sit down with my back against it.

"Comfy down there?"

"I like sitting on the floor." I shrug. I hate it actually. For so many years there was nowhere else to sit. I refused to sit on the mattress where things happened, so the floor was the only alternative. Now I have the option of chairs and beds, the floor is a last resort. It's necessary right now, though. I don't have the energy to drag a chair over, and it would look and sound weird if we are being bugged. I watch as Jimmy does a careful search of the room. Eventually he looks at me, frowning.

"I don't know why I'm sitting on the floor really. The chairs and sofa look lovely and soft." I nod towards the beige fabric lounge suite.

162

"They do, don't they?" He sits on the sofa and rummages around the back of the cushions. Suddenly he grins, and holds up a small black box. He mouths, "Bingo!"

I feel in the pocket of my jeans, where I deposited a pencil and paper before we left the bedroom. Extracting it, I write a few words and hand them over to Jimmy. He reads it and shakes his head. A wicked grin spreads across his face. He places the box just in front of the TV, and flicks the power switch. After few moments playing with the remote control, a kids' channel is blaring out cartoons at high volume.

He leans down and whispers in my ear. "Do you reckon they like *Scooby Doo*?"

I stifle a giggle.

"Come on, let's get out of here." I grab his hand and pull him out into the corridor. I'm just mentally congratulating us, when Karen emerges from the store room and stares at us.

"Well, look who's been hiding in the private lounge? What have you two been up to?"

I let go of Jimmy's hand and try not to look guilty. Judging from Karen's smirk, I fail abysmally. The only consolation is that her suspicion is way off target.

Chapter Twenty-Nine

Mel

I wake after a surprisingly good night's sleep. My headache is gone, and Emma is quiet. Panic grips me, and I stumble out of bed to check on her. She's lying peacefully in her cot. She seems to have discovered that thumbs are tasty, and she's sucking her right thumb as she slumbers. I smile down at her, my heart rate settling after the brief fright.

Why was I frightened? Mark won't let anyone come in here, and no one inside the Abbey would want to hurt her. I must try to relax. The health visitor told me that Emma will pick up on my anxiety, and it may upset her. I don't want that to happen, but there's a lot worrying me just now.

I leave her to rest while I shower and dress. My breasts have settled to a more normal size, and although there's still a bit of pain, it's loads better than yesterday. I'm about to leave the room when Mark comes in. He looks tired.

"Hi, come and sit down." I retreat back into the bedroom, and indicate the bed. He slumps onto the mattress, rubbing his eyes.

"Did you sleep well?" he asks me.

"Yes, great. Looks like you didn't, though. Are you okay?"

"I was up all night messing with the phone wires around the building – inside and out. It seemed sensible to sort them all out while it was quiet. Jimmy watched my back and so did Derek."

"Did you find anything?"

"Yeah. There was loads of evidence of bugs, and the phone junction boxes had been tampered with. I tried to sort it all out so they won't know we suspect them, but I can't guarantee it."

"Have you slept at all?" I ignore the lurch of fear in my stomach. I've enough to worry about without this.

Mark yawns. "No. But I wouldn't mind a nap now."

"Go to sleep. I'll take Em downstairs, and leave you to it until lunchtime. I'm sure we can hold the fort until then. Hang on, did you say Jimmy and Derek were up all night with you?"

"They took shifts. They'll be about this morning, and Derek's patrolling outside. There's nothing to worry about for the moment." He's getting his pyjamas on as he speaks.

"Great. Okay. Sleep well." I watch him get into bed, and turn on to his side. He's snoring gently by the time I've lifted our now stirring baby from her cot. I take her into the dressing room to get her changed and cleaned.

After Emma and I have both had breakfast – formula milk for her, Weetabix and buttered toast for me – we go to the old Cistercian common room for a bit of peace and quiet. But as I approach it, with Em in a papoose against my chest, there's a lot of noise coming from inside.

What on earth is going on in there?

I ease open the door and poke my head inside. The room is empty. The noise is coming from the TV, which is on loudly. There's a small box lying in front of the speaker. I add things up mentally, and retreat from the room.

Settled down a short while later in Mark's office, I've got Emma in her baby rocker-chair, and we're playing peek-a-boo, when there's a knock at the door. I grab my phone from the desk, and make sure I can call someone easily if there's a problem. Only then do I call out, "Come in."

The door opens and Greg walks in, followed by Shelley. I relax a fraction. There's no immediate danger. After the usual hellos, I invite them to sit down. I make sure Emma is strapped into the chair, with the toy bar fixed in front of her, so she can entertain herself with the rattles and keys while I talk to my guests.

"Can I get you a drink?" I point to the new drinks machine that Mark installed last week. "Hot drinks are on tap now." I grin at Greg. "No more calling out for willing volunteers to put the kettle on."

They come over to inspect the new gadget, and select drinks: white coffee for Greg, and a latte for Shelley. I delve in the cupboard for biscuits, and emerge with an unopened packet of chocolate digestives. I put some on a plate. Finally we're all settled down with drinks and snacks, but no one seems keen to come to the point.

After a minute's silence, I ask, "Is there something I can help with?" As soon as I ask, a flicker of activity in my brain prompts me to grab pen and paper from the drawer, and scribble a note, which I hand to Greg as being closest. He reads; his eyes widening, then he shows the note to Shelley.

"Well, I'll be brief. We've been trying to trace our trial subjects. Whilst I was excluded originally, Shelley realised she needed my help, as I was on the spot anyway. We've managed to trace all but Charles. We're following some leads on him, but the trail is lukewarm at the moment." He glances at his colleague, as if unsure how to continue.

"Greg, would you keep an eye on the baby for a while? I need to take Mel for a walk around the garden. The weather's nice out, and there are a few things that should be said woman to woman."

I look at Shelley in surprise. I wouldn't have thought she was the girly chat type, but then maybe she just wants a chance to speak without risk of being overheard. My note warned them not to speak too openly.

Five minutes later, I'm walking in the inner garden with Shelley, enjoying the late August sunshine. We avoid the more populated sections of the lawn, and also the garden benches. I'm becoming paranoid, but there's a risk that someone has placed a device under a bench or near a tree. We settle on a patch of grass pretty much in the middle of the garden, and as far as possible from walls, trees or garden furniture. The weather has been warm and dry since the day of the abduction, and the grass has dried out.

"Mel, I've been through those accountability records." She gives me a meaningful look, and my stomach lurches. My hands start to shake. "We've enough evidence to make a case against you, you know."

I fight the urge to throw up on the grass. Is everything about to crumble around me? I try to swallow past the huge lump now lodged in my throat.

"Oh yes, and I found this." She reaches into her pocket and extracts a folded piece of paper. I recognise it.

"How did you find it?" My voice sounds hoarse.

"It was found on the passage outside your room by one of your residents. She saw fit to give it to me." She notices my puzzled gaze. "Someone called Karen. Not a friend of yours, I believe."

"Wh-what are you g-going to do?" Fear tightens its grip on my throat and my chest, and suddenly I'm fighting for breath. Panic descends as I struggle to take in air.

"Calm down, Mel, take some deep breaths. Slowly. Come on, breathe in, one-two-three-four-five, and out, one-two-three-four-five, and in…"

I try to follow her instructions, and focus on my breathing, but thoughts are crowding in, and the terror won't go away. What if they take me to prison now? Are they going to charge me with Dominic's murder and keep me locked up, away from my baby and the rest of my family and friends? The idea of never seeing them again takes control of me, and I'm gasping for breath.

Slap!

The sting of Shelley's fingers on my cheek bring me back to reality.

"Breathe, Mel. Snap out of this. We need to talk properly, and we can't do that if you go into a meltdown." Shelley's voice is rough, but a little kinder than before. I try to calm myself and take a few deep breaths of my own accord. "As I said, there's evidence. I believe in justice, and I need to do some investigations of my own. Greg is adamant that you're innocent, but as he also said that you'd have been totally justified in killing Dominic, I'm afraid I can't totally trust his judgement on this."

"Do you want to put me in prison?" I somehow manage to keep some control this time, but it's fragile.

167

"No, of course not. But I do want your complete co-operation. And honesty. Greg might be right. You might have killed Dominic for what seemed to you like good reasons. If a jury would consider it justifiable homicide, you would get away with it. This letter certainly supports that you had some justification."

She spreads the letter in front of me, so I can read it, even though I know it almost off by heart:

Ben,

Stop being so bloody condemning. I've got Melissa under control. When she gives birth, you'll get the baby out of sight until I tell you. Think up some medical excuse for where the baby is. I don't give a damn what you tell her, but she can't get near that baby until the DNA tests are done. I've done the sums. She must have been pregnant before I slept with her. I don't know how; she's obviously a little slut, and she's just lost any privileges I allowed her. Thomas will have to do without his sneaky pleasures.

She deserves everything that's coming to her. Whoever she slept with will get it in the neck too. They'll never see that baby again.

There's the possibility she'll work out the truth. If she does, she may try to get at me. If anything happens to me, make sure she's implicated. She's such a bitch. She'll try to slide out of it somehow.

I know my meds aren't working as well as they did. I'm losing my temper more often, and the Almighty can't help me as much as He did. The voices don't make sense anymore.

I'm clinging on to the realities: Punish Melissa. Punish Mark. Kill Mark if he's the father. Get rid of the baby.

And don't forget, Ben, if you betray me, you'll be next in the firing line.

Dominic.

"So I have to go to trial?" My vision is blurring at the edges, and I struggle against faintness. Shelley must be able to tell, as she forces my head down between my knees, and keeps it there until blood is pounding in my ears. She finally allows me to sit up.

"There are two people who could corroborate your story about what happened to you in the weeks before Dominic died: Benedict Bishop and Thomas Tyler. Help me find them. I want you to write down as much as you remember of your time at the Abbey, from arriving here, until Dominic's death."

"How would that help?"

"Firstly, any information about those two might be useful. Secondly, when we do find them, they may be able to give further evidence against Dominic that would justify your actions, if it was you that killed him. The letter is suggestive, but is insufficient proof on its own."

I force myself to look at the policewoman at my side. Her usually jolly face is serious, but there's no malice in her expression. Can I trust her?

"Just supposing I did it – I'm not saying I did, but just suppose – what would happen?"

"It would have to go to court. In the current climate, and with the details of the case, your chances of acquittal on grounds of self-defence, diminished responsibility, or justifiable homicide, would not be great." She pauses, staring at the ground for a long moment. When she raises her head, she looks directly at me. "As a friend, I would recommend you not to admit to having killed anyone. Obviously, professionally, I can give you no such advice."

"Of course not," I reply. She is being kind after all. I relax a little. "How can I help you to find Benedict and Thomas? I thought Benedict was believed to be dead?"

"No body has been found. It's pretty suspicious – he's faked his own death once before. Provide me with that statement we talked about. Give as much detail about them as possible. Is there anyone else who would know anything about them?"

"Jimmy might know. Particularly about Len. Sorry, Benedict. I keep thinking of him as Len Harper." I pull up some grass and start shredding it with my fingers. "He and Dominic caused so much suffering. Did you know they had a man called Leonard killed? Just so they could protect Benedict's false identity?"

169

"Greg showed me the letter, yes. Do you think Jimmy knows more than the letter suggested?"

"I don't want to get him into trouble. He didn't know what he was doing. They told him to administer a painkilling injection to Leonard. It wasn't until the man died that Jimmy realised he'd been tricked into killing him."

"Thanks, Melissa, this is really helpful. The letter suggested that, but speaking to Jimmy might help. Other than the letter, we have very little information about Benedict."

"He reminded me of Dominic, but it wasn't until I read his letter that I realised why. I just thought it was his air of intimidation. He was a tall, scary man. I was a nurse before I came here. I knew Consultants with that same way of holding themselves, and of staring at you. He had this way of looking at you, and you wanted to sink through the floor. I suppose he had trained as a doctor originally, so maybe he picked up the mannerisms from his seniors."

"Most likely. Anyway, that's helpful. Who would be the best person to talk to about Thomas?"

"Apart from Alison, his sister-in-law?"

"We've spoken to Alison and Dawn, and been able to get many practical details, such as previous addresses, but it's character details that we're after."

I bow my head. I won't put Tina through this. I'm the only person who can and should throw Thomas to the lions.

"He saved my life. While I was imprisoned in the cellar, it was bitterly cold. He brought me food, clothes and heat. In exchange, all he wanted was sex. I don't want it on record. Please don't let Mark ever find out. I did it to survive. I'll let you decide if Thomas was being altruistic. He raped a friend of mine, on several occasions. I could do nothing to stop him, although he suggested that when I gave him my body in return for food, it enabled him to give my friend a reprieve." I know I've failed to keep the bitterness from my voice.

Shelley nods, and squeezes my hand sympathetically. "Did Dominic send Thomas to you?"

"I think so. It was part of the mind games he liked to play."

Suddenly, I spot Greg walking across the lawn, cradling Emma in his arms. I jump up, relieved at the end of this awful conversation.

"Is she okay?" I ask as he reaches us. The sound of soft crying tugs at my heart. I mustn't go to prison. Whatever the cost, I can't leave my baby.

"Just hungry I think. I've smelt her nappy, and there's no problem there." He laughs at my curious look. "My children are all grown up now, and have their own babies. I'm a dab hand at changing nappies, you know."

I take Emma from him. "I'd better go and feed her." Turning to Shelley, I ask, "Are we okay for now?"

"Yes, I think we're fine. Remember what I said, and give me a no-frills account that will help me catch Benedict and Thomas. Then we're good."

I think she's telling me there'll be no trial, as long as I don't confess. Maybe my account of Thomas's doings have convinced her. I don't want to count my blessings just yet, but perhaps we're safe on that front at least. Strangely, the letter seems to have helped. But I can't believe I dropped it.

By the time Emma's been fed and changed, and put down for her sleep, it's lunchtime. Mark woke up when I put Emma into her cot, but he looks a lot better for his nap. It hasn't got rid of the bags and worry-lines though. Another spear of guilt stabs me. His worry isn't going to be relieved for a while yet.

As we walk down to the dining hall, I force myself to concentrate on the present. My thoughts keep wandering back to the idea of prison, court cases, and the terror of leaving all this behind. Mark doesn't interrupt. He's either still tired, or too wrapped up in his own thoughts to notice my fears.

Jimmy and Jess are sitting together when we arrive, and a few other residents are sitting around at other tables. Jess appears to be teasing Jimmy about something, but she stops when we arrive.

"Hey, Mel; hey, Mark. Are you both okay?" Her voice is full of concern. I must look terrible. I know Mark does.

"It's been a tough few days. We probably need a bit of time to recover." There's no need to divulge the horrible revelations of this morning.

Other friends begin to arrive, and the residents on lunch duty bring out large dishes of salad, potatoes, salmon and quiche for each table. Jess gives me a sharp look – I don't think my answer fully satisfied her.

After lunch, I make a quick escape before she can ask more questions. I go back to my bedroom, so I can read whilst keeping an eye on Emma. I look regretfully at the romance novel on my bedside. One of the latest innovations at the Abbey is the library. This has been formed from our own books that had been kept hidden away from us in Brotherhood days. There is also a selection of used books that have been bought from charity shops by some of the security guards and the braver residents who venture into the nearby village and town on a semi-regular basis. Jane, the charity worker who befriended Jess, also visits regularly bringing literary contributions from her shop.

I turn instead to a letter from the refuge charity. Not surprisingly, they've heard what happened to Alison and Dawn, and even though it was only three days ago, have managed to write, post and ensure delivery. The letter is a brief note reminding me of my obligations to the residents, and advising that an inspection will follow within the next few weeks. My gut tightens in a painful cramp. I don't want to lose my ladies. Alison and Dawn were the first, but I've been able to offer a refuge place to two other families now – all women with children, ranging in age from six to fifteen – due to arrive in the next week. If I'm forced to close the Abbey, I will lose those families. There's a small income that comes with them, but that doesn't matter. It's the ability to help these people that counts. It eases some of the guilt inside.

The sound of *I will Survive* by Gloria Gaynor draws my attention. I click the *Answer* button on my mobile.

"Hello, Mel speaking."

"I think you're expecting me to call," says the female

voice. A cultured English accent. My heart drops into my shoes. Is this the inspector? Already? "I'm Beatrice. You were planning some counselling sessions I believe?"

It takes me several seconds before I register that she's not about to come and close me down. A sigh of relief escapes me.

"Yes, of course. What time did you have in mind?"

"I've a cancellation for this afternoon. I could do a group session, and then perhaps have a look around if that would be alright. Three pm?"

I check my watch just as Emma starts whimpering. It's just coming up to two-fifteen now. That would give me time to feed her, and be finished in time for the counsellor.

"Yes, that's fine. Thanks. Do you know where we are?"

"I'll find it easily enough. See you soon, dear."

She rings off, and I turn my attention to Emma.

Chapter Thirty

Jess

I've neglected my studies the last few days, so I made a conscious decision this morning to go online in the upstairs common room and start looking at some GCSE revision sites. It's ridiculous that at nearly twenty I don't have any qualifications. College is too daunting for now, but the possibility of doing courses online is very appealing.

I'm wading through the history syllabus and wondering if history is of any use to me, when Brie pops her head around the door.

"Jess, are you free? There's a counsellor here to do a group session with you, Tina and Dawn. Can you come down to the Franciscan lounge now?"

"Why didn't anyone tell me?"

"Mel said it only got arranged a short while ago, and she's been feeding Emma since the call came through. She's not quite finished, actually, and phoned me to ask if I could sort it all out. Can you come along?" Brie puts a friendly hand on my shoulder. "What are you looking at?"

"GCSEs. But I guess it can wait." I stand up and walk with Brie down to the allocated lounge.

"Thanks Jess. It's very sensible though. You're a bright girl. You should have a good range of GCSEs and A-Levels. I'm sure you could get into a university if you wanted, but there's no rush."

"I'm not ready to do anything that I have to leave the Abbey for. I'll settle for the online qualifications at the moment. Maybe, one day, I could have a look at an Open University course. But I don't know what I'd do." I can see the open door of the lounge, so I thank Brie, and head in by myself.

I've not spent much time in here, but the room appears to have been rearranged for the occasion. There are four squishy fabric armchairs set in a circle with a coffee table in the middle. On the table there's a plate of bourbons and jammy dodgers, and a jug with some glasses. Tina and Dawn occupy two of the chairs. The third contains an older woman, maybe in her late fifties, with grey hair in an immaculate bun. She turns at smiles at me, a thin-lipped, supercilious smirk that does nothing to ease the fluttering in my stomach.

"Sit down, dear. You're Jessica, aren't you?" She points to the empty chair.

"Yeah." I can't be bothered to correct her. No one ever calls me Jessica anymore. It was what He called me. I perch on the edge of the chair. Dawn and Tina are both sitting properly, with feet on the floor and hands in their laps. The stranger has a vaguely headmistress-like air. The biscuits remain untouched.

Tina glances at me, and compresses her lips into a grim smile. I don't think she's too impressed with our counsellor either – and the woman's barely said a word yet.

"Jess, this is Bea. She's going to be taking us for some group sessions apparently. Just us three." Tina indicates Dawn as being part of the group. My young friend looks up at Tina with wide, scared eyes. A long-sleeved shirt covers the bandages on Dawn's arm, but I know they're still there, as she keeps scratching at her arm. I know how much the damn things itch.

"Right, girls, enough of this. Let's settle down. Jessica, do you want a drink or a biscuit?"

I shake my head. The door opens, and Mel comes in.

"Sorry I'm late," she says to Bea. "I had to feed my baby daughter. I'm Mel. We spoke on the phone earlier."

"That's fine, Mel, thank you. But the explanation and your presence are both unnecessary. I find my sessions run better without authority figures in attendance."

My blood temperature rises a few notches. The woman's bloody rude.

175

"Mel's my sister. She's entitled to stay."

"It's okay, Jess. Maybe the first time it would be easier if I'm not here. You can speak freely." Mel looks wistful, and I twist round and hold out my hand to her over the back of the chair. She takes it in hers and leans over towards me.

"You'll be fine, Jess," she whispers in my ear. "If it doesn't work out, we'll find someone else, okay?"

I squeeze her hand. My sister gives me one more smile, taking in Tina and Dawn with that same sweet expression. Then she heads to the door.

Turning back, she glares at Bea. "Be careful. You're starting with my sister and two of my best friends. If you hurt them, you won't know what's hit you."

The door snaps firmly shut behind her as she leaves. I chuckle inwardly. I have a feeling she struggled to not slam it.

"Well, your sister has a bee in her bonnet about me. I can't think why. Let's get on with this anyway." She turns first to Tina and asks her a few basic questions about her life in the Abbey.

Tina's replies are brief and give nothing away about current conditions.

"How about before? I believe this used to be a religious cult?"

"Yes. But I don't want to discuss it."

She casts me a warning glance. I'm not sure what she's getting at, and I send her a puzzled look in reply.

"How can you expect to get better if you don't talk, girl?" Bea doesn't wait for an answer, but turns directly to me. "And how about you? Were you in this cult?"

"Haven't you read my file?" I ask. I've only ever heard second-hand about the sect (never referred to as a cult by any of my family or friends), and I won't be discussing it if Tina doesn't want me to.

"The session was arranged at short notice. I only had time to skim. I recall now, though. You arrived quite recently?"

"Yes. I escaped from... a place... a horrible place. And then I came here and found my sister and her family."

"What were you doing in this horrible place, Jessica?"

"I was taken there when I was a child. Taken from my home."

"By whom?"

"A man. I don't know his name. I don't know where I was. Not a million miles from here though." I shiver. The window in this room faces the main road and the driveway. There's a reason why I don't come here very often. The security guard, Euan, walks past and glances in through the window. He grins at me, and I give a wan smile back. At least someone is out there looking out for us.

"Focus, Jessica. On me, not outside, if you please." Bea's voice snaps my head back round to her.

My temper begins to slip, but I hold my tongue for the moment. Maybe this is her method of trying to help. But I'm not convinced.

"You were saying about the man. What did he do to you? Did he do anything, or were you just fed and watered and left alone?"

"What do you want to hear?" There's an edge to my voice now. I'm clinging to my temper by a cotton thread.

"The truth, girl, or as much of it as you can handle."

"As much as I can handle? You bloody bitch! I was beaten, raped and starved, and forced to watch other girls being turned into fucking drug addicts, and you want to know how much I can handle? Well, piss off and leave us alone. I don't know what kind of a bloody counsellor you are, but you're not coming near me again."

I don't remember leaving the room or climbing the stairs, but I find myself in a bathroom. There are no razors nearby, but I check out the cabinet above the sink, and locate a pair of nail scissors.

Chapter Thirty-One

Mel

Half an hour in the Cistercian lounge pretending to watch the News fails to settle the unease. I'd walked out of a lounge leaving a stranger to interview my sister and friends without supervision.

A sudden realisation that I'd never checked the woman's credentials has me running out of the room and along to where I'd left them. The room is empty. My phone buzzes in my pocket, and the familiar tune rings out. I check the display and answer immediately.

"Tina? Are you okay?"

"Mel, come to my room, please. Now." She sounds distraught.

I end the call and run.

Arriving in the girls' room a bare half a minute later, I find Tina pacing the room, Dawn biting her nails on the chair, and my sister lying unconscious on her bed. The quilt cover is splattered with red splodges. Again.

"Oh dear God! What happened?" I ask, as my fingers fumble to find a pulse in her neck. Silly question. I know what's happened. But I need to know why.

"I put her in the recovery position. She's alive. I've used my handkerchief to stop the bleeding. I didn't know what else to do." Tina's sobbing now, and sitting next to Jess with her hand stroking her shoulder. I've found the slow pulse, and spotted the red, sodden hankie tied over Jess's left wrist.

"Go down to the office and get the first aid kit," I tell Tina. As she leaves the room, I ask Dawn to come over to the bed and help me.

Dawn leans towards me and grabs some material from my

178

shoulder. The muslin. I hadn't removed it after Em's feed.

"Clever girl. Well done. Thank goodness someone's paying attention." I say. Between us, we manage to tie the muslin over Tina's soaked handkerchief, and I grip Jess's wrist, keeping up the pressure. With the wound in her arm kept above her chest, and the rest of her body in recovery, we manage to stem the flow of blood. When Tina arrives with Mark, Jimmy and the first aid kit, her eyes are beginning to open.

"Bloody hell, lass. Not again." Jimmy looks at my sister with frustrated affection. Now's not the time to ask what's going on between them, but the chemistry is obvious.

"I'm sorry," mutters Jess, and tries to move. She's hampered by me and Dawn holding her arm and keeping her in recovery. Dawn steps back, but I'm still holding Jess's wrist. Jimmy sits on the edge of the bed, and takes her arm.

I use the opportunity to check out the first aid kit. Now the immediate danger is over, I'm having trouble controlling my stomach. The urge to throw up is overwhelming, and I dump the kit in Mark's arms and run to the nearest bathroom.

Returning a few moments later with slightly wobbly legs and an emptied stomach, I see that Mark and Tina are dressing Jess's wounds properly while she lies back and looks anxiously at Jimmy.

When they finish, Jimmy looks at me. "I'll stay here and look after this young lass. I reckon we need to get to the bottom of what sparked this off, don't you?"

"Yes, of course." My brain clears. "Dawn and Tina, why don't we go and have a chat? What happened to that woman? Has she gone?"

"Oh yes," Tina gives a grim laugh. "We got Derek to escort her off the premises. She won't be back. Then we came back and found Jess."

I glance at my sister, and see her relax visibly at this news. I drop a kiss on her forehead.

"I'll be back in a bit, honey. Jimmy will look after you for now, okay?"

She nods, and I usher the other girls out of the room.

"Right, shall we go to my room? I need to check on Emma anyway. She's usually awake by now."

When we get to my room, my daughter is awake and crying for attention.

"Sorry, darling. Mummy had to sort out your auntie. Let's get you out for a play now."

"Give her to me, Mel. I've not had a cuddle for a few days." Tina takes Em from me and starts whispering to her. I watch them for a moment. If I get taken to prison, Tina would be very involved in my baby's upbringing. I shut the door on that thought, as it threatens to overwhelm me.

I make sure Tina and Dawn are sitting comfortably on cushions on the floor, then open a drawer under the bed.

"Wow, Mel!" Dawn peers in to the drawer. "How long have you been hoarding all that chocolate? Where do you get it from?"

"I have an arrangement with the security guards. They all adore Emma. They get to give her cuddles in return for chocolate for her mummy."

"Does Mark know?" says Tina. I feel a twinge of annoyance.

"Yes." Mark and I had an argument about this last week, and it's time to change the subject. "So what happened with that woman?" I hand them each a KitKat, and close the drawer. I don't take one for myself. My stomach is churning.

Tina gives a brief outline of the conversation leading up to Jess storming out of the room. Then she pauses and looks warily at me.

"What happened, Tina? What don't you want to tell me?"

She shakes her head and smiles. "You can always read me, can't you? Okay, as you insist on knowing: Bea, if that's her real name, wanted us to show her around the Abbey. When we refused, she turned nasty, and started saying horrible things about you and Jess."

"What sort of horrible things? How on earth would she know anything?"

"That I don't know, but there was stuff in there... If it was true, I don't think you'd want it repeated to Mark." Tina hands me half her KitKat and I eat it, hardly tasting the chocolate. Perhaps I needed it, as my stomach settles a little, despite what I've just heard.

My mind is running amok. What could she know? Did she know Dominic? Did he tell her about me?

"Mel?" Dawn's watching me, her eyes wide like a frightened doe. I try to smile at her, but I fear it comes out more like a grimace. "I don't think Bea really knows anything. She said horrible stuff, but it didn't sound like you. I can't imagine you betraying Mark anyway."

"Thanks, honey, that's sweet of you to say." I take a deep breath. I'm not sure how much danger we're in from the fake counsellor (I'm now sure she's a fraud), but perhaps it's safer if the girls know there might be some truth there after all. "Sometimes, when people are in unbearable situations they do unspeakable things in order to survive. Earlier this year, I did some awful things. I'll always regret them, but even now I don't think I had a choice at the time."

"Why are you telling us?" says Dawn.

"Because maybe it's safer for you to know that we all have secrets: things which are dangerous if the wrong people know about them."

A sudden image pops into my head, and I jump up from the floor and start searching the room. A frantic look behind curtains, under the bed, and behind and under all the furniture ensues, while Tina and Dawn watch in bemusement. When I'm finally sure that there are no bugs, I sit back on the cushion. But I can't stop shaking. Tina passes Emma to Dawn, and comes over and puts her arm round me.

"I've just realised what that was all about. Even if there had been anything, you've not said anything they could get hold of." She rubs my back.

A feeling of exhaustion overtakes me. Hardly surprising after the day I've had so far. I rest my head on Tina's shoulder. Despite my occasional jealous bouts, she's still my best friend, and she's grown hugely over the last months. Dawn sings softly to Emma, while I rest for a moment, so all is settled when Mark comes in.

"Everything okay?" He doesn't wait for us to answer, but swoops down and pulls me up from the cushion. "Bed!" He guides me to the divan and helps me lie down, fully-clothed, on top of the duvet.

I watch as he takes Emma from Dawn, and dismisses the girls politely but firmly. He waits for the door to close behind them.

"Jess told me what happened. I'm not surprised she freaked out. I can't believe you let that woman come here without checking her out."

"Give it a break, Mark." I can't face recriminations right now.

"No, Mel. I won't. It was bloody irresponsible, and if they shut us down as a refuge, I won't blame them." He's standing in the middle of the room, with Em in his arms. She starts to cry, probably sensing his anger.

I get up and take her from him, cuddling her to my chest and rubbing her back in a soothing motion. I try to keep calm, not wanting to aggravate her any further.

"That woman caught me at a bad time. I wasn't thinking straight."

I swallow hard. It's time I told Mark about this morning's conversation. I can hardly believe it was only this morning.

"Greg arrived with Shelley this morning. She took me to one side and hinted that she suspects me of killing Dominic. She wants me to help her find Thomas and Benedict."

"Why would you be able to help?" He sits on the bed, and beckons me to sit next to him. Relieved that he's no longer yelling at me, I comply. Emma murmurs and becomes heavy in my arms as she begins to doze off.

"I don't know that I can help, but if I find them, they'll be able to give evidence against Dominic."

"How does that help you, Mel? It sounds to me as though it just tightens the case against you." He looks away. "I know I'm not as supportive as I should be, but I don't think I could handle it if they took you to prison."

"Now you know why I was distracted when that woman phoned."

"Bloody hell. Okay. Sorry I shouted. You had a good reason. I'm a selfish bastard."

"We're both tired." I stand up and take Emma to her cot. She's fast asleep, and doesn't stir when I lie her down. "I'm going to check on Jess, then I'll bring up some toast or something and we can get an early night."

"I'll get some food sorted. Come back here after you've seen Jess. I might be able to rustle up something from the kitchen. Hugo said I can get takeaway from him any time. I think he was doing a Bolognese for tonight, with a second choice of pizza."

"Pizza will do me. Just a slice though. I'm too tired and worried to be hungry."

I'm opening the door when Mark reaches me. He grabs my wrist and pulls me to him, holding me close for a few precious seconds. He drops a kiss on the top of my head before letting me go.

Chapter Thirty-Two

Jess

My arm is sore. Again.

Why the hell do I keep doing this to myself? I'm such a bloody idiot.

Jimmy wasn't sympathetic yesterday when he sat with me. In fact, he gave me a good talking-to, although he didn't say anything I wouldn't be saying to myself anyway. I'm great at knowing what I should have done, but at the time…

I lost it with that woman. Mel said last night that she reckoned the woman was a fake, but God alone knows who she really is and why she was here. Either way, she freaked the shit out of me.

Tina's asleep. It's not quite seven yet, and there's no need to be up for another hour or so. Neither of us are on breakfast duty today, and I reckon she deserves her rest anyway. She always seems to keep calm. Amazing girl. Especially after what she's been through. I should try to be more like her.

A soft laugh escapes me. Although we look alike, I'll never manage to achieve her calm self-control. I'll just keep wishing.

I must have dozed off, because next thing I know, Brie is at our bedroom door.

"Jess, are you okay this morning?"

"Yeah, thanks." I look at my watch on the bedside table – 8.15. Tina's no longer in bed. She must have got up while I was asleep.

"The real counsellor has called. All credentials checked, and totally kosher. Her name's Petra, and she'll be here at ten."

"Seriously? Not another group session?"

"She wants to speak to you. I would say alone, but actually she's happy for you to have me or Mel with you. Who would you prefer?"

"If she's the real deal, I'll talk to her by myself. I should be able to handle it. As long as I can walk out if I need to."

"How about I come with you to meet her, and then you can let me know if you're okay for me to leave? I think we should leave Mel to rest this morning. She had a tough day yesterday." Brie puts her head on one side, as if she's considering me. "You know she takes on the guilt of everything that goes wrong. Your sister is far too sensitive really. If you want to help her, have a think about that next time you see something sharp."

I bite back a rude response. She means well.

"I'll try, but rational thought doesn't happen when I'm having a meltdown."

"I know – just something for you to think about though. Maybe practising controlling your thoughts would be a good start. I guess that's what the counsellor is for. Anyway, get yourself dressed, and get down to breakfast. I'll meet you outside Mark's office at ten to ten, okay?"

I manage to eat some toast and jam. It's normal sliced bread, so doesn't have the same effect as the fresh bread that freaked me out so much. Alison makes the fresh bread at least once a week and I'm gradually getting used to it. But it still sparks memories.

Today, it's as much as I can do to eat standard toast. There's a gnawing feeling in my stomach. I don't know if it's a reaction from yesterday. That woman totally got to me. I guess that's obvious from my reaction. Now I've got to talk to someone else. What if she's horrible too?

I sit in near silence at breakfast, taking some comfort from Jimmy's presence next to me. At least he doesn't expect me to chat. We had a bit of a natter yesterday, but I wasn't really able to tell him what freaked me out. I suppose any time I have to delve into my past, I get upset and reach for something sharp.

At ten o'clock, I'm still sitting in the dining room, toying with the crusts of my toast, and sipping cold tea. Brie calls to me from the door.

"Jess, come on. You're late, and the counsellor's here."

I reluctantly get up and leave the table. I join Brie and head towards the office.

"Mark's vacating his office for you and the counsellor to meet in private. He's removed all insects from the room." Brie's face is bland, and it takes me a minute to realise she's not talking about the six-legged varieties.

"When did he do that?" I realise as the words come out that I shouldn't be making a big deal of it. "Never mind, forget it."

Brie nods in approval. "All you need to know is they're gone."

"Thanks." I take a deep breath as we approach the office, and scratch my nose as Brie knocks on the door. "Why are you knocking?" I ask.

Mark answers, standing there in jeans and a t-shirt – a bit less formal than his usual clothes, but still fairly smart.

"Jess, meet Petra. Petra, this is my sister-in-law, Jessica." Mark grins at me, and then escapes through the door, closing it behind him. He says something to Brie on the other side, but I don't quite catch it. I'm having trouble not staring at Petra.

"Sorry, duck. I know I'm a bit of a shock. Let's have a seat, and we can have a proper chat."

Anyone less like the woman yesterday would be hard to imagine. My real counsellor is of African origin, but with a thick Brummie accent, multi-coloured braided hair, and a pink t-shirt with ripped, faded jeans. I ignore her suggestion of sitting down, and stand there staring at her.

"How old are you?" The words slip out before I can stop them. She looks about the same age as me.

"I was thirty-two last month. I've got twin babes at home. My hubby looks after them during the day, and does a night-shift at the factory while I'm asleep." She laughs at my helpless look of surprise. She must be quite clever to be in

186

her position. You can't be a counsellor if you're thick.

"Isn't that a bit of a dead-end job?"

"Don't be so quick to judge, duck. He's doing an OU degree in Law during the day when the twins are asleep. He'll graduate next year. He was at Uni when I got pregnant, and it wasn't going to work out, so he dropped out and used his credits towards the OU."

"Sorry, it was none of my business anyway. He sounds like a hard worker."

"He is. I'm very lucky. I got one of the good ones. Not like some of the girls I see. In my line of work, there's a lot who've been seduced by a real charmer. Then they get married, and find the guy's a right bastard behind closed doors. Places like this are a godsend to women like that. It gives them somewhere to come to. Isn't it your sister that opened it up?"

"Yes." I'm getting accustomed to the unusual appearance of this young woman, but my gaze keeps wandering to those colourful braids. They seem to be coloured randomly rather than in a pattern, but the compulsion to check them out is overwhelming.

Petra laughs again. "Alright, let's get this out of the way, then you can give me your full attention. I've got six colours in there – red, purple, blue, green, yellow, and orange. The hairdresser wanted to put them in some kind of order, but I told her I wanted them random." She smirks. "I got out my phone, and did this random colour generator thing on it. She had to follow the pattern the phone app created. It took hours. I had to get my mum to look after the twins that day, so Simon could sleep."

At a gesture, I get up and look more closely at the arrangement. It's a relief, and once I've examined it closely, I feel a lot better. I also realise I'm not nervous any more. This unusual woman, with the amazing hair, friendly manner and casual clothes, appeals to me hugely.

"Come on, let's grab a drink from that fancy machine over there, and then we'll get on with the job, shall we?"

We select drinks from the machine: a latte for me, and a

chai tea for Petra. Armed with beverages, we sit back down by the table, using the corner, so we're not quite next to each other, but we can face each other comfortably. Petra digs into a bag next to her, a canvas affair that's nearly as bright as her hair. She pulls out a buff file and a pad and pen.

"What's in the file?"

"Police reports, duck. I got called in by Greg. He's an old mate. We've worked together a lot over the years. I sometimes freelance as a family liaison officer when they're short-staffed, or if they get a case where they need someone like me."

"Did Greg decide you were the right person to talk to me?"

"Yeah. Don't you agree?" She looks at me with curiosity and some concern. Her eyes are dark brown and filled with warmth.

"Yes, I think I do. Greg's a good guy."

"Definitely. So, do you want to tell me about yesterday?" she says, suddenly stepping into business mode. I sense a gear shift, but the friendly warmth is still there.

I repeat the conversation as well as I can remember, but dry up as soon as I mention storming out of the room. I expect her to quiz me about the scissors.

"Let's back up a bit. You said she kept asking about where you were kept during your abduction? Why do you think she was doing that?" Petra takes a sip of her tea, but is watching me with those big brown eyes.

I force myself to think back, trying to ignore the fear that grips my stomach and sets off a cold sweat.

"There was something about her. She was kind of insistent. Like she had to know what it was like, but as though it was for her benefit, not for mine." Reaching out for my cup, I take a convulsive swallow of coffee.

"Have you thought about who she might be, Jess?"

I frown and shake my head.

"Okay, let's move on then. You obviously told her some stuff, when she dragged it out of you. How did she react?"

"I don't know. These are really weird questions though.

Almost as weird as hers."

"Okay, sorry. I should have explained properly. I thought by telling you Greg sent me, that you'd realise he's asked me to help him out. But we both want to help you too. What's the thing you want most in the world?"

"For the man who took me to get caught and put away for ever." There's no hesitation there. I don't even have to think about it. Briefly, an image of Jimmy flicks into my head, but even that's secondary to getting Him locked up.

"Good. Because that's what I want, and that's what Greg wants. I've worked with a lot of girls who've been victims of rape, abuse, abduction, all sorts of crimes like that – they all want to feel safe, more than anything else. And the only way to feel safe is to get those bastards put in prison for a long, long time. We're all working for the same thing, duck, so let's go back to my earlier question. How did that woman react when you told her?"

"At the time, I didn't really notice. I was so busy freaking out, but looking back… she looked weird. Kind of smug but angry. Does that make sense?" I frown. It doesn't make sense to me, but maybe Petra can come up with a reason.

"Greg had a theory about who Bea might actually be. Excuse the pun." She laughs apologetically.

"Who does he think she is?"

"Well, it kind of fits with her reaction, so I think he might have a point. What if Bea is your abductor's wife?"

Bloody hell. I wish people wouldn't give me shocks like that. My whole body reacts to the theory: cold sweat, pounding heart, shortness of breath… If I was older, I'd think I was having a heart attack. Stuff older – I am seriously struggling to breathe.

"Sorry, duck." Petra gets off her chair and comes round to my side. She begins rubbing my back gently. "Take some nice deep breaths now, slow and steady."

I try, but it's getting increasingly difficult. The room blurs.

I wake up on the floor in the recovery position. I know the name of the pose because Tina's been teaching me first aid. My breathing seems to have returned to normal. Petra is sitting cross-legged on the floor in front of me.

"Not the best way to cure a panic attack, duck, but it seemed to work. Do you want to stay in that position, while I tell you the rest of Greg's theory? You seem safer on the floor." She grins.

"Yeah probably." I feel a bit numb now. Weak and wobbly, like I've been ill, but emotion has subsided.

She takes my hand in hers, and starts talking again, this time in a more gentle tone.

"Okay. So before I carry on, I want you to take a few slow deep breaths." My counsellor watches as I obey. "Right, good. Greg reckons he knows the identity of your abductor, but there are a few questions he needs to know the answers to about timing. He said if you're okay with it, can he come and talk to you later?"

"Yeah sure." I should have got over the shock by then. "Tell me who he thinks it is."

"I'm not sure how much your sister's told you about the Infirmary and the trials that went on there?"

"Not a lot. Just that she met Greg when he was pretending to be a trial patient. I think she also mentioned something about a trial that went wrong."

"That's right. Greg was undercover, investigating Dominic's brother, when this trial went tits-up, and a man called Frank nearly died. In fact, he did die, but not until several months later."

"Because of the trial?" My curiosity is surfacing, and with the interest of the story, I sit up and face Petra on the floor.

"Kind of. Turns out he was murdered – most likely, anyway. The point is, the only one who seemed to have a motive at the time was a guy called Charles."

I'm not sure why, but a shiver runs through me.

"What was the motive?"

"Apparently Frank was mouthing off about an affair he'd been having with Charles's wife, Beryl." She's watching me as the name of the wife is revealed. I don't know anyone called Beryl, but...

"What, do you reckon Bea is Charles's wife?" This is not

quite adding up yet. "And if she is, what's that got to do with me?"

"Charles is the only member of that group of trial subjects who hasn't been traced. He gave a false address, a name of a GP who's never heard of anyone called Charles Lindon, and every lead so far has led to a dead end. Why would he do that if he had nothing to hide?"

"You think he's my abductor?"

"Did you ever have times when he'd leave you alone for a week or two?"

"Yes. Right near the end, just before I escaped. There was a girl with me. Kylie. He'd turned her into a heroin addict, and she needed a fix, but he disappeared for over a week. After a few days, she died of severe heroin withdrawal." A huge lump fills my throat, and I can't speak for a moment. Only the unspoken sympathy in Petra's eyes helps me to block out the pain. I know it's a temporary block, but I guess it's a relief to have told her.

I take another deep breath. "Her body was with me for three days. When he came back and started to remove the body, I used the opportunity to run. That's how I escaped."

"Was that the only time he left you?"

"No. He went out about once or twice a year after the first few years. He'd come back each time with another girl. Company for me, I thought. Then he'd start them on the drugs. The others got taken away though. I don't know if he killed them or left them somewhere to be rescued. I don't suppose I'll ever know." My voice sounds hard, but it's as much as I can do to stop myself sobbing.

I reckon Petra understands, because she gives me another of those sympathetic looks, but otherwise ignores my impending distress. It allows me to maintain fragile control.

"Okay. When Greg comes, you can give him times and rough dates? I don't suppose you had a calendar there?"

"No. But I did have a pencil and an encyclopaedia. He brought it down for me after a couple of years, and in the page about calendars, I wrote in a new number for each day afterwards. I got up to 2,523. That was the day I ran. I had little codes that I used. A P was for every day when I had a period. An F was for each day I had company from a friend. I did a teardrop for the day each friend was taken from me. And for the days he didn't appear, there was a smiley face."

Tears are running down Petra's face, and I realise the enormity of what I've done to survive and stay relatively sane. I put my knuckles in my mouth and bite, trying to find the courage for what I need to say next.

"The days I cut myself, I wrote an X; like a pair of scissors." There. It's out now.

"Did you have codes for anything else?"

"No. The days when he did stuff to me were days I didn't want to remember. They were so frequent anyway. It was almost routine. He went through phases. Always when I was alone, or just after a new arrival. Like he wanted to show the new girl what to expect. Then, a few days in, it would always be her, and I was expected to watch. He'd ask me questions afterwards, and hit me if I didn't answer. It became easier to watch and answer his sodding questions, than to avoid it."

"How did you not get pregnant?"

"He was dead careful about wearing a condom every time. It didn't seem weird, but looking back I guess it is. I don't suppose I knew any different, but one of the girls asked him about it once. She got hit for it, but then he said he didn't want to catch anything. But he must have known he couldn't catch anything from me."

"I appreciate you telling me all this. Apart from making it easier to catch the bastard, it will help you to recover, and help me to assist you. Trust me, duck. You will get better, and I am going to help you."

Chapter Thirty-Three

Mel

Emma's been crying all night, and Calpol has only worked for short periods. By the time Mark stomps down to his office at six-thirty, I'm bleary-eyed, and unable to think clearly.

I get out the thermometer strip for the hundredth time and lay it across Em's forehead. Thirty-nine degrees. Probably not enough to worry about, but it was over forty when I checked an hour ago. I suppose the Calpol is starting to take effect. If only she'll sleep…

After another twenty minutes of carrying her around the room, I sense she's getting dozy, as her weight settles against my shoulder. I lay her down, and wait a moment for her eyes to flick open as they have so many times in the last eight hours. When they don't, I retreat to bed and close my own eyes.

When I wake, the sun is streaming through the window. I look at the clock next to the bed. Eleven-thirty. I've slept half the day. I glance over at the cot. Emma's still sleeping peacefully.

I drag myself out of bed and into the shower. Once I'm clean and dressed, I feel a bit more awake, although still a bit fuzzy-headed. I wish I could get a professional to check on my baby, but Paul's still away. I slip out of the room, so as not to wake her up. I phone Brie on my mobile. It's not always easy to guess where she'd be at this time of day.

"Mel, are you okay? I've not seen you all day."

"Em's been up all night. I've just managed to get a bit of sleep now."

"Ahh, that explains why Mark was snoring in his office when I popped my head round an hour ago." She chuckles.

"It doesn't surprise me. He was very stroppy when he left the room this morning. Like it was my fault."

"Let's hope a nap will do him some good. Do you want me to keep an eye on Emma while you get some work done?"

"Thanks, but I'm wondering if we could get anyone in to have a look at her. I'm a bit worried. Her temp's settled, but she's had such a bad night."

"I don't know," says Brie. "Paul's not here. Your nurse friend, Emily, is in Spain with her mum and dad, otherwise I'd give her a call. She only went yesterday as well, so she won't be back for nearly a fortnight. You might have to give the surgery a call." She hesitates – I can sense something on her mind.

"What?"

"It's just that Mark's been so picky about visitors, and about residents coming and going since the fiasco with the so-called counsellor last week, I can't imagine him agreeing to anything at the moment." Brie pauses again. "Why don't you see how Em is later? We can always call the emergency doctor if there's a real problem."

She's talking sense, so I try to calm down. I accept her offer of babysitting, so I can go down and get something to eat. It's lunchtime now, and as usual, there's a lovely selection of salads and sandwiches laid out in the dining room. Lunch is a relaxed meal, with people grabbing a plate, filling it, and then sitting wherever they want – often wandering out to a common room to watch some daytime TV. Jess is sitting at the table on the far left of the room, with Jimmy next to her and Tina and Dawn opposite. There are a few other groups of people dotted around the dining room, but only about half the residents of the Abbey. Mark's nowhere to be seen. I decide to check on him later.

After grabbing a plate and some egg and cress sandwiches, I go and join my sister and friends at their table.

"Alright, Mel? You look exhausted." Jess frowns at me. I must look bad. "And where's my niece?"

"Asleep. She's had a bad night." I can't face going into

detail again. "How are you? Has Petra been today?"

"Yeah. Greg came too. He said he's still trying to track Bea, but he's now pretty sure she's Charles's wife, Beryl."

Jess had explained to me after Petra's first visit about Greg's theory of Charles being Jess's abductor. It sounds crazy, but the dates seem to work out, and now Charles has completely disappeared. Why would he have given a false address if he had nothing to hide?

Meanwhile, Greg and Shelley haven't been to see me since she threatened me with prison. That's perhaps an exaggeration, but I feel the threat of it hanging ominously in the air. I have tried to find clues as to Benedict's whereabouts. I even spent an afternoon a couple of days ago searching his old rooms in the Infirmary. The manager kindly let me in to explore, as long as I stayed away from the clinical areas.

Benedict's room is now an office – open-plan, used for four secretaries. One of them, a pleasant-faced girl, showed me to a cabinet.

"This is where we put all the papers and other bits and bobs that were here when we arrived. There's only two boxes, but you're welcome to take them back to the Abbey. Do you want a hand?"

I accepted her offer, and we carried the boxes to the room where I first discovered the accountability books. It's now a cosy sitting room with a couple of chairs, desks and computers. I know Tina and Jess sometimes come here to study in peace.

I went through those boxes, reading every note, opening every page of every book, and feeling in pockets of the three pairs of trousers and two jackets that he'd left behind when he ran. I found nothing that would exonerate me, or help to find their owner.

"Mel! You're staring into space, lass. Sit down and eat, otherwise you'll be falling over." Jimmy's deep Glaswegian tones bring me back to the present, and I sit down with an apologetic smile. But the memory has given me an idea. I can ask the Infirmary staff for help with Emma.

The conversation turns to the history that Jess and Tina are hoping to study for their GCSEs starting in September. They've found a distance learning course, and seem to be looking forward to it. But I let the chatter drift over my head, as I nibble at my sandwich, and alternate between worrying about Emma's health and the terrifying prospect of prison if Benedict or Thomas can't be found.

I return to the bedroom a short while later, to find Brie sitting in the rocking chair with Emma awake on Brie's knee, and Mark preparing a bottle.

"How is she?"

Brie looks up and smiles. "She's not too bad. Maybe a bit grumpy, but that's to be expected after such a bad night."

I go over and take her in my arms. She's still wearing the cotton baby-grow that I put her to bed in. I hold her up and sniff near her nappy.

"She should be clean, Mel. I only changed her a few minutes before you came in." Mark comes over with the bottle and hands it to me. Brie offers me her place on the rocker and I sit down to feed my baby, while they stand and watch.

Emma fusses, taking a few small mouthfuls and then pushing it away. I try her again, but she doesn't seem interested, and her body begins to feel hot through her clothes. I look up at my critics.

"Her temperature's going up again. It's time for some more Calpol. And I really think I should take her to the doctors."

"No!" Mark starts pacing around the room. "After what happened last time you left the Abbey? Seriously, Mel, are you crackers?"

"No, I'm just worried about our daughter." Out of the corner of my eye, I notice Brie slip quietly from the room, tactful as ever. "Aren't you?"

Mark stops in the middle of the room, rubs his eyes, glares at me, then carries on pacing. I have another go at nudging the teat of the bottle into Emma's mouth. She turns away. I get up and hand her to her dad.

"Take her. I'm getting the Calpol. If that doesn't settle her down, I'm getting the doctor whether you like it or not."

After an hour of crying (from Emma), muttering and more pacing (from Mark), and growing irritation (from me), the medicine finally kicks in, and Em agrees to drink her milk. I burp her, and cuddle her until she grows drowsy and falls asleep. Relieved, I put her back in the cot, and usher Mark out of the room. I put the receiver end of the baby monitor in my pocket, before following him out.

He turns to face me in the passage outside our room. "If she's not better in the morning, you can call a doctor out to come here. Make sure they bring their credentials. You are not taking her there, under any circumstances."

I shake my head slowly. I don't know if he thinks I'm agreeing with him. I'm not. I'll try the Infirmary tomorrow, but if I can't get a doctor to her, and she's no better, I'll find a way to get her to the surgery.

After a solid night's sleep, Emma wakes with her temperature down. Mark's gone from the room when I awake, but we've barely exchanged a word since yesterday afternoon. A terse 'Goodnight' was the extent of our conversation, and I am left with a cold emptiness in my chest.

Emma smiles at me as I lift her from the cot. I don't know whether to get the doctor, but perhaps I can leave it for a while and see how she goes.

But by ten o'clock her temperature's gone up again. I put her in the papoose and carry her through to the Infirmary. I'm greeted by the secretary from my previous visit.

"Hello. Are you okay? They've promoted me to receptionist." She gives me a grin.

"Congratulations."

"They haven't really," she says. "The real receptionist is off with her baby. Apparently there's a lot of whooping cough going round, and her baby's poorly. She's taken him to the doctor."

"I'm a bit worried myself. Emma's been unwell, and she's starting with a cough. I'm really concerned, but it's difficult for me to get to the surgery at the moment. Is there a doctor here who could have a look at her?"

"Oh Mel, I'm sorry. We've not got any clinics on today. Only a physio and audiologist are in to see patients. But I can ring around and see if anyone could pop into see your baby. Would that help?"

"If you don't mind, that would be a great help. Thanks." I leave her with my mobile number in case she manages to get hold of someone. Meanwhile, Emma's dozed off. I carry her back to my room and lie on the bed with her snuggled up on my chest. She feels warm, but I don't want to wake her.

It's gone eleven-thirty when my mobile rings; I glance at the screen before answering. It's an unknown number. I sit up carefully, trying not to disturb my sleeping baby.

"Hello?"

"Mrs Winterton-Jones," says the voice on the other end of the phone. "I'm the health visitor at the surgery. I'm calling about whooping cough vaccine."

This must be in response to my chat over at the Infirmary earlier.

"I'm worried that my baby might have whooping cough."

"You should bring her in to see me."

"It's difficult for me to get to the surgery," I say. I'm reluctant to explain too much to this woman, even if she is the health visitor.

"Well, you should get her vaccinated against whooping cough. There's a lot going round at the moment. You need to bring her in as soon as possible."

"My daughter's not been well the last couple of days. Nothing specific, but just a temperature. She seems a bit better today, but I don't think she's up to a vaccination."

"All the more reason why you should bring her in. I'll get her checked out, and if there's anything worrying we can get you an immediate appointment with the doctor. Can you come in at three o'clock this afternoon?"

"I'm not sure. I need to check about lifts."

She gives me an address for where to take Emma.

"Why are you not at the surgery?"

"All the clinic rooms are full. We often use a room at the community centre for vaccination sessions. I can examine your daughter there. That's the address I just gave you. I'll see you there at three."

She hangs up. The churning in my stomach makes me want to throw up. How am I going to explain to Mark that I've made an appointment to take Em outside the Abbey? Particularly as he's not actually talking to me at the moment.

I wish I'd taken the number for the woman. I look up the number for the surgery on Google, and call up. It's engaged. I try again several times, but can't get through. I suppose if there's a lot of whooping cough going round, there'll be a lot of anxious mums calling in.

I give the Infirmary a quick call, but there's no answer. It must have been my new friend that set up the appointment. All the listening bugs are gone now. No one else outside the Abbey would have known Em was poorly.

Emma wakes and starts crying. She's hot again, so I dose her with more Calpol. She coughs a couple more times while I'm measuring the medicine into the syringe. What if it is whooping cough? Panic fills me, and after dosing her up, I cuddle her to my chest as I pace the room. I can't lose her. Not after everything that's happened. If I have to defy Mark and go to this community centre without his permission, so be it. I'll go. He shouldn't be so bloody stubborn anyway.

I put Emma into a papoose that I sometimes use to carry her around the Abbey with me, and go downstairs to find a driver. Euan is in the kitchen having a coffee while he watches Alison peeling the potatoes.

"Are you okay, Alison?" I ask. Our relationship has been civil but fragile since their awful experience and its many consequences.

"Yeah, fine." She clearly isn't. Her tone is curt and unfriendly, but she adds, "How's Emma?"

"Up and down with her temperature. I don't really know what to do, but I've got an appointment to take her to the health visitor at three today." I figure Alison won't know Mark's edict.

"Mark's forbidden anyone to leave the Abbey without permission. He didn't give much of a reason, except that there's 'stuff going on' and 'it's not safe out there at the moment'. He'll go ape if you ignore him, Mel."

Okay. So Alison does know. I'll have to trust her, and hope she won't tell on me.

"I have to take her. The health visitor said it might be the start of whooping cough; there's a lot going round." I put my arms protectively round my daughter, even though she's safely cocooned in her papoose.

Alison turns to look at me. There's a slight thaw in her expression. "You'd better take her then. I guess they'll give her something to stop it getting any further if that's what she's sickening for." She glances at Euan. "Would you be able to drive her there and back? Where is it, Mel? The Surgery?"

"No, it's at a community centre on the edge of the village." I give the address.

"I'll take you. What time have you got to be there?" Euan rubs his nose. "Did you say three o'clock? I go off at half two, so if you're ready to leave then, we can get going with your hubby being none the wiser. I can drop you off, then pop into the pub for a quick half. Then I'll pop back about half three and pick you up. We can be back here before your old man's even noticed you've gone."

"Thanks, Euan. That's great. Thanks, Alison." I give her a smile, which she returns. We seem to have reached a truce of sorts. I arrange a place to meet Euan, and then head back upstairs to put Emma back down for a nap. She's sleeping so much at the moment, but it's not surprising while she's poorly.

I manage to avoid Mark until it's time to leave. He's emerging from his office, a black scowl on his face, as I round the corner with Emma in her summer coat, sitting in her car seat. The weather is grey, drizzling and windy. A cold and horrible August day. He's looking the other way, and I back quickly into a common room. I watch from the doorway as he heads down the corridor towards the dining room. I'm guessing he hasn't eaten yet. That might account for the scowl, possibly.

When he's out of sight, I slip out of the room, and run to the front door. Opening it as quietly as I can, I go outside, manoeuvring the car seat so it doesn't bang against the door.

Chapter Thirty-Four

Jess

Following advice from Petra, I'm writing down some of my experiences during abduction. I tried this morning to talk to her about it, but apart from the bare bones, I can't get the words out. They get stuck in my throat every time. Putting pen to paper is a different matter, and the words seem to flow out of my pen. I've not decided whether to show her or not, but it does seem to help a bit to write them down.

I'm sitting on my bed with the writing pad on my knee, writing about the day when Kylie was brought in. She was so terrified. Fifteen years old, and she'd been snatched from the woods between her home and school. She kept asking me what was going to happen, and I couldn't bring myself to tell her. How do you warn a teenage girl that she's about to be raped repeatedly, and that eventually she'd get dumped somewhere? Although I never knew if they were dumped dead or alive. He never told me what happened to the previous girls, and I could never bring myself to ask. So I evaded Kylie's questions that first day. We were locked into the room together, with no electric light, just a greyness seeping in from the grate between us and the greenhouse. I remember her barely able to cry, the terror was so intense. By the time He came back in to the room, my new room-mate was pale, shaking and silent. He took one look at her and turned to me.

"Take her clothes off, Jessica." He laughed mockingly as I looked back at him in horror. "Unless you want me to beat her first. It will be worse for both of you if you don't obey me."

I was shaking myself as I went to undress her, slowly unbuttoning her blouse, pleading with my eyes for her forgiveness.

A knock on the door makes me jump, and the pad falls to the floor.

"Come in." I pick the pad up and shove it under my pillow as the door opens. Mark walks in. His brow is furrowed, and his lips are in a thin line. I take a deep breath, waiting for the explosion, but he speaks calmly, although it's clearly an effort.

"Have you seen your sister this afternoon?"

"No. Have you tried calling her? She doesn't go anywhere without her mobile."

"I've been trying to call her for about an hour – since about half three." He slams the door and starts pacing the room. "We had a row. Emma's been poorly and I wouldn't let her arrange an appointment to go to the doctors."

"Do you think she's ignoring you? If she's angry or upset, she…" I trail off at the fury in Mark's face. Blimey – I'd ignore him right now if I could!

"She wouldn't keep ignoring me. She certainly wouldn't hide from me, and I've searched every room in the bloody Abbey."

I refrain from asking why I was his last resort. Perhaps he wasn't being literal.

"Should I try ringing her from my phone?" My suggestion is tentative. I don't want to make him even more angry, although I know from experience now that he won't do anything violent, however livid he gets. I have a lot of respect for his self-control, however much I hate it when he gets angry. A sudden flash of insight tells me that I want him to care about me, and when he gets mad, I worry that he doesn't like me anymore. Stupid really. It's most likely that he does care.

At the moment, though, his fury is directed at Mel. I want to protect her, but I'm a bit concerned myself. It's not like her to disappear.

When he nods, I find her number on my phone and hit the green *Start call* button. It rings, and goes on ringing, until after about a minute, the voicemail kicks in. I listen to the automated voice asking if I want to leave a message.

"Mel, It's Jess. Please call and let us know you're okay. As soon as you get this. Please?"

When I hang up, a clenching in my gut almost stops me breathing. I get why she might ignore Mark if they've argued, but why would she not answer my call? Something doesn't feel right.

Mark stops pacing and goes to my dressing table. I watch in amazement as he straightens all the bottles, turning them so all the labels face the front.

"What are you doing? Is that going to help to find Mel?"

"Sorry – it's just a thing. I do it when I'm stressed. It helps me think."

"So, what do we do next? While we wait?" I glare at him. He came to me for answers, but now he's got me worried, and I don't know what to do. Although… I get my phone out again, and select Jimmy's number. Life in the Abbey has been a lot easier in some ways since Mark issued everyone with a mobile phone. Jimmy answers on the second ring.

"Hi, it's Jess."

"So I see. Are you okay, lass?"

"Kind of. Mel's missing."

"Is she no' back yet?"

"What do you mean, back?"

"Brie told me she took the baby to see if she's picked up one of those kiddy illnesses – measles or whooping cough or something. I think one of the security guards drove her there."

"Hang on." I tell Mark what Jimmy's said.

He grabs the phone from me. "Who drove her there? ... Is he back yet? ... Ok, find out and call me back. Or come and find us. We're in Jess's room. Thanks."

"Well? What did he say?" I reach out for my phone.

Mark hands it over reluctantly. "Apparently Euan took her. He's not back yet." He slumps into the chair next to my bed. We sit in silence for a few minutes until the ringtone has me fumbling for the *Answer* button.

"Hi Jimmy, what did you find out? Hang on a sec. I'll put you on speaker." I press the right button and put the phone on the bed between us. "Okay. We can both hear you now."

"They left just after two-thirty. Mel's appointment was at three. Euan drove her. Brie's on the phone to him now, to find out where he is, and why he's no' brought her back."

"Where's Brie?" says Mark.

"We're in the common room opposite the dining room. Used to be the Dominicans'."

"Why there?" It seems a strange question from Mark, but I'm fairly curious as well. Our little crowd has a few favourite hidey-holes, and that's not one of them.

"It was the only empty room we could find, and some things are best not overheard."

"Shall we come down to you?" I ask.

"Aye, sure. See you soon. Better meet in the office though. This won't stay empty for long."

"Cheers, Jimmy. I'll bring Jess, and we'll see you in a minute."

I don't need bringing, but I let it pass. There are more important things going on. Like *Where the hell is my sister?*

When we reach the office, we find Jimmy, Brie and Tina sitting round the table with hot drinks in front of them. There are two other full coffee cups on the table. Brie passes one to each of us.

"You probably want something stronger, but I reckon you might need your wits about you, so we'll stick with caffeine for now."

"Thanks." I manage to smile at her, despite the fear gripping my insides. "What can you tell us?"

She glances at Mark with some anxiety, before addressing me. "Mel was worried about Emma. She knew that Paul and Emily were unavailable to help, so when the health visitor rang, she jumped at the chance. She was due to meet the woman at the community centre in the village, and as we knew it was inappropriate for her to go alone, we arranged for Euan to take her."

Mark stands up. He's directly opposite Brie, and glares at her. I wouldn't like to be on the receiving end of that look.

"Are you telling me that you helped to organise this little

expedition? Do you know how bloody dangerous it is for any of us out there at the moment, let alone for my wife and daughter? And yet, you helped her to leave the premises, purely because Emma had a bit of a temperature?"

I wince at the sarcastic tones, and cast an anxious look at Brie.

She gets to her own feet, and says, "Yes, Mark. I helped her to get your daughter some professional attention due to a whooping cough scare. Combined with Emma's temperature, there was enough concern for us to defy your orders and get her to seek proper advice."

"And how do you know it's proper advice, and that it's not some trap?" Their voices have been steadily increasing, but at this, Brie slumps down in her chair.

"God help me. I don't. I did what I thought best at the time, but now I'm not sure it was the right thing. And don't glare at me like that. I love Mel too. I can't bear the thought…" She trails off.

Tina gets up and goes to Brie, putting an arm round her shoulders. "We all love Mel, and Emma," she says in her soft voice. "We need to stop making accusations and spreading blame, and work out what's happened."

"Aye. We've not been able to get hold of Euan, so if you'll let me, I'll bob down to the community centre and see if I can pick up any clues. Mel might be there for all we know. The mobile signal in the village is a bit patchy at times." Jimmy turns to me. "Jess, will you come with me? I'll keep you safe, you know I will."

I nod my head. There's not many people I would leave the Abbey with, or for, but I need to know what's happened to my sister. I down the rest of my cooling coffee in one gulp. The combination of caffeine and adrenaline should keep me going for a while. Jimmy stands as soon as I put the mug down, and I get to my feet too. My hands are shaking, but I put them behind my back as I turn to face my brother-in-law.

"We'll come back with Mel, hopefully. See you soon."

"Jess, stay with Jimmy, and don't put yourselves in danger, okay?" Mark comes over to me, and pats me heavily on my shoulder.

I nod. My throat has become a bit clogged. "Thanks," I manage to growl in a low tone, before escaping from the room.

Going to the front door takes a huge effort. I want to go and help Mel, but my legs are telling me 'No'. Jimmy's at the door already, and he turns to find me several feet behind. He reaches out to me, and gives me the courage to walk forward and take his hand.

"Come on, lass. No one ever said this was going to be easy. You've no' stepped foot out of the door since you tried going to the pub with that daft bitch." Holding my clammy hand in his, he leads me to a battered car on the drive. "Mark bought this for me a few weeks ago – shortly before those lasses got into trouble in Macc. Just as well, as it turned out. Do you trust me to drive?"

"Of course. Better you than me anyway." As I've never had the chance to learn to drive, this isn't saying much, but he grins, and opens the passenger door for me. I get in, and signal for him to get in himself. I'm capable of shutting the door, and we shouldn't waste time. He nods, and is in the driver's seat in a second.

It only takes five minutes to get into the village, and we're soon outside the community centre. It's obvious at a glance that it's locked and empty.

"Jess, I'm no' going to stop here. Let's drive on to the pub where Euan said he'd gone. When we've rounded him up, the three of us can walk back and have a wee look round. But I don't want to park the car outside the community centre in case there's something dodgy about it."

"Okay. Sounds sensible." My voice is a bit strange, and Jimmy glances at me as he parks the car in the pub car park.

"You okay?"

"Yeah. Fine." I force a quick smile, and undo my seat belt. Opening the door, I pray my legs will hold me up. They feel as if the bones have dissolved.

As I get out, I'm nearly blown off my feet. The wind is cold for August, and bites through the thin cardigan I'm wearing. In the Abbey, it's always a bit chilly, but jeans, a shirt and cardigan are my standard clothing, with comfy sandals, and no socks. The straps on the sandals offer little protection, and my feet are seriously chilled by the time we've made the short walk to the pub.

Inside, I thaw out a bit, but my heart is hammering painfully against my chest as we enter the crowded bar area. I stall. I don't think I can walk in there. I've not been in a crowd since… probably when I was ten, before I got taken by Him.

Jimmy takes my hand again. "Come on, lass. You can do this. For Mel and Emma?"

He's right. I can do it for them. I clench my jaw and force myself to march forward.

I look around, and spot Euan in a corner by himself with what I assume to be a nearly empty pint of beer and a packet of crisps. I'm sure about the crisps, but I don't see beer in the Abbey. Occasionally wine, but no other alcohol.

Jimmy looks at me; then, still holding my hand, leads me over to where Euan is sitting. He glances round. We're slightly out of the crowd here, and I relax a fraction.

Jimmy prods Euan in the shoulder. "What the fuck do you think you're doing, pal? Where's Mel?"

"I'm having my pint. It's my afternoon off. I only brought her into the village as a favour."

Jimmy takes a deep breath, and I can see the struggle to control his temper. He sits down opposite the other man, and indicates me to sit on the remaining stool.

"Are you a fucking idiot?" The disgust in his voice makes me wince, even though I'm inclined to agree with the assessment. "Did you check when you dropped them off that she was in the right place; that it was safe; and she wasn't walking into a trap?"

"That wasn't my instructions. They said I was to drop her and drive off."

"What?" Anger overcomes my fear, and I interrupt. "Who told you to do that?"

Euan starts looking around, panic in his eyes. "I can't say."

"So it wasn't Mel or Brie that told you to do that?" I ask.

"No."

"Was it anyone else from the Abbey?" I'm leading the questions now.

"Yeah. It was that girl. The one you used to be friends with. She said she owed you this favour, and asked if I'd sort it out. Said she'd overheard that the boss's wife needed a lift to the docs, and I should volunteer." He looks angry. "It's not my fault. She said she'd make it worth my while if I did it proper, like she told me to, but if I didn't, she and her boyfriend'd make sure I never work again. I couldn't have that. I've a wife and kid to support."

"So, let me get this straight. Karen approached you and asked you to take my sister and niece to the doctors, but just to drop them and drive off? Is that right?"

"Yeah. I suppose."

"Did she say what would happen to them when you dropped them off?"

"No. Just to, like, get the hell out of there as fast as I could, and don't look back."

I turn to Jimmy. "Let's leave this piece of shit. I don't think he's going to be able to help us any more."

"Aye." He leans over the table and grabs Euan's t-shirt at the neck. "You are in such fucking shit! If you know anything else, say it now. It might just reduce your time in the nick."

"She didn't say anything else... except... If you let go of me, I'll tell you."

Jimmy releases his fist, and with it the material at Euan's throat.

"She just said something about 'Once Charles had them they wouldn't be quite so pretty.' But I don't know who Charles is."

I do.

My blood freezes for a second in my veins. I don't know how, but if Greg was right, my abductor has taken my sister and her baby.

209

In a daze, I'm aware of Jimmy picking me up and carrying me out to the car, and laying me across the back seat in the recovery position. I don't think I fainted, but perhaps I came close. His voice is close by, and I look around to see him crouched by the open back door.

"Okay, lass. We need to get back to the Abbey now. You stay lying down. You look as if a brisk wind would take you out, and there's plenty of that going round. I'll drive us back. We'll be there in a minute. That plan alright with you?"

"Don't you think we should check out the community centre?"

"I've got people I trust who can do that. It's more important to get you back and get on to Greg. We need to find out where Charles lives."

I'm about to protest that no one knows yet, when Jimmy's phone rings. He answers it quickly.

"Aye. What? A note? Shit. We're coming back now. See you in five." He leaps into the driver's seat, and revs the engine.

I sit up and put my seat belt on. Adrenaline has kicked the faintness out of the window. I glance at Jimmy's face in the mirror. He looks horrified.

Chapter Thirty-Five

Mel

I wake to find I'm lying on a hard floor. I open my eyes, but the room is spinning, and I close them again quickly. Am I having a nightmare? Is this a flashback to Brotherhood days? A sense of *déjà vu* prevails, and I'm not sure if the nausea and headache are an effect of the terror I feel. Is Dominic here? I try to move my hand to feel for clothes, but both hands are fastened behind my back. I wriggle my wrist and it chafes against the rope.

I try to get my senses in order. I'm reasonably warm. The sensation of fabric against me is reassuring. I force my eyes open again. The room is still moving, but less violently. The light is dim, but I can make out Emma in the baby chair, just out of reach. She appears to be in a deep sleep. I glance at myself. I'm dressed in the same clothes as when I left the Abbey: black trousers and a pale green blouse. I wanted to look like a smart capable mum for the health visitor.

The health visitor! I don't remember seeing anyone. In fact, I don't remember much after Euan dropped us just out of sight of the community centre and then drove off without arranging to pick us up. I vaguely recall feeling uncomfortable about that, and then picking up the car seat with Em safely fastened in. Then what? My head hurts as I try to remember more details. It's a complete fog, and I have to give up.

What do I know? I'm tied up – fully clothed, thank God – on a hard floor in a dark room. I seem to have been drugged at some point, otherwise why would I be unconscious? Unless they hit me over the head? But the headache feels more general than that. When I got hit on the head by one of

Dominic's minions, it felt sore at a particular spot. This feels different. So, drugs. I rack my fuzzy brain for a likely solution – digging into my long-forgotten nurse training – and somewhere from the depths an answer surfaces. Chloroform. Easy to administer via a handkerchief or scarf. The after-effects tie in. Dizziness, nausea, headache.

For a moment I watch Emma sleeping. Her head is resting against the support in the car seat, but would otherwise be lolling against the side. I think whoever brought us here gave her a whiff of chloroform as well. But I can't be sure. I will need to get her checked out when we get out of here. I ignore the small voice in my head that says '*If* we ever get out of here'. Not getting out is unthinkable.

A door opens behind me. I try to turn to see, but I'm hampered by the awkwardness of hands tied behind me. Heavy footsteps bring the intruder round to where I can see him. Even in the dim light, I recognise Charles from his time as trial participant in the Abbey Infirmary. Why would Charles kidnap me?

He leans against the wall and watches me silently as I gather my thoughts.

"Did you kill Frank?" *Wow, Mel! That was clever. He's really going to let us go if we know he's a murderer.* "Sorry. Forget I asked."

"Why should I forget, Melissa? You think I'm a murderer, do you?"

"I don't know. Maybe it was an accident."

"Let's leave it at that for the moment, shall we?" he says.

I nod, and wince as the pain in my head gets worse with the movement.

"Why did you bring us here?" It seems a safer question.

"Numerous reasons. Would you like to hear them?"

"Yes please." Manners might seem incongruous here, but I vividly remember being punished by Dominic for not saying please. I don't want to tempt fate here. I might not be comfortable, but the immediate risk of harm is moderate rather than high. I want to keep it that way, or reduce the risk if possible.

"The first reason is very selfish. I've been missing your sister, and want to entice her back here." He laughs at my shocked expression.

I'd dismissed Greg and Petra's suspicions as too far-fetched. How could the man suspected of murdering Frank be the abductor of my sister? It seems ludicrous. And yet, he's just admitted it. I've heard people say '*My skin crawled*', and dismissed it as a cliché, but I now feel as though I have a thousand insects crawling over my body. I fight down the bile that fills my throat.

"How do you plan to do that?" My voice is faint, so I repeat the question, with a little more strength.

"I've sent a letter, Melissa. A nice little note, giving an address for your sister and husband to come to rescue you. I thought you might like to see your husband before you both die."

Air leaves my lungs in an explosive sound, and my whole body turns weak. It suddenly hits me: I've walked into an elaborate trap, and now we'll all be killed as a result. I want to scream with frustration and fear, but I reckon it would be a bad idea. I try to gain some semblance of control, and squeeze my eyes shut before opening them again. I take a deep breath, and attempt to look back at him calmly.

"You have courage. I'll give you that," he goes on. "Do you still want to hear the other reasons, or shall I save those for when your husband gets here? I think he might like to hear them too." He pauses. "Yes, I think I'll wait. I'll leave you now, while I go and await our guests."

He disappears from in front of me, and I hear the door close a few seconds later. I listen out for his breathing, but there's silence except for Emma's quiet steady breaths.

The mixed emotions get the better of me, and I succumb to tears for a few moments, before telling myself that they won't do any good. I need to use my time to formulate a plan.

I got us into this mess. God knows how, but I need to find a way to get us all out of here safely.

Chapter Thirty-Six

Jess

As soon as we reach the Abbey, I summon all my energy and jump out of the car, even before Jimmy's turned off the engine. I run to the front door. It's opened immediately, and I reckon Mark's been looking out for us, because he's right there behind the door. Jimmy's only a second behind me.

"At least you both got back here safely. You'd better come into the office. Tina and Brie are still there. We need to decide what to do. I have to rescue them." Mark looks and sounds distraught.

I glance around the entrance hall. There are a few residents hovering, looking curious.

"Let's get into the office, and we can discuss it there." I smile and nod at the onlookers, and try to look nonchalant as I follow Jimmy and Mark. I wait until we get inside, then turn to my brother-in-law. "Okay, what's this about a note?"

Mark hesitates, and Brie comes over and puts an arm round me. "Sit down, Jess, this might be a bit of a shock."

"We know it's Charles," I tell Brie. "Euan told us."

"How the hell does Euan know?" Mark interrupts, as I sit down. My legs do feel a bit wobbly again. I let Jimmy answer, as I don't trust my voice to stay steady. Brie sits next to me.

"Acting on Karen's instructions," Jimmy says, as he walks over and puts his hand on my shoulder. "When I let go of his throat, he let on that Charles had instigated the whole set-up. So what does this letter say, and what are we doing about it?"

"It pretty much gives an address and says Mark and Jess are to go. No one else. No police to be involved." Brie looks at me, then up at Jimmy. "I recognise the handwriting from

214

when we saw that letter to Jess. There's no doubt that Charles is…" She stops, clearly unsure of what to say.

"I know. Don't worry." Why I'm telling her not to worry is beyond me. I'm bloody terrified. I'm sure my clammy hands and trembling limbs are giving me away, but no one says anything about it.

"I think I should go instead of Jess." Tina's quiet voice from the chair near the coffee machine startles me.

"Don't be daft. He wants me there. If that's what's needed to get Mel and Emma to safety, I have to go. Thank you for offering. I'll be forever grateful, but I can't let you."

"Jess is right. The note says her and me, and that's who it'll have to be." Mark's voice quivers, but his stance is firm. He's hiding his fear as well as he can.

"Aye, I'm really going to let the two of you walk into that place. You might never walk out again."

"Thanks, Jimmy. Your reassurance is a great help. What do you suggest?"

"I'm coming with you. I want to beat that bastard to a pulp." He squeezes my shoulder.

"You'll get your chance, Jimmy. But for the moment I need you here." Brie smiles – a grim smile that would chill my blood if it could get any colder. "Mark, you and Jess will have to go in, but you will have back up on the way very quickly. Before you go, you need to eat something. We know you're walking into a trap, so although we're going to spring it, it might take a while to rescue you. There's no point in you being hungry while you wait. You might need your strength."

Tina leaves the room, and returns a few minutes later with a trolley, laden with pizza and cans of coke.

"Junk food, but I guess it'll provide the energy we need. Come on, Jess. The sooner we eat, the sooner we can get to Mel and Emma." Mark hands me a plate and a can, and I take a single slice of pizza.

My stomach feels as though someone has clamped it shut, and I honestly don't know how I'll be able to eat. I nibble on a corner, and manage to force it down my throat, and then somehow, I manage another bite, bigger this time. Before long the combination of caffeine and carbs takes effect, and I eat a second slice of pizza before looking up at Mark.

"I'm ready."

"Me too," he says, taking a final swig of coke. He's polished off four slices, judging from the neat pile of crusts on the edge of his plate. I don't know how we managed to eat, but we both accept it's necessary.

I go over to Jimmy, who's sitting at the other side of the table watching me, while he shovels food into his mouth. He puts down the slice as I approach, and wipes his fingers on a paper towel. He grabs my hand.

"Now, lass, you know what you need to do?"

"No. I'm bloody terrified," I whisper so only he can hear.

"Just keep the conversation going. Do whatever you have to do to keep everyone alive and safe until I get there."

Right, no pressure. But he's correct – it probably is down to me. I'm the one Charles wants. He's set this up to ensnare me. I need to find the inner strength to do this.

I nod. I can't speak.

Jimmy gets up, holds me close, drops something into my pocket and whispers in my ear. "Love you, Jess. Get back here safely, okay."

Tears spring to my eyes, and I find my voice. "I love you too." I give him a quick kiss on his cheek. I don't know what this means for our relationship, but he's just given me something to hang on to: something worth living for, and worth escaping for.

"Come on, Jess," Mark says. "We need to be going. I'll drive. We can't risk anyone else being seen to join us. We'll take the car with the sat nav in the glove compartment, otherwise we'll never get there."

Mark looks better for the food, but he's still pale. We're walking into a trap, and no one knows if we'll ever make it back here.

Chapter Thirty-Seven

Mel

Charles hasn't been gone long when Emma wakes up and starts crying. She's out of reach and my arms are still tied behind my back, so all I can do is talk to her, and try to keep her calm. She cries louder, and a whiff of smelly nappy drifts to my nostrils.

"Oh Emma, why now? I can't sort this out just now, sweetheart." Her cries get louder. I pray they can't be heard by Charles, but a few minutes later, I hear the door open behind me. The footsteps are softer than previously, but I'm still shocked when Bea appears in front of me.

"Was Greg right then? Are you Charles's wife?"

"Shh, keep your voice down. He doesn't know I'm here. I'm supposed to be in the bath, out of the way." She looks towards the door, and even in the dull light I can see bruises on her face. She's wearing a pale-coloured long-sleeved blouse and dark trousers. Returning her gaze to my face, she says, "Yes, I'm Beryl. We need to get your baby to safety." I can barely hear her above Emma's cries.

"Could you free us both?"

"No, he'll kill me if I let you go, but if we don't get her out of here, he'll lose his temper. He could never stand noise. She's in serious danger. Will you let me take her?" Beryl goes over to the car seat, unfastens the straps and lifts her up. "Yeurghh, is that her nappy?" She wrinkles her nose.

"I'm afraid so. Where will you take her? Why should I trust you?"

"I can take her into a neighbour, and they'll get her to the police. Your friend Greg will get you reunited, assuming you get out of here safely. Otherwise, he'll get her to someone in the Abbey who can look after her. Don't worry about her. You have to trust me. If I don't get her away now, she'll die here. I'm sure you don't want that."

I shudder. I'm reminded of why I disliked Bea so much. There's no warmth in her voice, but what she says makes sense. Emma's cries can inflame the tempers of those her love her; she has no chance against Charles.

"Okay. Please get her to safety. Will you be safe too? You look as though you need help as well?"

"Charles is angry with me because although I managed to speak to your sister in the Abbey, I wasn't able to find a way to get her away from there. I failed him, and he's been taking it out on me since." She's rubbing Emma's back as she speaks, and the cries soften a little. "I'm off now. I'll look after your little girl. She'll be fine."

A minute later the room is silent; empty except for me.

There are so many questions I should have asked her. *Did she know about the girls Charles kept here? Why did she try to help him get Jess back? Does she know what Charles plans to do with us all?*

The dim light fades, and my fear increases. I've never liked the dark, and months in the cellars of the Abbey didn't help. I'm now bereft of my beloved baby, and the only thought preventing utter panic is the faint hope that she'll be safer away from this house.

To stave off the mounting terror, I focus on logistics. It's late August, so if it's getting darker, either a lot more time has passed than I thought, or it's going to rain. Charles said he left a note, so Jess and Mark should be arriving soon.

Muffled sounds from upstairs interrupt my thoughts. I start to sweat as my heart seems to hammer out of my chest. What's going on? Is Emma safe? They can't have been gone more than fifteen minutes, although that's purely a guess – with my arms tied, I can't see my watch. Maybe Mark and Jess have arrived.

I swallow, but my mouth is dry. Horrible images scurry around my head: Mark being killed, my sister raped, and Emma injured or even… I block that one before it takes hold.

I try to breathe. Dots are dancing in front of my eyes. I must breathe. I concentrate on taking a slow inhalation through my nose. I breathe out through my mouth, then repeat. The dots recede, and the panic eases a touch. I keep focussing on the breathing process. I know that as soon as I let those images back in, I'll completely lose it.

Meanwhile, I wait to find out what's going on.

Chapter Thirty-Eight

Jess

It's gone six by the time Mark pulls up outside the house. It's a house that looks perfectly ordinary on the outside: situated on a quiet leafy road, with a garden gate and a neat lawn. It's a house that almost paralyses me with terror.

My physical reaction to the building is off the scale. The hairs on the back of my neck are not just standing up, they're stiff and immoveable. My heart rate is probably way over two hundred, and sweat is oozing from pores I didn't know I had. I feel too ill to get out of the car, but Mark puts his hand over mine.

"Jess, are you ready?" There's a catch in his throat, and I glance at his face. His terror is for Mel and Emma, and it gives me the courage to ignore my physical reaction. I have to do this.

"Okay. Come on." My voice is feeble, but the intention is there. I force my hand to open the car door, doing it quietly and gently. We decided that an element of surprise might help us, if we can throw Charles off guard. I'm not convinced, but it's worth a try.

My legs nearly give way, as my feet hit the floor, and I cling to the car for a moment, gathering my strength. Being incapacitated by fear is not going to help anyone. I shut my eyes for a moment, and picture Jimmy holding me, and his final words. They gave me confidence then, and they do so again. Energy flows through me as the adrenaline creates a positive effect.

I open my eyes, and let go of the car. Walking slowly but steadily, I go round to where Mark is standing, staring at the house.

"Mel and Emma are in there. Let's go. Do you know where they'll be?"

"Probably in the cellar. That's where I was for all those years."

He glances at me. "Sorry, Jess. Are you okay?" He looks concerned, and I'm grateful, but I can't afford to think about it.

"Yeah. Come on. Do we go to the front door and ring the bell, or try to effect a rescue? From experience, we haven't a hope in hell of getting them out without being spotted. I think we'll have to leave the rescuing to Jimmy and Brie, and whatever their plan is."

"I suppose so. Front door then?"

I nod, and gesture for him to lead the way. He opens the gate and I follow him up the garden path to the front door. Mark glances at me before ringing the bell.

"Are you sure you're okay with this?"

"No, so get on with it before I bail out." I try to grin to show it's at least half a joke, but I think it comes out as more of a grimace.

He pats me on the shoulder, takes a deep breath, and presses the doorbell. There's a low buzz. I guess Charles wouldn't want to be startled in the middle of anything critical. I never heard a bell ringing in the nine years I was there, so probably Mel can't hear it either. I hold my breath.

When He opens the door, the physical reaction returns, and I fight down an urge to throw up.

"Jessica! Welcome back. Mark, nice to meet you at last. Do come in." He sounds as though He's welcoming us to a party.

Battling my fear, I take a curious look at Him. Although his voice is horrifyingly familiar, I've never seen his face close up. The profile with the prominent Adam's apple is not new, but the clean-shaven, narrow, almost horse-like face is strange to me. His thin lips and straight nose fit well with the rest of the features, but overall He looks normal. If I'd bumped into him in a street, I wouldn't give him a second glance.

He holds the door open until we're inside, and then shuts and locks it behind us. The slither of the bolt as it slides into place paralyses me for a moment. How will Jimmy be able to rescue us? I glance at Mark, but he seems unconcerned. I take a slow breath, trying to calm myself. I'll be no use to anyone if I faint.

"So can I see my wife and daughter now?" says Mark, as we enter a lounge that I've never seen before.

"You'll be able to see your wife in a moment. Your daughter isn't here just now. You'll find out more about that in good time. But before we go down…" Charles pulls me back into the hall, shuts Mark into the lounge, and gripping the door handle, pushes me against the wall. He presses himself against me, his free hand at my throat, ready to squeeze if I don't behave myself. His mouth forces mine open and his slimy tongue invades. I'd blanked out how vile this was, but it's as much as I can do not to vomit. Bile fills my throat, burning.

He pulls back and sneers, a disgusted look on his face. "I forgot about that little trick of yours. It's still revolting. But there are plenty of other ways to make you suffer, now I've got you back." He grabs my breast and kneads it until pain shoots through my chest.

I wince, but He clearly doesn't care. We've probably only been alone for a couple of minutes, but it feels like ages until Mark forces the lounge door open.

"What the hell's going on here? Hey!" Mark fastens his hand around Charles's arm, and yanks him away from me. "Leave her alone. Jess isn't your toy anymore. She's my sister-in-law and she's under my protection."

"You seriously think you're going to get out of here alive? When you've seen my face? Do you think I'm stupid?"

I interrupt. "Yes. You must be stupid. You left a note for us with your address. Greg already knew that you killed Frank. Now he knows where you live. Do you not think the police will be here soon? You don't have a chance of getting out of here without a prison sentence. That would be ironic, wouldn't it?"

"If I go down, I take you all with me. Greg will arrive to find three dead bodies. He'll be too late to save any of you." Charles smirks at me, and something strange happens.

My fear ebbs away. I don't know how. I never want Him near me again. He still makes me feel sick. I don't really have time to analyse this feeling, but the thought flashes into my head that the worst He can do is kill me.

I'd rather not die. I've discovered there are people I love, who are not totally screwed up, and are not dependent on a madman for survival. Although, at this moment, two of the people I most care about are very dependent on the madman. My legs buckle. Perhaps I should focus on something else. But I know that my fear is of losing people, not of Him. Maybe seeing his face has helped. He's no longer the faceless bogeyman.

"Perhaps you could take us to see my sister? Or better still, bring her up here?"

"I'm not that stupid, my dear. And the police are welcome to try to find you. I have the house surrounded. Friends of yours I believe, Mark. Or at least – previous employers?"

Colour leaves Mark's face. "How? What have they got to do with you?"

"We've been collaborating for quite some time now. They helped to bring your wife and child here. They've probably caught and killed my wife as she tried to escape with your baby. They were responsible for the capture of your friends from the Abbey. My new friend, Jason, had great pleasure with the younger one, what was her name? Debbie? Dorothy? Ah, no, Dawn. That was it. I believe it's given him a taste. I could take him on as my apprentice."

Poor Dawn. None of this was her fault. This sick piece of shit has got in with Mark's enemies, and they've just targeted us all.

"I seem to have built up quite a network of people who have it in for you all. There's Karen and her boyfriend, Geoff – now close personal friends of mine – and Simon, who I believe has inveigled your doctor friend into a delightful tangle."

"What have you done with Paul?"

"I've done nothing, Mark. But my friend Simon has been keeping Paul Griffiths busy whilst I needed Melissa to be kept away from easy access to medical professionals. Karen has been working well on the inside for me. The occasional compound in the baby's bottle – just enough to cause alarm without doing any permanent damage – assisted in the building of the trap that your wife recently jumped into."

He looks from Mark to me, and then opens a door. Behind the door are steps downwards. My stomach contracts.

"Shall we go down and visit Melissa now?"

Chapter Thirty-Nine

Mel

I hear the door open behind me and turn my head. I try to sit up, but it's difficult with my hands still fastened behind my back. My arms ache from the awkward position.

Mark is first down the steps. My heart contracts with joy at seeing him, but it's immediately replaced by guilt that I've led him into such danger.

"I'm so sorry." I would say more, but he's on his knees next to me. He pulls me into a sitting position, and throws his arms around me."

"God, Mel. There's no need to apologise, my love. It's not your fault. You were manipulated. He even got Karen to dope Emma so you'd seek help. It's not for you to say sorry." He punctuates his speech with kisses – on my lips, forehead, cheeks – and then holds me tight against him.

"I can't hug you back. Sorry."

"Mel, are you okay?" Jess crouches down next to us, and bends her head to my ear. "We'll get out of here alive. I promise," she whispers.

I nod. Charles is at the top of the stairs, watching with a sneer on his face.

"Such a touching scene. It's a shame I need to kill you all really. But at least you'll be joining your daughter very soon."

Mark steps away from me and dives towards the steps. He stops suddenly when Charles extracts a gun from his pocket.

"I would stay down there if I were you, Mark. Maybe you didn't hear me earlier when I said your baby and my wife would have been stopped by my associates – your enemies. They're under instruction to let no one leave the house alive – except me of course."

Jess stands up and stares at Charles. "This is a residential road. You can't just go around shooting people in the area. Your wife and Emma are probably fine."

Bless the girl. She's doing her best to ease my mind. But it's not working. The huge lump of lead in my chest seems to get heavier each time I let in the thought that my baby might be dead. After all we've been through, how could I have let this happen?

I see my sister glance at me. She rests her hand on my shoulder and squeezes gently.

"So what other revelations have you got for us? You've told us you're in with Mark's ex-boss, and Paul's tormentor, and with Karen and Geoff. How the hell did you manage to get together with that lot, and stay out of Greg's reach?"

"You're very sharp today, Jessica? Why don't you work it out for yourself?"

My feisty sister gives him a quelling look. She's not afraid of him anymore. Pride fills me for a moment, before the fear of loss brings me back down.

"Just tell us, okay. You know you want to." There's a strange note in her voice.

I study her expression, as much as I can in the dim light. I can see a grim determination in her face. She's got something in her mind – maybe even a plan. I sit still and allow her to focus on the man with the gun.

"Maybe you're right. I do want you to know how clever I am before you die." Charles lowers the gun, but doesn't return it to his pocket. Maybe he reckons he's safe at the top of the stairs. "You've forgotten a key player. Do you remember Thomas?"

Mark and Jess are looking puzzled, so I speak up. "What's he got to do with anything?"

"Everything. You see, Thomas is an old friend. We met before he went into the Abbey, and he's always kept me apprised of events since. As a group head, he had many privileges. His older brother married your new friend, Alison, who gave birth to Dawn. I was delighted when I found out that they'd been sent to the Abbey to join my young friend,

Jessica. It made everything so neat. Of course, it would have been too much of a coincidence to have happened naturally, but Thomas had contacts within the refuge charity. A bit of pressure, a little gentle blackmail, and the thing was done."

Jess gives him an evil glare.

"How did you find out?" I ask.

"When Thomas left the Abbey in such a hurry, he came here for a night. He explained he wouldn't be staying, saying he was wanted for some trumped-up charge of rape and possibly murder. It was two days after Jessica escaped, so I was a little distracted. I missed some of the details he gave me, but he provided a couple of names of people who were in contact with him. He'd been given mobile phones by a chap named Geoff, so Karen could keep him updated on the goings-on inside the Abbey. Thomas gave me Geoff's contact details, and told me to keep in touch. I decided it would be beneficial to know what was happening, so I left instructions with Geoff that I was to be updated on everything to do with the key members of The Brotherhood. Thomas had told me that Dominic had died in suspicious circumstances. He mentioned you of course, Melissa, but it wasn't until Karen told me of Jessica's arrival that I realised you were her sister."

"Geoff and Karen? I'd forgotten they're in cahoots," I say.

Jess grimaces before replying, "They've been together for months. She was hoping to meet up with him that night she dragged me to the pub." She turns to Charles. "How did you get involved with the guys that were after Mark?"

Charles' thin-lipped smile sends shivers through me. "Well now. That was a bit of luck. A chance meeting with an old associate, a few comments he let fall in passing, and I became aware that he had a grudge. I inquired who the villain was, and it turned out to be Mark. How fortuitous, when I was seeking as many links as possible to the Abbey. My associate was willing to collaborate, and an allegiance was formed. He wanted to punish Mark. I wanted Jessica back. We could see that working together would achieve both ends. Perfect."

I glance at Jess. Her face shows a brief glimpse of the same revulsion I feel, before she assumes a mask – expressionless and calm. I'm near enough to hear her heartbeat, and it's pounding fit to burst. But she's focusing on Charles.

"So, all our enemies seemed to fall into your lap?"

"Yes, that would describe it rather well." He smirks. My fist clenches behind my back. I try to concentrate on what's going on, but my brain is screaming at me now: *Emma might be dead!*

Why did I let Beryl take her away? If they've walked into the arms of Mark's old boss and his gang, they're dead. Dead!

My throat constricts. I can't breathe. This would be a really bad time to faint. *Pull yourself together, Mel. They might be alive.* I cling desperately to that thought, and my breathing returns to normal. I force myself to look around. Jess and Mark are both watching me with concern.

Our host is laughing. "Are you feeling a little better now, Melissa? Yes, there's a small chance they might be alive. Beryl was always a sneaky bitch. She would work for me for a while, then turn against me. I tried to keep her from knowing about my girls, but every now and again she would see me taking food down. One night she found me taking one of the girls away. I'd drugged her. I can't remember her name now. I think it was the first I brought to keep you company, Jessica."

"Lisa," mumbles Jess.

"What was that? Ah yes, Lisa. Well, I was going to take her to the woods and kill her, but Beryl interfered. She was angry with me. She'd discovered I liked to use the girls for sex, and became jealous. She drove the girl off somewhere. She never told me where – just said the girl would be safe now. I have no idea if Lisa survived. I don't particularly care. She had her uses, and then she didn't. It's irrelevant to me where she is now. She wouldn't be able to give evidence against me. She never saw my face."

"I don't think that matters," says Jess in a hard voice. "The police know where you live. They know some of the things you've done. If you kill us now, that would just add to your sentence." Her glance flicks towards the gun in his hand.

"If the police find me here, I will be arrested and imprisoned for life. My plan was to kill you, and use my accomplices to get out. Jason has a car waiting for me, with a suitcase and a lot of money. I've no doubt if I was to get caught, you'd make things as difficult for me as you could. I saw the look of hatred in your face as I carried out the body of the last girl. I know you think I killed her."

He looks amused, but Jess now seems to be struggling to keep it together. Her face is flushed and fists are twitching. She inhales deeply, and releases her fists. Her hands go to the front of her blouse and she undoes the top button before speaking. Charles watches her; his expression suddenly greedy and lustful. He descends the stairs and rests the gun on the top step.

"How about one last time then, Charles, before you kill me? I can see you want me still." Her fingers work down her red blouse, and when she's finished she pulls it open showing a black lacy bra.

Mark averts his eyes from Jess, looking over at Charles instead. Neither of us interfere. My sister clearly has a plan.

Charles hesitates, seeming to wrestle with himself, until she deliberately touches her breasts, stroking them. It's not something I want to see my sister doing.

I focus on Charles. He heads towards her, gun seemingly forgotten, and hands outstretched towards Jess. His hands go to her breasts and his head bends towards them.

I can't believe she's allowing this. Suddenly, her hands move so quickly there's a blur of activity. Her hand travels to her pocket, then upwards to his neck. There's a slicing action, and then blood is spurting from beneath his jaw. He staggers back, his hand going to the wound before falling and cracking his head against the stone stairs.

There's a moment's silence, broken only by the sound of metal hitting the floor. Jess sits heavily next to me. She tries to do her blouse back up but her hands are shaking too much.

She settles for wrapping it around her and folding her arms across her chest.

"I'm sorry. I couldn't think of another way." She rests her head against my shoulder. I wish I could put my arm around her, but the only means of cutting through the ropes is the Swiss army knife that was used to slash arteries. I would prefer for it to stay on the floor.

Mark watches us. He hasn't moved from his spot near the bottom of the stairwell, but after a few moments, he takes his phone from his pocket.

"Greg? Yeah, we're here... Me, Mel and Jess... Apparently Charles's wife Beryl left with our baby. She might have been caught. There are supposedly members of that gang surrounding the house... Oh, yeah, Charles is dead. Self-defence. He had a gun." Mark pauses for longer this time. Greg's probably giving instructions, or at least reacting to what he's been told. "Yes, sure. Mel's tied up. Get here as soon as you can. Are Jimmy and Brie on their way? Okay, thanks. See you soon." He puts the phone back. "Jimmy's on his way. Apparently he wouldn't allow Brie to come. Greg's crew have captured the Boss' cronies... Jess, are you okay?"

Of course she's not okay. She's throwing up violently, leaning away from me as she heaves in reaction to what's just happened. I know to some extent how she feels. The horror of killing someone, even when they've been tormenting you for months (years in her case), is unimaginable. I still have nightmares about it. The horror is mixed with overwhelming relief, overlaid with guilt at feeling relief that someone is dead at your own hand.

But as I watch her being sick, I realise we still don't know if Emma's alive. My stomach contracts, and I have to take some deep breaths to stop myself joining my sister.

Chapter Forty

Jess

Vomiting seems to be a reflex action to what's just happened. Apart from the pain in my gut, the shakes, nausea and the shivers, I feel numb inside. My body is processing the events, but my brain is incapable of thought. Except for one thing: Jimmy's on his way. I cling to that knowledge as my body expels all the food I've eaten today. The heaving continues beyond the point where there's nothing left to come up.

I'm aware of Mark joining me on the floor, and patting my shoulder awkwardly every so often. Eventually, my stomach must realise that it's empty, and it stops contracting. I lean back against the wall, exhausted.

Mel is also leaning back, but her arms are still behind her back.

"Mark, go and find the kitchen, and see if you can find something to cut those ropes with." My voice is pathetic after my efforts, but Mel must be in a lot of pain with her arms like that for so long. While we wait for him to return, Mel and I sit in silence. We exchange weak smiles. I think we understand each other, but there's too much to process right now.

Then the sound of a doorbell rouses me from my lethargy. Is that Jimmy? My heartrate doubles in the space of a beat, and I'm suddenly conscious that I reek of sick, and I'm covered in splatters of Charles's blood. Perhaps not the best way to impress the man I love.

There are footsteps in the hall upstairs. Mark left the cellar door open, so we can hear muffled voices, but it's not clear who, or how many people. Then I hear Jimmy.

"Where's Jess? Through there?" Half a minute later,

Jimmy appears at the top of the stairs – where only a short time ago, Charles stood with his gun.

"Oh my God, lass, are you okay?" Jimmy leaps down towards me, taking the stairs two or three at a time, and he's in front of me in seconds. "You found the knife, then," he whispers. His arms go around me, and he pulls me against his chest. I cling to him, feeling safe for the first time since I arrived here. Perhaps for the first time in nearly ten years.

But it can't last. I'm not sure how long we're hugging each other for, but the peace is broken by the arrival of Greg, Shelley and Mark. Jimmy pulls me up to him, and we go and sit on the other side of the cellar, away from vomit and blood. As we sit down, I notice that Shelley's arms are full. There's a shriek from my sister, as she takes in the sight: her daughter, alive and well, and resting in the arms of the police officer.

Mark goes to Mel, and cuts the ropes using a bread knife. It takes a few minutes, because the rope's thick, but as soon as she's free, Mel gets up (wincing – her arms have been confined for hours) and goes to her daughter, dropping excited kisses on Emma's head.

"I'm not going to let you hold her yet, Mel. Sorry, but you'd probably drop her." Shelley nods towards Mel's trembling limbs. Even her legs are wobbly.

"SOCO are on the way," says Greg. "They'll be here in a couple of minutes. As soon as they've taken photos of everything, including your clothes, Jess, I think we should leave, and get back to the Abbey. I'm sure we'll all be more comfortable there than at the station. We will need to fingerprint everyone, and take all your clothes for evidence. Better to be safe than sorry. But we can do that at the Abbey."

Mark reaches into his pocket, and pulls out his phone. "There's a recording on here that might be useful. It contains Charles threatening to kill us all. You might find it relevant to the case."

Greg extracts a plastic bag from his own pocket, and opens it for Mark to drop the phone into. I glance at Jimmy, who grins reassuringly at me. Facts are slotting together.

SOCO, my clothes, Mark's phone, fingerprints, and the interviews that Greg has only implied so far; all suggest there will be a court case. I killed Charles. He deserved it. To all intents and purposes it was self-defence. But I still killed him.

I slip my hand into Jimmy's, and he squeezes it.

Epilogue

Mel - one year later

It's been a horrible court case, and several times I thought we were going to lose. Greg's been helping us because he's retired from the police force. He now works as a private investigator – and has been helping Jess and her legal team with her plea of self-defence.

Jess's defence was complicated. She had been imprisoned by the 'victim' for nine years; she'd seen him murder Kylie, and he had been stalking her since her escape. So the jury had plenty of evidence of motive. But the murder weapon was a Swiss army knife. With my sister's history of cutting herself, it was considered possible that she'd carry one around with her.

We got through it mainly because of Jess's demeanour. In court, her vulnerability and her obvious love for us all was on display for all to see.

In between sessions, she admitted to me that she hadn't meant to love me. It had taken her a long time to let go of the anger, but the bond was too strong. We had too many things in common. By the time I was stupid enough to walk into that trap, she had no choice but to come and rescue us.

That came across clearly in court, but the most valuable piece of evidence was Mark's phone, which had 'accidentally' been set to record before they entered the house to rescue me and Emma.

Charles's recorded admissions of abduction, rape, incitement to murder, and intent to kill Jess, Mark and myself swung the jury completely. I think they would have acquitted my sister even if she'd walked in with a gun and shot Charles through the head.

We've all had a challenging year. For a while, Shelley was sorely tempted by her love of the justice system to get me tried too. Ironically, it was the letter from the Clinical Trial box that clinched it; the letter that I found, and hid. Karen admitted to going through my drawers, extracting it, and giving it to Shelley to get me into trouble.

During that fateful evening, Thomas was captured, together with the gang that had plagued Mark. The police caught Geoff and Karen afterwards, and questioned them closely. Their testimony seemed to tie all the loose ends of the plot together.

Karen had delved into many situations to cause trouble. She'd helped Thomas from afar, and was very complicit in Charles's activities. She'd placed many of the bugs around the Abbey, and did a lot of listening at doors to supplement the devices. Geoff was a general dogsbody, thug, and passer-on of information. They've both been charged with numerous crimes. Their relationship collapsed under the pressure of the trial.

Thomas gave a statement against Dominic. He confirmed everything I'd been through, and shared his opinion that the leader of The Brotherhood was '*a complete crackpot that could easily have done himself in to make a point*'. He also verified that Dominic was known by the inner circle to be on medication, although he didn't know what for. Greg told me Thomas showed little surprise when told that his leader had been schizophrenic.

In return for Thomas's assistance, some allowances were made in his sentencing, but my lovely friend Tina cried with relief when Shelley told her he wouldn't be out of prison within fifteen years. Shelley accepted Thomas's statement as sufficient, and Dominic's suicide is now on the record as fact.

Alison and Dawn have made their home here in the Abbey. Alison is in a relationship with Derek, but is too traumatised to make a definite commitment. I'm told their arguments can be heard in the local village pub when the wind is in the right direction. Dawn, with the help of counselling from Petra, is slowly coming to terms with her rape.

Petra has been invaluable helping Jess to recover from all that's happened to her. The court case set off several episodes of cutting. One of them resulted in a hospital admission, and my poor sister was sectioned for two weeks. The judge adjourned the trial for that time.

Mark has had to give evidence in two separate court cases: Jess's defence, and the prosecution of the scum who were threatening him. My poor husband is on medication at the moment for high blood pressure and an ulcer, but he is a lot more relaxed now that all court cases have ended with the right result.

Emma is growing into a beautiful, happy toddler. Thank goodness she was too young to remember anything about that day. I was told she'd been taken into the next-door neighbour's house by Beryl, so she escaped the more traumatic events.

Beryl broke down on the day the trial began, and admitted that her life with Charles had been nearly unbearable much of the time. She had nowhere to go to escape, and therefore had to obey his strange demands, including helping to retrieve Jess. But she did provide valuable information to the police which helped them gather evidence. She confirmed that Lisa was returned to a location near her parent's house, and is alive and well.

Paul Griffiths returned to us. He was shocked to discover he'd also been duped in order to get at me, Jess and Mark. He's settled back into his hours at the surgery, but takes plenty of time to help out with our little community.

The Refuge has grown. We have a thriving community of women and children who need us, and all measures are in place to make sure everyone has the right help from legitimate people.

My own guilt has never lifted, and perhaps never will. I've done so many things I regret; whether through stupidity, desperation or temporary insanity, I can't tell. Petra is helping me too, and I'm gradually learning to embrace the good things: the solid love of my family and closest friends, the joy of watching my daughter growing up, and the blessing of the new life growing inside me. Emma's brother is expected to make an appearance next month.

I stand now by Jess's side as she makes her marriage vows in the local village church. She is glowing in health, beauty and happiness, and I have never seen anyone look as proud and adoring as Jimmy. He has stood by her throughout her ordeals of the last year, and I know they are both looking forward to a happy life together.

THE END

Fantastic Books
Great Authors

CROOKED
CAT

Meet our authors and discover
our exciting range:

- Gripping Thrillers
- Cosy Mysteries
- Romantic Chick-Lit
- Fascinating Historicals
- Exciting Fantasy
- Young Adult and Children's
  Adventures
- Non-Fiction

Visit us at:
www.crookedcatbooks.com

Join us on facebook:
www.facebook.com/crookedcatbooks

40520282R00146

Printed in Poland
by Amazon Fulfillment
Poland Sp. z o.o., Wrocław